Sir Griswold was doing something he never did when sober. He was boasting. While a good deal of what he said was lost in a haze of alcohol, the general gist managed to find its way through to Dimmot's weary brain.

' . . . 'Twas the time when I did find myself betwixt a maiden fair of face and a dragon of the darkest countenance, with lips afire and eyes that did blaze in crimson and green. While she did lie at my back the creature towered above me, screeching and sending down flames upon my meagre shield. But I did not yield. And, when it seemed the monster would overwhelm us both, my blade did find its vitals. I struck again and again until the vile being fell before me, screaming and roaring and shaking the ground so that the rocks and trees trembled.'

Griswold belched.

'And with that I did gather up the fair maid and did away with her to a nearby glade, bordered by a lake that did shimmer in the warmth of the sun. And I did put my lips to hers . . . '

'But she did not yield,' mumbled Dimmot sleepily.

'Indeed she did,' retorted Griswold indignantly. 'Oft and plentifully.'

'Isn't that bloody typical,' thought Dimmot.

COLLIN WEBBER

MERLIN
and the
LAST TRUMP

VGSF

To Mo, Tris, Dids
and Wob

First published in Great Britain 1993
by Victor Gollancz Ltd

First VGSF edition published 1994
by Victor Gollancz
A Cassell imprint
Villiers House, 41/47 Strand, London WC2N 5JE

© Collin Webber 1993

The right of Collin Webber to be identified
as author of this work has been asserted by him
in accordance with the Copyright, Designs
and Patents Act, 1988.

A catalogue record for this book is
available from the British Library.

ISBN 0 575 05718 1

Printed and bound in Great Britain
by Cox & Wyman Ltd, Reading, Berks

It is quite clear that everything this man wrote about Arthur and his successors, or indeed his predecessors, was made up partly by himself and partly by others, either from an inordinate love of lying or for the sake of pleasing the Britons.

William of Newburgh,
concerning Geoffrey of Monmouth,
Historia, 1190

Acknowledgements

I would like to thank Marion Hough who fired the hot-air balloon of my creativity with her faith and enthusiasm.

Without her I'd have never left the ground.

And Tricia, Pam, Jean, Ann and Linda for keeping me soaring when I wanted to pack it in.

And Mo for waiting until I came back to Earth.

Prologue

During the twelfth century AD the self-styled historian Geoffrey of Monmouth wrote a treatise on the Kings and Queens of England, recorded in great detail and accuracy. It included a tale that had been handed down through the ages to Geoffrey by the most reliable sources, telling of the death of Sir Lancelot at the hands of another knight, Sir Griswold des Arbres.

On the eve of beginning the last page of this extensive work, Geoffrey retired exhausted to his bedchamber, wherein he slept the deepest, most dream-filled sleep of his life.

When first light came, he awoke, locked himself in his library and worked feverishly for weeks, pausing only to stave off death with frugal meals consumed while he worked.

When he had finished, the revised version, bearing no mention of Sir Griswold, was spread abroad and passed down through the centuries to become the tale of King Arthur's compassion and forgiveness in the face of his wife Guinevere's infidelity with Lancelot, his best friend.

Though this revised work, presenting Arthur as the epitome of goodness to which all men may aspire, has for centuries been accepted as the definitive record of those events, some have had their doubts concerning the finer details.

But then, it was a long time ago and there *were* other things going on.

Chapter 1

AD 570

Now though a mechanist whose skill
Defies the degenerate grasp of modern science
Grave Merlin (and belike the more
For practising occult and perilous lore)
Was subject to a freakish will,
That sapped good thoughts, or scared them with defiance.

William Wordsworth

'Dolt,' screeched Merlin, his voice echoing over the sunlit woodlands and sending clouds of starlings clattering into the blue skies.

'Fool,' roared Merlin, and in the distant meadows flocks of sheep unfurled and rumbled like bleating storm clouds.

'Ragwort. Thou art ragwort,' thundered Merlin.

Across the valley the people of Camelot, wandering through the market eyeing vegetables and livestock, mumbled idly, 'Ribwash. Thou art ribwash.'

'Ribwash,' hissed Merlin. 'Thou art ribwash.'

He glared up with ice-blue eyes that could burn through oak and asked, 'What hast thou to say?'

The armoured man standing before him stared down at his feet and toyed with the plumed helmet in his hands. He shrugged his massive shoulders, sniffed and mumbled casually, 'I did become a little over-zealous.'

They were standing in a clearing in front of Merlin's cottage, an unassuming little dwelling that did as much to belie the character of its owner as did the simple tunic and leggings that covered his tiny frame, and the untidy straggle of sparse, white hair that crowned it. Merlin had, to all intents, abandoned the traditional

9

cave and trappings long ago. At his age the more demanding studies of wizardry required warmth, comfort and freedom from lumbago.

A pained expression came over his sharp, porcelained features. 'Over-zealous?' He sniggered and glanced around as though addressing an imaginary audience.

Sir Griswold des Arbres groaned inwardly. Here we go, he thought.

Merlin looked towards the tall oaks flanking the cottage and raised a veined hand as if in supplication.

He paused for effect. 'Didst hear what sayeth this lad?' he whispered.

The trees murmured in the still air. He cocked an eye at the wooden bucket standing by the well. His eyebrows rose.

'Didst understand? Didst comprehend?'

He chuckled. The water in the bucket gently bubbled.

Griswold squinted under his black eyebrows at the distant hills and sighed quietly, not moving lest his armour creak.

The old man scampered off a few paces, crouched over and addressed one of the many bright crocuses that grew around the cottage throughout the year.

'The oaf,' he smiled gently, 'became a little over-zealous. He did mount his steed. He did take up his lance. And with curdling cry and abandon most gay did he thunderhoof upon the king's favourite knight and skewer him like a sucking pig.'

The crocus grinned in the knowing way that crocuses round wizards' cottages do.

Before the knight could catch his tongue he'd growled something into his beard, Merlin stepped back, staring at the little flower.

'What! Didst thou speak, my pretty? I heard words and thou art the only creature of wit within my compass, yet thy voice is wondrous gruff for one so small.'

'I said,' snapped Griswold, 'that Lancelot was an arrogant oxhead.'

Merlin frowned at the crocus.

'Arrogant? Oxhead? Oh.'

He appeared to ponder this.

He stroked his wispy beard.

'I suppose it might be termed arrogant of Lancelot to stand by his queen and ward off thy crude comments regarding her, what shall we say . . .' He looked up quizzically, 'remarkable lack of attraction?'

'He would not . . .' began Griswold.

'Was it arrogant of him to make formal request that thou stay thy words before he was forced to challenge thee to combat?'

'But he would not . . .'

'I suppose,' growled Merlin, arching his thick white eyebrows at the little crocus, 'thou thinkest it arrogant that, when thou didst insist upon pursuing thy ill-conceived course, he did even lay aside his formidable sword and offer thee choice or arms,' his voice rose, 'in fond belief that thou wouldst choose fist or stave and so avoid undue bloodshed, unwarranted demise or dismemberment of a king's knight, *and* the end of an alliance that Lancelot obviously valued infinitely more than did thee!'

The crocus cowered dutifully before the little wizard's onslaught.

Merlin turned to peer round his shoulder, his eyebrows raised questioningly.

'Well, boy, what hast thou to say? Canst thou justify this latest idiocy?'

Griswold stared thoughtfully at the crocus. The sudden scrape of his armour broke the stillness as he dropped his arms to his side and strolled over to where the old man crouched. Merlin's eyes narrowed suspiciously.

Griswold bent down awkwardly beside him and smiled broadly. As he did so the jagged scar that ran down his right cheek and disappeared under the black foliage of his beard stretched into a soft pink curve.

'A fit of pique,' he said.

'What?' Merlin's voice was dangerously soft.

Griswold raised his helmet and held the black plume under Merlin's nose. 'I did covet his prissy white feathers.'

The flaring of Merlin's nostrils indicated that he was less than impressed.

'Wilt thou take nothing seriously, fool?' he snapped. 'Dost thou not begin to conceive the import of thine actions?'

'I have slain another knight. 'Tis nothing unusual.'

'Lancelot was not just another knight. He was the king's favourite.'

'Not to mention the queen's.' Griswold smiled.

'Thou pup! Thou durgeon brain! Dost know what Arthur will do when he hears of this?'

Griswold sat back on his haunches, his armour groaning as he adopted a pose for which it was not designed. He gazed casually down the hill to the valley and the bustling market and gave a shrug.

'I did nothing except defend myself in fair combat.'

'A combat that would never have taken place had ye not chosen to commit a minor indiscretion.'

'Indiscre . . .'

'Ye insulted the Queen of England!'

'Ah. No . . .'

'Ye said that her neck was too scrawny, that her teeth did protrude, and that she was a trifle cross-eyed.'

'Ah. Yes . . .'

'And are these not insults?'

'If ye put it like that, yes, but . . .'

'How else would one put it?' spluttered Merlin.

'As I would have put it, had the queen's horny lover stayed his hand long enough to hear me out,' retorted Griswold.

'Go on,' said Merlin thinly.

'He, she, everyone would have heard me say that, though she did indeed exhibit the attributes thou hast mentioned, by some miracle of divine alchemy they had been combined in such a way as to produce a countenance of truly rare beauty, a fairness of face that kings might forfeit their thrones for, that priests might renounce their vows for, that men might give up their very lives for.'

'One did,' said Merlin drily.

'Because he was a fool.'

'Lancelot was thine ally and thou hadst choice of arms. Who is the fool?'

'My lance was taken up for a king who deserved neither an unfaithful wife nor a disloyal knight.'

'Perhaps so,' acknowledged Merlin. 'But that is not the way *this* king will see it. Unless I can persuade him otherwise I fear thou wilt pay a heavy price for thy folly.'

'And what form will this price take?' Griswold was unconcerned. 'Will I be banished from the next crusade? Or confined to the ladies' quarters as a bodyguard?' he added with interest. Then, more thoughtfully, 'Perhaps Arthur will take back my knighthood.'

'Thy knighthood,' replied Merlin in disbelief. 'Thy knigh . . . it's not thy knighthood that he will have,' he snapped. 'Hogscobblers, boy, it's thy head that he'll have.'

Griswold sucked at a tooth.

'Then the ladies may have to wait a while for my services.'

He frowned. It appeared that circumstances were about to become a little troublesome. He barely noticed Merlin hovering before him, his eyes flashing in multi-coloured hues. One or two of the Enchanter's powers tended to acquire a life of their own when he lost control of himself.

'In the name of Abaddon,' shrilled Merlin, 'art thou not listening? Wilt thou not take me seriously?'

'Nobody,' replied Griswold, 'takes thee seriously.'

He was snapped out of his pondering as, with a strangled oath and a crack of thunder, Merlin vanished. In the space left by the wizard was a cloud of black vapour which was rapidly disappearing as if being sucked into a tiny hole at its centre. A smell of ozone touched Griswold's nostrils.

All was still. The sun beat gently down on the big knight, warming his shaggy head and heavy armour. The oak leaves glittered above him and, from the distant hillside, the occasional bleat of sheep, now quietly grazing, floated up to his ears.

He waited with a warrior's patience.

When after some while Merlin did not reappear, Griswold sighed in the warm sunlight and moved at last. His leather and armour creaked into life as he ambled over to the well and sat awkwardly on the low wall. Casting his eyes over the valley and woodlands he laid down his helmet, unbuckled his sword and leaned it carefully against the wall, close at hand. He reached down, drew the ladle from the wooden bucket and brought it to his lips. The water was warm, but it dispelled the dryness in his mouth. Licking his whiskers he glanced about him.

At the top of the neighbouring hill stood Camelot castle, its battlements rising from the surrounding moat, pale grey in the sunlight, heavy and dark in the shadows with the hillside beneath it shaved bare of all trees that might protect any invading hordes.

Griswold sniffed.

Life, he thought to himself, can be very confusing.

Merlin's wrath and capricious disappearance, both of which had become more common of late, were worrying. The little wizard might be gone for days, even weeks. His ways had become increasingly strange over the past few months.

Griswold plunged the ladle into the bucket and lifted it high above his head, letting the water cascade over him, slapping off his shoulder-plates like a waterfall on flat rocks.

Then, sliding to the ground, back to the wall, he settled down to wait a little longer. The water drops glistened on his beard and trickled down his armour. Closing his eyes he rested his head against the stone. The stillness caressed his ears. The summer smells drifted in his nose. The sweet, gentle scent of flowers, the warmth that sent a calmness right down to the belly, the smell of leather, familiar yet still exciting to the senses, creaking as it did under the strain of one's muscles during battles in distant lands against strangely garbed adversaries.

As his mind wandered Griswold began to hum drowsily. Though no more than a vague intonation to start with, the hum gradually became a poignant, haunting melody that seemed to take his thoughts and carry them along, mingling with them until the melody became the thoughts, the thoughts the melody, a strange, alien tune that Griswold didn't know that he knew.

A tune never heard in these parts before.

The chirps of summer sparrows sparkled against the dark, velvet baritone of his voice for a while before the tune drifted off into a mumble, then silence.

Chapter 2

Uther, once king of all England, is more renowned for the deceitful way in which in AD 527 he did beget his son Arthur, most famous monarch of all time, than for all his other deeds and victories put together.

In his middling years, wifeless and lusty, he fell for one Lady Igraine, wife of the powerful Duke of Cornwall. Suffice to say that Uther did covet said duke's lady with all his heart, soul and loins, so much so that he did invite them both up to his castle, ostensibly to enter into peace agreements with the duke, but in fact so that he might enter into a particularly peaceful agreement with the lady herself.

Lady Igraine, however, was a passing good woman and wasn't having any. In fact, once she got the measure of Uther, so to speak, she persuaded her husband to take her home forthwith and in secret, which he did.

On discovering their absence, Uther, wondrously wroth, went out and laid siege to the duke's castle. During the course of the battle, Merlin, Uther's personal magician at the time, knowing of the lady's beauty and the old king's lust, made a rather immoral deal with his monarch.

The nature of the deal was that, while the duke was out leading his troops against those of King Uther, said king, changed by Merlin's magic into the spitting image of the duke, would enter the castle, make his way to fair Lady Igraine's private chamber and, with a bit of luck . . .

In return, should this deception bear fruit (which of course Merlin knew it would), the wizard would get custody thereof for reasons of his own.

During the battle the duke received a fatal blow, which left him wheezing his life away on the battlefield. Meanwhile his deceitful monarch, who should have been facing him midst mud and arrows, lay panting in the arms of the lady who thought that her husband had just dropped in for a short break from the fighting.

The deception was short-lived for, before Uther had time to adjust his dress, a messenger entered bearing news of the duke's death. A confused and by now pregnant Igraine wept, wailed, cut her losses and married the king.

Seven months and two weeks later a spindly baby was born prematurely.

Igraine called it Arthur. Uther called it a skinned rabbit and, denouncing it as hardly monarch material, willingly handed it over to Merlin. For the next fifteen years, the Enchanter quietly and secretly prepared it for its monarchical role in ways that would have been impossible within the politically petty atmosphere of the Royal Court during those Dark Ages.

Despite losing her husband and now her child at Uther's hand, Igraine, passing wise and philosophical, appeared to live happily with the king. On his untimely death from a mysterious malady some years later, Igraine mourned publicly and held her peace.

So, in his sixtieth year, Uther yielded up the ghost and set about exploring Eternity in spiritual bliss. He wandered through time, space and various other dimensions, meeting spirits of infinite varieties, chatting with such deities as he encountered, studying the common source of good and evil, etc., in fact doing all the usual things that spirits do with time on their hands.

He wandered far and wide, but never strayed from his beloved homeland for long. He'd waft on a whim, delving into England's green and pleasant past or nosing around its future, beady eyes wide with wonder, mouth metaphorically agape. Being, in death as in life, boisterous, loud and lusty, he developed a fondness for the late twentieth century, spending much of his time exploring the large cities and particularly the capital that he knew when it was little more than a Roman-built village.

Sometimes he travelled alone, sometimes with spirits of different sexes. There were a whole host of ethereal liaisons to be explored.

It was not a bad Afterlife.

Then, some twenty years after his demise, Merlin called him up.

'We have a problem,' said the Enchanter. 'I need thy help.'

'I *am* rather busy at the moment,' grumbled Uther.

'This is a matter of life and death,' replied Merlin.

'Whose?'

'Everyone's.'

Chapter 3

There the wise Merlin whilom wont they say,
To make his (dwelling) low underneath the ground,
In a deep delve, far from the view of day,
That of no living wight he might be found,
When so he counselled with his sprites encompassed around.

Edmund Spenser, *The Faerie Queene*

Ten miles north-east of Camelot lie the Mendip Hills. They are riddled with caves, the characters of which are as different as chalk and cheese. Some, like Swildon's Hole, are awash with rushing water, lively, exciting, often extremely noisy. Some, like Eastwater Swallet, are forbidding, malevolent and silent, except when the boulders move.

The cave in which Merlin materialized and which, fifteen centuries later, would be known as Goatchurch Cavern, could be summed up in one word . . . dreary.

'Dammit, Merlin,' bawled Uther who had been waiting, in spirit if not in body, for the wizard to appear. 'It's about time ye tarted this place up a bit. 'Tis like a morgue.'

'Then it should suit thee well, thou long dead king,' Merlin's voice snapped back, hollow and distorted in the tiny cavern. The Enchanter was having trouble dragging the last strands of his molecular structure into place. He ruefully acknowledged to himself that half a lifetime's experience of telekinesis appeared to be yielding to the debility of old age.

It is easy enough to disassemble one's material being, for that accords with the way of cosmic entropy, but reversing the process requires considerable reserves of internal energy. Merlin felt that these reserves had become considerably less during recent months.

18

He had a sneaking suspicion that, if he wasn't careful, he might one day find himself trapped in some ethereal limbo without the power to rematerialize.

In view of the immense task before him and the recent escapade involving Griswold, he felt that a certain shortness of temper was acceptable.

Uther, to whom the contents of Merlin's mind were at present a closed book, was less than sympathetic.

'I trust,' leered the spirit, 'now that ye have . . . pulled y'self together . . .'

He tried to continue but, overcome by his own remarkable wit, he fell about the floor, hands clasped over his stomach, filling the cavern with shrieks of laughter.

'Oh, Lord,' groaned Merlin.

Ignoring Uther's antics, he sat down gingerly on the low ledge that occupied one of the dimly glowing walls. With a grimace of pain he mentally prodded around his insides, while Uther, unable to control himself, tumbled out of the present, leaving an abrupt silence behind him.

The intestine, thought Merlin, finding the source of the trouble. Always the damned intestine. Toes and noses and such have a habit of falling into place naturally when one rematerializes. They're never any trouble. But intestines are another matter entirely. Oh, how simple it would be to spirit oneself hither and yon if it were not for the irritating tendency of things knottable to become knotted.

He remembered, as he often did at times like this, the words of his teacher when he was a child over a century ago. It was during his first crude attempt to change his hand into a claw prior to becoming a raven. He had been practising for hours and the pain was becoming unbearable.

'I don't want to be a wizard. It hurts too much.'

The eyes of his teacher blazed, though not unkindly.

'All men are wizards, Merlin, though few know it. Their wizardly powers lie deep within them waiting to be released, but these powers will only be released when the time is right. Thy time is now.'

'And when will *their* time be?' he'd asked with all the earnestness of a child trying to delay further discomfort.

'When their hearts, minds and bodies are ready to weather the immense forces that these powers will bring with them. And, hopefully, only when their spirits are pure enough to allow those powers to emerge naturally from their love and their need to help their fellow men.'

'And *how* will this come about?'

'Nature will see to it.'

Merlin remembered the bullying he'd received from some of the village boys the day before and wondered if he could learn to become a bear.

'But,' continued his teacher as if he'd read the boy's thoughts, 'if thy will is sapped by malice thy powers will turn to evil. Thou, Merlin, must be above evil at all times for thy destiny accords with the fate and future of all Mankind.'

Then, placing long delicate fingers on the boy's shoulder, he stared deep into Merlin's eyes.

'Thou art wizard. Thou wast born wizard, of daemon father, of human mother. There is no other way for thee and, in spite of the pain in thy body and the turmoil in thy young head, thou wilt learn thy craft as Nature demands. Thy responsibilities are great, perhaps greater than one man deserves, but remember this: while other men strive and fail to find even a tiny part of their powers, for thee the powers are within thy reach and the privilege is beyond price.'

Seeing the reluctance still lingering in the young child's eyes, he added wisely, 'One might say that thou art the most important little boy in the entire world.'

'And the whole village?'

'And the whole village.'

Merlin never cried at the pain again. Much later, when he learned that no one is that important, but that, to make a child reach for the stars, one must at times be a little devious, Merlin was glad that his teacher had lied through his teeth.

He began to unravel his intestine.

The cavern burst into life as Uther reappeared.

'Sometimes I think I'll be the death of me,' he cackled and vanished.

The tiny chamber echoed only to the sound of Merlin's laboured breathing as he bent to his irksome and painful task. The spectre appeared again just as Merlin was finishing and sat down on the ledge gasping for breath that he hadn't needed for nearly twenty years, old habits having a tendency to live on.

He cocked an eye at the wizard. 'Innards playing up again?'

'No.'

'The sooner you're able to give up the ghost and join me on my travels the better. You can go where and when you like and not suffer a whit. Look at me. Not a day's illness in my life since I died.'

He sniggered. Uther never tired of life and death jokes.

'The day of my demise must be delayed a while,' said Merlin without humour. 'There is much to do and no time in which to do it.' He cocked an eye at Uther. 'Thou hast news for me?'

The old king nodded. 'I have found the one we seek.'

Merlin's eyes lit up. 'Where?'

Uther leaned towards Merlin. He wiped the tears from his eyes, his mirth forgotten.

'Not a hundred miles from here. In London itself. By horse, two days' journey at most.'

Merlin nodded grimly. Then he hesitated.

'When?'

'In the year of our Lord . . . one thousand, nine hundred and fifty-six,' said Uther, adding unnecessarily, 'a little under fourteen hundred years hence.'

At this Merlin's face drained. The old shoulders sagged.

'Too far,' he whispered. 'Too far.'

He sat in silence, his head bowed. Uther waited patiently.

How scornful is Fate, thought Merlin, of men's welfare. How uncaring of their destiny, to put the one I seek in the best possible place in time to serve Mankind, knowing that that very time, the Time of the First Unborn, is utterly beyond my reach.

After a while he looked up.

'Is there no one else? No one nearer?'

Uther shook his head.

'There are others, but they're of no use to us. They come from different eras, from earlier times. They are rife in four or five hundred years from now, but none has the power to reach the twentieth century.'

He laid a gentle, ghostly hand on Merlin's shoulder.

21

'You must find a way to reach this man y'self. It all lies with you.'

Merlin remained silent. It suddenly seemed to him that all his life people had been laying gentle hands on his shoulders and exhorting him to remember his responsibilities. The periods in his life were long and many when he had felt alone, but never more so than now.

'Dammit, Merlin, all men are alone,' chided Uther, for the wizard had left his mind open and unguarded in the presence of his friend.

Merlin stared for a while at Uther shimmering in the darkness with the cavern walls dimly visible through his body.

'Indeed,' he said. 'Well then . . .'

He straightened up and took a long, deep breath. When the air left his lungs, he was again Merlin the Enchanter.

'What of this man? The one we seek?'

'His name is Dimmot,' said Uther.

Merlin knew that, while he might possibly reach his destination, there would be little left of him to be of service. After a few centuries' travel, the atoms of his body would start to slough off and, long before he arrived, the thoughts and feelings that made up his being would become distorted and dissipated throughout the intervening depths of time. All that would be left would be a few sluggish and brittle tendrils of thought squirming around like summer-dried worms on a dusty cart-track.

Merlin wondered if that might be enough.

'No way,' said Uther. 'Dimmot has the one skill, but his mind is no greater than those of today. Thy dried worms will be of no use to him.'

Merlin clenched his teeth in anger.

'Were I but thirty years younger I might have had strength enough to make the journey and still arrive with my powers intact. If only I had some way of travelling without recourse to my own energies . . .'

Uther grunted. 'That would require the services of another enchanter and there is none living that can hold a candle to you . . . to thee.'

'I know. I know,' said Merlin.

His gaze wandered round the cavern walls as if seeking to find an answer written on the damp limestone. Uther sat beside him pondering. The old king shifted his weightless weight and said hesitantly, 'There is another possibility.'

Something in the tone of his thoughts sent a warning shiver through Merlin's body. The wizard realized with mild surprise how cold he was feeling after the long hours they had spent in the tomb-like cave. He had magicked it out of the solid rock some ten years ago.

That was when the visions had started to haunt his nights and burden his days with a deep-felt concern. Soon after they began to appear he realized that, though they came from many centuries hence, he could not ignore them. He would do what he always did when confronted with any evil that threatened harm to his fellow men. He would find a way to help.

So it was that, resorting to the darker aspects of his craft, he had dragged King Uther away from his Eternal travels to find out from whence came the visions and what was their meaning.

At first Uther was reluctant. There were much more interesting things to do, he wasn't spending time travelling ridiculous distances just to look round any dreary Dark Age. He wasn't some sort of messenger boy, was he, he was a King of England (deceased).

So, for a second time in history, Merlin had struck a deal with King Uther.

This time, however, it was a double-edged deal, the sort that had been discovered by the Romans and would be perfected by the Sicilians and practised throughout the world in centuries to come. On the one hand, said Merlin, if Uther agreed to Merlin's request, he would have the wizard's assurance that King Arthur of England and the Round Table would be immortalized throughout history and would be remembered and revered as the most noble king in all Christendom. (Since this had been Merlin's aim anyway, for reasons of his own, this was pretty sneaky, but Uther didn't know that.)

'And on the other hand?' said Uther suspiciously.

'On the other hand, if thou decline . . . I will bring thee back to life.'

'Sounds like an offer I can't refuse,' Uther had grumbled. Now, ten years later, the wizard had an uneasy feeling that *he* was about to receive a similar offer. Suddenly he wished that he could simply turn his back on the whole thing and spend the rest of his days, bereft of his powers, responsibilities and obligations, just fishing, studying and enjoying the company of his friends and the fellowship of his beloved people of Camelot.

But, above and beyond all, and knowing in his heart of hearts that he must go on no matter what lay ahead, he wished with all his might that he had the quiet strength of Sir Griswold at his side.

Chapter 4

Griswold awoke with a start. His hand darted instinctively to the sword at his side.

Squinting uncomfortably in the strong sunlight, he glanced quickly round.

No one was in sight.

He heaved himself to his feet, buckled on his sword and picked up his helmet. The sun told him that he'd been asleep for an hour. Now he was sure that Merlin would not be returning today at least.

He was about to walk back down to Camelot when, glancing idly at the cottage, he wondered if possibly Merlin had returned and gone inside. The unpredictable old devil might well have let Griswold sleep under his watchful eye.

'Master Merlin?'

There was no reply, so the knight placed his fingers on the door and gently pushed it ajar. Although the stillness told him that the wizard wasn't there, he put his head round the door and looked inside. A frown creased his rugged features. It was some months since he'd last visited the cottage and he was surprised to see how untidy it was.

The door opened into the main room in which Merlin lived, practised his craft and received such friends as were welcome. Off to one side was a smaller door leading to his bedroom. That door was always locked.

The paraphernalia that Merlin used for his wizardly arts was scattered about the room – his books, charts bearing weird and unintelligible signs, some unfamiliar objects that appeared to be instruments, though what they measured was beyond Griswold's comprehension. The familiar fragrance of magician's herbs, some deadly, some remedial, scented the air with a mixture of mint, musk and lavender.

As Griswold gazed around he became increasingly concerned. Normally the place was tidy and spotless. Now it was in disarray. Everything was, for the most part, scattered haphazardly, spilling off the table, stools and shelves on to the floor.

Several books were left open. The ashes remained untended in the hearth and, most disturbingly, bowls of broth stood on the table and window sills, their contents cold and untouched. When Merlin went off his food it was a sure sign that things were seriously wrong. Griswold gazed round the room in silence.

In the sunlight gleaming through the window motes of dust hung motionless as if time in that small room had been suspended. There was stillness that felt to Griswold as if things hadn't changed inside the cottage for a hundred years. It was a feeling quite unlike the warmth and cosiness he had known in the past. For the first time in his life he felt unwelcome in the room.

He went in. Even in his weighty armour he walked like a cat, lightly, with the casual grace of highly toned muscles with no hint of surplus flesh on them. He wandered round the room looking for some clue as to what the wizard was up to.

It was strange that Merlin had not confided the nature of his worries to Griswold. He glanced at the various books that lay open, reading what he could without turning any of the pages. Little of what he read made any sense and many of the words, although vaguely familiar, seemed to be in a completely foreign language. As he turned away from the table a piece of half-burned parchment in the hearth caught his eye. Tucking his helmet under his arm he squatted down and squinted at what remained. The right-hand side of the parchment was gone, leaving just a few part-words and some figures.

He made out what looked like a list of names.

Geoffrey of M
11

Malor
d. 1472

Wordswo
1770–18

Einste
1897–195

The list went on for another dozen lines. Each name, if that is what they were, had been crossed through. They meant nothing to him.

Suddenly he felt like an intruder in the old man's private world. Without more ado he left the cottage.

Stepping out into the sunlight he closed the door carefully behind him.

'Sir Griswold des Arbres!'

The tone of the voice had Griswold's sword out of its scabbard before he'd even assessed the extent of the danger. He whirled round keeping his back to the cottage door.

Six men on horseback waited in the clearing. He recognized them as King Arthur's guards headed by the sergeant-at-arms, all in mailed armour with heavy shields.

Griswold was puzzled. Their stealth told him that they could conceivably be a health hazard. The sergeant who had spoken urged his horse forward a few paces and the other soldiers spread out either side, placing themselves where they could converge on Griswold without getting in each other's way.

They were well trained, experienced and efficient. And, more's the pity, they were loyal.

Griswold hoped he wouldn't have to kill any of them.

'Sir Griswold,' called the sergeant.

'Belkin?' said Griswold.

Sergeant Belkin was short, stocky and grey-whiskered. Under his helmet Griswold knew that his hair was cropped short to prevent it from being grabbed. His face was leathered from the suns of many lands, his eyes small and coolly alert. Sergeant Belkin was about forty, old as soldiers go, and probably the most experienced man on the battlefield that Griswold had ever met.

Belkin was a miserable sod. He hated the Saxons. He hated the Romans. He hated the Picts and he hated the Welsh. He appeared to hate his troops, one could not be sure. And he hated knights

27

with all the contempt of the lower rank soldier who sees himself superior in both intelligence and ability on the field of battle.

Knights were a great source of amusement to him. He was glad that he was not privy to the dubious honour of knighthood with all its pleasures and privileges. He was a fighting man, not some prissy poet or raven-haired young 'warrior' with his thees and thous, and with pages to help him dress and wipe his arse.

Sergeant Belkin had two loves. He loved his monarch, for which reason many a knight standing by the king on the battlefield owed his life to Sergeant Belkin. That same knight, however, would have been asked to draw his sword, had they met on a narrow street and should one have had to stand aside for the other to pass.

Sergeant Belkin's other love was horses. The only time his voice changed from the gruff arrogance with which he addressed peasants, troops and monarch alike was when he talked quietly and gently to his horses.

He stared coldly down at Griswold. 'Is the wizard within?'

Griswold shook his head.

'Where then?'

With a shrug the knight made a loose fist and tossed it into the air, splaying the fingers and glancing skywards.

'Poof,' he mouthed.

'I think not,' Belkin smiled mirthlessly. 'Those days are long past. Merlin's powers were on the wane before ye were born, sir knight.'

Griswold shrugged a 'You're no fool, are you,' sort of shrug.

Belkin glanced around the clearing. 'I see your horse is somewhat conspicuous by its absence. The old man has left you to walk home, perhaps?'

'When Merlin summons, one does not come by horse,' said Griswold with feeling.

'Oh, so he still has the power to make a young knight's balls tremble with fear, then.'

The soldiers behind him sniggered a casual five-against-one snigger.

'Not fear,' said Griswold evenly. 'Respect.'

The sniggers died, for the tone of the conversation had suddenly

28

become more business-like. The lone knight was saying, 'Stop flapping thy petticoats and say what thou hast to say.'

Without further ado Belkin said, 'We have come to escort you to the castle.'

'For what purpose?'

'To answer for the slaying of Sir Lancelot du Lac.'

'I do not understand,' replied Griswold. 'I answer only to the king.'

'Of course,' said Belkin. 'And 'tis to the king that you shall answer.'

Griswold frowned. 'But he is two days away.'

'And the queen is just across the valley.' The sergeant smiled thinly.

Guinevere was a good woman but for two weaknesses, her eternal concern over her looks and her constant desire to feel the ground beneath her bare buttocks.

And now, derided in public *and* deprived of her lover by the same man, she wanted to wreak her revenge. Griswold had a rough idea as to the form her revenge would take and he preferred to avoid it.

'With respect, Sergeant,' he said, 'the order for my arrest can come only from the king. Thou art not a man to take the law into thine own hands.'

'We come not to arrest you, sire.' Belkin smiled humourlessly. 'The queen asks that ye return to the castle to await his majesty's pleasure.'

'Since when dost thou answer to a woman?' asked Griswold quietly.

'I am a common soldier,' replied Belkin in a tone that implied just the opposite. ''Tis not for me to distinguish between man and woman where the monarchy is concerned. In the absence of the king, the queen rules and whosoever rules England commands me and my troops.'

He walked his horse forward a few more paces just out of earshot of his men and leaned towards Griswold.

'Besides,' he added, granting Griswold the rare privilege of talking to him as though the knight might actually be his equal, 'hers is the tongue of a woman denied the pleasure of giving copiously to a very demanding knight. A pleasure which she is

29

loath to be denied. For myself, sir knight, I cannot help but condone your action. When a man becomes ruled by his loins rather than his honour he becomes little more than a randy stallion. Without the stallion's nobility, of course.'

His jaw hardened. He straightened up.

'I am a soldier. I know nothing else. I wish to remain a soldier, so the queen's word is my command.'

Then, so that his troops could hear him, he spoke out.

'Now kindly sheathe thy sword, sire, and come with us peacefully.'

In spite of himself Griswold felt sympathy for the sergeant. Death, however, was not too appealing to him at that moment. For all his allegiance to his king, and for all his sense of honour, there was another to whom he felt a greater loyalty and who would surely be needing his help. Griswold would be of little use to Merlin dead.

With a swift movement he rammed his helmet on his head and leapt towards Belkin, seeking to unseat the sergeant and make his escape on the other's horse. However, Belkin reined in without attempting to draw his sword and skilfully avoided Griswold's grasp. Then he urged his steed forward, sending the knight tumbling with a shuddering blow to his shoulders from its heavy-muscled chest.

In spite of the shock Griswold rolled away easily, holding his sword away from him and coming to his feet with his blade at the ready.

'Aclides,' called Belkin and from their belts his soldiers each drew a short club comprised of a thick, wooden handle with a spiked ball at the end. They were not good weapons against a sword, but in the hands of six men with shields, quick and effective in bringing a man to the ground without killing or sorely wounding him.

The queen obviously wanted Griswold alive . . . at least for the time being.

The soldiers casually encircled him. He would use the flat of his sword until he gained a horse or threatened to fall under the other's weapons.

Before they could pen him in he sprinted for the nearest gap, then swerved to the right, round a horse and, grabbing the rider's ankle, wrenched the man's foot from the stirrup. With the flat of his blade he sent the man tumbling. The soldier fell with a crash and lay still. Quickly the other men moved in before Griswold had time to mount the empty steed and suddenly the air was alive with the familiar sensations of battle. At once Griswold was in the midst of shuffling, startled hooves, twisting and ducking, parrying and striking, his ears filled with the snorts and whinnies of wild-eyed horses mingling with the slap of leather, the scrape and clash of metal and the oaths of men with their blood rising. Instinctively his senses burst and bloomed as he became one with his danger and reacted with his whole being, his body generating the power and speed needed for his survival. Each breath became a roar, each roar became a blow.

Another man went down, his horse bounding away from the fray and out of reach. Griswold's task was made more awkward by his need to squint up at his opponents as they span and turned above him, trying to strike down at him with the sun flashing at their backs, now hidden, now glaring in his eyes. But the real difficulty came from his refusal to turn his blade on man or horse.

As he fought, one part of his mind registered the fact that Sergeant Belkin was sitting quietly astride his horse watching the mêlée and making no attempt of his own to bring him down. Griswold blocked a blow aimed at his head and drove the hilt of his sword into a mounted knee, then he struck upwards in a continuous motion as the contorted face dropped towards him. His metal-clad fist struck bone with a jarring thud. He dodged away and turned as the stricken soldier slumped to the ground. He was sweating and his breathing was becoming difficult. Still men and horses swirled round him, blows whistled about his head, some missing, some glancing off his helmet, blade or shoulder-plates. If he did not gain horse soon he would succumb to the blows of the three remaining soldiers.

Still the sergeant made no move to assist his men. Instead he called above the noise, 'Dismount.'

One man pulled away from Griswold and galloped towards Belkin, who took the reins of his horse. The man dismounted and ran back to the fight.

Another withdrew and did the same. Griswold flashed a glance

31

of respect at Belkin, acknowledging the skill and discipline of his soldiers' tactics. The sergeant nodded.

In a few moments the men faced Griswold on three sides while Belkin held the horses out of the knight's reach. As the men circled warily he called to Griswold.

'Ye fight well, sir knight, but to what end? Without a horse you are lost. Should ye, perchance, defeat my remaining men, you'll not reach me while I'm on horse.'

Griswold ducked a swinging blow to his head and, grasping the lower edge of his attacker's shield, jerked it upwards. The shield swung over the man's arm, the upper edge smashing into his jaw. Griswold followed up with a crashing blow to the head and dodged quickly away as two more strokes cut through the air where he had been.

Now he could afford to go on the attack.

He bounded towards one man, sending him scuttling backwards under a rain of blows. The soldier stumbled and fell, but before Griswold could disable him, the other one was close behind. Griswold turned, falling to one knee. As the man's aclide skimmed over his helmet he swung his sword low, smashing an ankle. He rose as the man fell and thrust a metal-clad foot at the exposed jaw. In two strides he was upon the last soldier, stamping his club hand into the ground with a crack of knuckles, then laying him cold with the flat of his blade.

He stood amidst the silence and carnage, catching his breath, his gaze turned towards the sergeant.

Belkin let go the horses' reins and dismounted. He walked towards Griswold, thumbs in belt, his sword still undrawn.

Griswold watched him closely. Belkin looked around the clearing.

'Ye've made a fair mess of my troops,' he said.

'They'll live,' answered Griswold. 'But for now it's me and thee. Wilt thou draw thy blade? As ye see I'll not surrender and thy club will avail thee little against my sword.'

Instead of doing as he was bid, Belkin glanced over his shoulder to where the horses stood grazing quietly.

'The steed on the right next to mine. He has the legs of the others both in speed and distance. He'll carry you fast and far.'

Griswold frowned. 'Thou wouldst let me escape?'

Though he stood over a foot taller than the sergeant, the other was a brave and ferocious fighter and, being fresh, might well have been Griswold's equal at that moment. By way of answer Belkin waved his hand around the clearing. 'Ye are, without doubt, a most worthy warrior and an honourable knight. Better that you lie low for a while. Ye can return when King Arthur is back. He may be more lenient to you than the Lady Guinevere.'

Then, with what might have been a smile, he said, 'Begone if ye will, sir knight, before my men awake and bear witness to my unsoldierly conduct.'

Without another word Griswold sheathed his sword and approached the horses. Carefully he mounted the one that Belkin had indicated, getting the feel of the steed and gently asserting his authority. He nudged the horse forward.

'Thy reasons escape me for the moment, Sergeant Belkin, but I hope that one day soon we may share a sup of ale and the secret of this encounter. I thank thee.'

With this he urged the horse into a gallop and rode swiftly away down the hill.

The sergeant stood looking after him for a while until a slight movement to one side caught his eye. One of his soldiers was regaining consciousness and raising himself dazedly from the ground.

Belkin ambled over to him and, as the soldier turned bleary eyes towards the sound of receding hoofbeats, he lifted off the man's helmet.

'For the treacherous Lancelot,' he murmured, raising the helmet high into the air.

'And,' he added as the dull thud of metal on bone rang across the clearing, 'for the horses.'

Chapter 5

It was nearing midnight when Merlin silently reappeared in the clearing. A large, white moon hung low in the sky, etching the trees, rocks and distant castle in silver relief against their own shadows.

The sheep in the valley were silent and all was very still.

On the dark side of the castle a candle glow dimly outlined one of the tiny windows on the upper floor. Merlin wondered briefly who was giving Lady Guinevere nocturnal solace at this hour of mourning. He stood quietly turning over the thoughts of the last few hours.

Uther had given him the only option left.

''Tis plain ye'll not make it in one piece if ye use your traditional way of blundering hither and yon,' he chided, referring to the wizard's method of travelling through space and time.

'So?'

'So, ye must forsake the direct approach. You'll have to take the long way round.'

When Merlin finally understood what the old king was driving at, his heart chilled. He'd faced many terrors, many forms of death in his earlier days with unfaltering courage (most of the time) and had stood over the corpses of the most formidable enemies, both human and otherwise.

He'd made many journeys through snows and over deserts with his powers at their lowest ebb and only his legs and iron will to carry him on.

This journey, however, was something else. There would be no struggle against the elements, no venting of rage, no mortal combat to bring one's will and one's courage within easy reach.

No way of fighting the terrors that might crawl into his unguarded mind. Just the sitting and the waiting.

And the centuries.

Merlin shivered in the night air, folded his arms across his small chest and scurried into his cottage. For a second he hesitated just inside, staring into the moonlit room, a puzzled frown on his face. Then he latched the door, reached into his pocket and pulled out a key, weaving his way across the untidy room as he did so. He unlocked the bedroom door and went in.

There was a click as he locked the door behind him.

Inside all was in blackness for Merlin had no prying window to let in the light, but then the room brightened as the candle by his bedside came to life quietly and unobtrusively like a faithful servant. Like Merlin it was very old, gnarled and wrinkled, but unlike the wizard, whose bearing was upright and proud, the candle languished squat and ugly from years of service, bearing its flame with surly determination. Merlin walked over and stared sadly down at it.

'This may be the last time thou'lt shine for me, old friend. Tomorrow I must begin a journey that will take me farther than ever before and there is, I fear, only the faintest chance that I will reach my destination, let alone return alive.'

The candle's flame flickered for a brief instant, almost threatening to snuff out. Then, as if fired by a stoic pride, the flame grew straight and steady and Merlin realized ashamedly how much he'd taken for granted, how much he'd had to neglect in pursuit of his mission. Friends had been forgotten. The king had gone wanting for his magician's wisdom.

And Griswold.

The lad had suffered his slights and tantrums with staunch patience and would never know how much Merlin had wanted to share his dread secret with him.

Merlin sighed. 'Serve me well tonight, little greasy one. I have a demanding task to perform before I sleep and I need thee to light my way through a veritable labyrinth.'

He stepped across the small room and stood before a sturdy shelf. After a moment's hesitation he reached out and pulled down a huge, stiffly bound book. It bore no title or hint of its contents and it was very dusty, for it was not a book to be opened

35

on a whim. The binding was a strange form of grey hide and, although it was heavy in Merlin's arms, the book had an elusive quality as though, given good reason, it would fade in his grasp and return to some other rightful and unimaginable dimension. It exuded a faint malevolence, reminding him that it remained in his possession only under considerable sufferance.

Casually he blew across the cover, masking his unease with a scowl and a careless wave at the billowing dust.

'No doubt thou wouldst wish to remain aloof and undisturbed by the crude probings of mere men, oh vessel of wisdom and knowledge.' The eyebrows arched. 'But thou wast, presumably, created to serve Man, and for all time. I trust, therefore, that thou wilt forgive the disturbance if I presume upon thee for the means whereby I can fulfil my part in such a service.'

The book was unmoved by sarcasm. Its pages remained blank.

Merlin hefted it over to the bed, sat himself cross-legged on the hard straw mattress and laid it open before him. He squinted down at the first page, peering through the outer surface of the thick parchment to the words buried inside, beyond the reach of normal eyes. The old candle burned more brightly, lighting the page for him and throwing his crouching figure harshly over the wall.

The words were few and appeared to make little sense as they stood, but their meaning and the method employed to make use of them were well known to Merlin, though he had used the phrase only once before, long ago. It read thus:

Man is Man is every Man is Man is all the men who ever were are Man is Man.

This was the key to unlocking the secrets held by the disturbing volume. But, while their meaning might make sense to someone with the gift of perceiving them, a man could chant the words until his tongue wore away and still the book's pages would not reveal those secrets. They would come to light only when the words were shared in a specified manner by two such adepts.

Or read by a wizard with the gift of double tongues, the ability to say two separate things simultaneously.

Merlin knew that to conjure false voices out of the air and command them to chant the key would bring a terrifying and fiery destruction upon the being who sought to deceive.

The Book would heed only the voice of Man.

Laying it aside, Merlin shut his eyes. Face furrowed in concentration he attempted, by way of practice, two tentative phrases at once: 'Thou art Merlin the Wizard' and 'I'll fight the good fight.'

He winced, peering under one half-opened eyelid at the Book. Though it gave no sign he felt that it would not take kindly to 'Thou'll fart the Moodlin Gizard right.' Therefore a little practice was in order. He stuck out his tongue and peered awkwardly down at it. He wiggled it up and down. Sideways.

The gift of double tongues is not so much a gift as a product of many years' practice in muscle control with, of course, the extra touch of wizardry to effect the desired results.

He wagged it in a circle, first one way, then the other. The candle sniggered, sending his shadow skittering across the wall. With tongue still squirming Merlin turned to throw a withering glance over his shoulder.

The flame steadied. His shadow returned to its deathly stillness save for the frantic jiggling of the creature protruding from its flat face.

He made the tongue ripple from root to tip in a series of slow waves. He'd not used this technique for many years. His coordination faltered and the tongue waggled uncertainly like a worm sniffing curiously at the sunlight.

He scowled, took a breath and started again slowly.

Once mastered, the double tongue could be useful in many ways. Anyone adept in its use could simulate the sound of two or more people talking at once, sometimes in different accents. A magician might master the art of talking in two languages simultaneously. He could give the impression of arguing with himself or of being a large group of fearsome warriors, which could prove very handy if being pursued by a smaller group of fearsome warriors.

Merlin worked faster and faster until his tongue was a blur, then he stopped the left side and rippled the right. Then the left. Then the right. One side backwards while the other went forwards. Before long the soft, pink muscle had regained its memory and was flowing, rippling, curling and waving like a skilled and agile dancer.

Suddenly he stopped breathlessly, satisfaction glinting in his eyes. Confidently he tossed off the two phrases that had eluded him earlier and it was as if two men were speaking at once, each word, each inflection falling from his lips complete in itself, each phrase quite independent of the other.

Perfect.

He realized with some surprise that he was covered in sweat and his body ached from the sheer effort of concentration. No matter. He hauled the Book before him again and opened the cover. The phrase appeared before his intense gaze. Softly he intoned the words in a dark minor key, his two voices splitting into harmonies as he did so. The notes of his song rose from the tonic, gathered intensity as they reached their peak and dropped back for the final note.

'Man is Man . . . Man is Man . . . All the men who ever were are Man.'
'Man is every Man . . . Man is all the men who ever were . . . Man is Man.'

Without stopping he repeated the phrase, his voices weaving harmonies through the silence.

As Merlin chanted the last word a soft minor chord rose from nowhere, swelling rapidly, threatening to drown his voice with its volume. The Book and the Enchanter held the chord for a few seconds. For a third time Merlin sang, louder, more slowly, more intensely as the Book accompanied his fugue with crashing minor chords, the sounds frightening in their unearthly discipline, somehow organlike, somehow not. Chimes interspersed the harmonies, vibrating, oscillating, threatening to burst within the wizard's head and scatter his brain all over the shaking walls, while glittering arpeggios screeched and swirled around each word.

In the midst of this sat Merlin, his mind fighting to remain calm within his shaking body, knowing that to falter would bring about a noisy and unmusical finale to the singer and the song.

Each chord exploded about him, its remnants showering down in a cascade of tiny, glittering barbs on his shoulders, threatening to drag him into the very ground, scraping at his face, his cheeks, trying to catch at his tongue so that it might stumble and plunge him screaming into the Earth's molten bowels.

But the wizard sang on.

At last he reached the final note and, as if echoing his victory, the music emanating from the terrible Book modulated from the minor key into a thunderous and triumphant major chord. For long seconds the two held the chord between them. Then, as if by some mutual signal, they ceased.

Silence rang around the little room.

Merlin sagged gratefully against the wall, his eyelids drooped. His body trembled.

After a few moments the Book spoke.

'Thy courage is without equal, Merlin,' it whispered, 'though thy singing has hardly improved since we last met.'

'And thy subtlety leaves something to be desired,' murmured Merlin tiredly.

'Ah, well, if it were up to me . . . but I must do as I am bid.'

The old man nodded.

'Besides,' continued the Book, 'thou must earn thine entry to the secrets herein. A choir of nuns warbling hosannas would hardly constitute a challenge to thy formidible powers of survival.'

'Have I passed the test?' asked Merlin impatiently.

'Indeed. Ask what thou wilt.'

With some effort Merlin sat up and began to explain at length all that he wanted to know. For a while the Book remained silent. Merlin imagined that he could feel a faint disturbance as if something were searching stealthily through his mind, sifting all he had said, and weighing up the most appropriate answers.

Then it replied much as Merlin expected.

'Is thine eyesight still as good as ever?'

'It is perfect,' said Merlin stiffly.

'Good. Then I have no more to say to thee. Until we meet again, brave Merlin.'

And the Book was silent.

Merlin gave a grunt and squinted round the side of the Book at the edges of the pages. A misty glow emerged from somewhere near the middle. He leafed through until he found the glowing page, noting without surprise that the other leaves remained blank.

He opened the page to find the glow swirling around and through it, revealing brief snatches of a longish poem, but never showing him the whole text at once. He knew that he had to catch and keep the glimpses in his mind and piece them all together to complete the picture.

This contrary object does not give up its secrets easily, he thought sourly.

'Thou couldst at least make some allowance for old age,' he grumbled aloud, but the mist did not abate. Beside him the candle's flame rose with renewed vigour as his old eyes creased painfully trying to catch the elusive phrases.

When the mist had revealed all of the poem it quickly dissipated, merging into the parchment until it had vanished completely. The glow died and the page was blank, but now the poem was engraved as if in granite within the wizard's mind.

He shut his eyes and read it through.

> The goal that lies beyond thy powers
> Cannot be reached by travelling,
> But comes, like sunlight, to the flower's
> Patient seed who, with no need
> For haste or speed, nor yet for any urge indeed,
> Must wait for Time's unravelling.
>
> The goal that lies beyond thy powers
> Cannot be reached by climbing
> But with the crumbling of the towers
> Of Time's dark castle, years will pass
> Until at last the future will become the past,
> The spires will fall in time. In
>
> Distant years beyond thy powers
> Waits he whom thou art seeking.
> He knows of thee and often scours
> The books of yore and history for
> Some hint of thy grave mechanist skills
>   and perilous lore.
> With him thou must be speaking.

This one who lies beyond thy powers
Must needs be reached by waiting,
For, though in future times he cowers,
He'll come to thee if thou wilt be
Completely free from forces of Infinity
By means of thy creating

A deathless time, a timeless death,
A breathless life, a lifeless breath,
A stillness that moves constantly
Throughout the dark eternity
By virtue of just being still,
While time flows through thy being till

Thou take a breath, thou bid thy heart
To rise from death, to beat, to start.
The flow of life stirs in thy soul.
Awake
And thou'lt have reached thy goal.

So, Merlin thought, the old king was right. What Uther in his simple way had guessed, the Book now confirmed beyond doubt. There was no other way.

So be it.

With a last distasteful glance at the poem Merlin muttered, 'Hardly Wordsworth,' and, opening his eyes, he turned to the next page. It was entitled 'Ye Ancient and Timeless Methode whereby a Man may be Suspended from All Living Functions for Many Centuries, Thereby, in Essence, Transcending the Barrier of Time, For the Explicit Purpose of Benefiting Mankind.'

The title was longer than the instructions that followed: 'Sit alone, cross-legged with eyes closed. Think once only of the time in which thou wouldst awaken. Allow the Timeless Formula to fill thy mind completely, *Don't forget the potion.*' Like the poem, the Timeless Formula was revealed piece by piece from within a swirling mist. By the time Merlin had read it through, memorized it perfectly and failed completely to understand it, another hour had passed and the flame was beginning to flicker.

Closing the Book on the fading words Merlin realized sadly that the old candle had burnt itself out in order that he could finish his task. It was, after a century's faithful service, about to sputter its last.

Laying the Book aside, Merlin leaned over and pulled the candle holder towards him. He lifted it carefully so as not to extinguish the dwindling flame and cupped it gently in his hands.

'Thou hast served me well, little one,' he said. 'My task is complete and now I must sleep, for tomorrow my journey begins and thou canst rest from thy labours. No doubt we shall meet again in spirit and it will honour me greatly if I can be of service to thee as thou hast . . .'

He sat for a long time in the blackness, the holder in his hands, his smile tender and salted with tears.

Chapter 6

'If you haven't made it by now, forget it.'

Broadcast from Radio Essex Jambuster plane,
somewhere over London, winter 1987

James Dimmot could wait no longer. He felt as if he'd been waiting for centuries for something to give his life a purpose. A trail of failures marked the paths he had followed during his thirty-eight largely miserable years. A trail littered with uncompleted manuscripts, unfinished bookshelves and unfulfilled relationships. Unpaid cheques (numerous), unfaithful ex-wives (two) and unsympathetic employers.

He sat on the snow-swept parapet of Tower Bridge at 2 a.m., 13 January 1987, his slippered feet dangling over the Thames. Below him ponderous blocks of ice flowed down to the sea, bobbing and chuckling amid the effluent, for it was the worst and the coldest winter for many decades. The grey gabardine raincoat that was his only other clothing did less to protect him from the icy blizzard than did the lethally high alcohol content in his bloodstream.

But James Dimmot was unconcerned.

Flinging back his head he drained the dregs from the bottle in his hand, flipped it casually away into the black water and leaned forward until he toppled from the parapet, leaving as the only sign of his passing a thin layer of skin from buttocks frozen to the unfeeling ironwork.

Chapter 7

It was nearing midnight and Sir Griswold des Arbres was in the very last place on Earth that one would expect, doing the very last thing that one would imagine.

'If thou please, Sir Griswold,' whispered Queen Guinevere, the languorous quality of her breathing beginning to give way to a sharper, more irregular rhythm. 'A touch faster perhaps.'

'My pleasure, your majesty,' replied Griswold, applying himself dutifully and with much practised skill.

That afternoon, as he rode away from Sergeant Belkin, he had realized that, if he were to retain King Arthur's favour and remain in a position to help Merlin the Enchanter, he could not avoid the queen's lust for vengeance.

His only alternative was to confront the queen face to face using a simple and direct weapon. One to which she would find it difficult not to yield.

Sir Lancelot had once told him, in the early days before that great knight had succumbed to evil thoughts and deeds, 'Thine enemy's weakness is thy most powerful weapon. Carry that knowledge with thee all thy days . . .'

And Griswold did.

'And use it whenever the need arises.'

And Griswold was using it.

'Sire, I wonder if thou couldst . . .' Guinevere took Griswold's hand from her cheek and steered it hopefully down past her long neck. Griswold placed his massive fingers where they would have the most effect.

'Like this, my lady?' he asked rhetorically.

His fingers barely moved, but the breath hissed from Guinevere's lips and the languor in her eyes disappeared completely under clenched lids, re-emerging seconds later in the guise of glazed anticipation.

With some difficulty the queen whispered, 'Oh yes, sire,' and added with a gulp, 'That would be very pleasant.'

Griswold moved his fingers softly, imposing a gentle cross rhythm on the slow, undulating movement of their naked bodies . . .

. . . Lancelot's mistake, really, had been to underestimate Griswold's potential. At first, as Griswold became more skilled, Lancelot viewed him with a degree of warmth and in time they became friends and allies, often standing back to back, against diverse enemies of different lands. As he grew in prowess and his stature in the eyes of Arthur and Guinevere increased, a wariness crept into their relationship. Merlin had once warned Griswold that Sir Lancelot was destined to become a victim of his own desires and a dangerous and unpredictable adversary to anyone who threatened them. So, in time, the two men, while maintaining a healthy respect for each other, tacitly acknowledged their rivalry and agreed to avoid any confrontation which might disrupt their combined strength and weaken the protection they afforded the king. Things might have lasted many years thus had not . . .

. . . 'Sir Griswold, my love. It would please me greatly if we could . . .'

She pushed gently, if a trifle impatiently, with her hand on his ribs.

'Of course, Lady Guinevere,' he smiled. 'Whatever thou ask, it shall be thine.'

He emphasized the word 'ask' and rolled on to his back carefully so as not to risk breaking the link between her desire and his tenuous dominance. Gratefully she sat upright, proud and beautiful, although the nature of her position precluded any pretence at regal splendour and the grey-green eyes whose individual tendencies were a constant blight to her vanity now converged unashamedly beneath drooping eyelids as she imitated the action one might make when urging one's horse into a trot. Griswold, however, was not prepared to trot until he could ensure that Guinevere would break into her final gallop before he did. Guinevere's devotion and Griswold's life could well depend on his self-control. His hands continued to work their magic . . .

. . . Things might have lasted many years thus, had not Merlin's predictions come true. In time Lancelot grew so besotted with, and desirous of, Guinevere that he became blinded to all reason. Guinevere, for her part, being easily flattered and with a voracious appetite left unsatisfied by her husband's attentions, did little to discourage Lancelot's approaches.

In time a story that was to endure for centuries became a fact. The illicit love of Lancelot and Guinevere had a profound effect on life in and around Camelot and already half-truths, lies and myths began to sprout from its seed.

Perhaps even more gossips and legends might have blossomed, had not a roguish knight sought to flatter the queen one day and had not a jealous warrior thrown down his challenge too quickly, thus sealing his own doom and depriving the queen of her most ardent admirer.

So Griswold had headed across the valley that afternoon, skirting the southern border of Camelot town and ensuring that he was seen by some of the villagers. Many of them waved as he clattered past with the sound of armour and leather shattering the still afternoon. The men grinned and raised the clenched fist of victory, for neither the secret of Lancelot's treachery nor the significance of the casual questions of sergeants leading small bands of soldiers had escaped them.

A few did not wave but watched narrow-eyed as he passed.

He'd struck out across the country with the lengthening shadows of the trees pointing his way towards the east. After an hour's ride, he'd turned north and circled round, driving his lathering horse back to Camelot, squinting into the red sun and safe in the knowledge that any troops ordered to pursue him would be far to his south by now.

Dusk was well on its way as he approached the castle through rapidly darkening woods that he'd known as a boy. Releasing his horse, he continued on foot, reaching the castle about an hour before midnight. After discarding all but his breeches, he'd avoided the castle guards by slipping into the moat then scaling the castle wall to the battlements. He knew the castle well and getting into the queen's bedroom was easy. Getting into the queen's bed was only marginally more difficult . . .

. . . In the candlelight the sheen on Guinevere's upper lip, together with the uncontrolled urgency of her movements, indicated that it was time for Griswold to give his attention to the matter in hand. First, however, it was necessary for him to reassume his dominance for it was vital that her forthcoming fulfilment was felt to be completely due to him.

With a grunt and a heave he reversed their positions and set to with a will, although in one small part of his mind, some curious, somewhat musical sounds drifting through the window threatened to break his concentration.

Dimly he realized that the music had been going on for some while and, from its unearthly quality, it was clear that Merlin was back at the cottage.

No doubt the old man is celebrating another wizardly victory, thought Griswold, picturing Merlin jigging around triumphantly as he did on such occasions to his own musical accompaniment. He trusted that the wizard's victory would be as fruitful as his own . . . and as pleasant.

And with that he abandoned all thoughts of Merlin and all grip on self-control, as Guinevere entwined her limbs gratefully round him and thought not of Lancelot, nor of Arthur, nor least of all of England.

'Ah! Yes, yes, yes. Oh, mmmm!'

He continued.

'Oh, Griswold. Faster, faster.'

He went faster.

She also went faster, and in remarkable unison, considering the indiscriminate urgency of her foregoing convolutions.

'Ooooh . . . Ooooh. Yes. Oh. Mmmm. YES. Ohh, Gris — WULK?'

She gulped. She frowned.

Something was amiss. Where the exquisite, about-to-burst completeness had just been . . . there was nothing. Where the deep-muscled chest had burned against hers there was but a cool draught flickering over her naked body.

She opened her eyes.

No craggy face. No burning eyes.

She raised her head up and stared through encircled arms within which there were no rippling shoulders, between hovering knees

47

and locked ankles beneath which there were no pumping buttocks. She stared at nothing but the bolted oak door in the far wall.

Sir Griswold had vanished.

Lady Guinevere, very confused and not a little peeved, abandoned woman's most ungainly and powerful posture, rolled on to her knees and leaned over to peer under the bed. Neither sadist nor jester met her eyes. She leaned a little further, squinting into the dusty gloom. Frustration and disbelief gave way to rage as she leaned too far and, with a scrabbling of long limbs, toppled off the bed.

As she lay sprawled on the stone floor it was some while before she understood that her shivering was not due to a lively and singularly frustrating dream, but to the fact that beneath her naked body lay a pair of very cold and soggy breeches.

History does not record that Queen Guinevere, destined up to this particular moment in time to become King Arthur's successor to the throne of England, had waited nearly twenty years since their first meeting to be seduced by the man for whom Sir Lancelot was but a barely adequate second best.

Nor does history relate that, just as her true motive for his capture was about to be realized, Sir Griswold was being sucked through the depths of Time on his way towards fulfilling the desire of another being.

Which was quite remarkable, for the being in question had been and gone long before Griswold had been born, while the desire in question would not be born for many centuries.

History is very confusing until seen in retrospect.

Chapter 8

Merlin the Enchanter awoke with the birds, ate a hearty breakfast and stepped out from his cottage into the heavy-misted morn. Over his tunic and breeches he wore a thick cloak beneath which was hidden a leather purse of belongings. He closed the door behind him, waved vaguely at the cottage with one hand and strode away without a backward glance, down the hill towards the town.

The cottage waited until the old man had disappeared round the curve of the hill. Then it faded into nowhere and settled down to wait for his return.

The cold mist became thicker as he neared the floor of the valley. It allowed only the nearest trees and bushes into view and stripped them of all colour, leaving them grey and lifeless, receding into lighter greys before disappearing from sight. The grim symbolism, though coincidental, was not lost on him. He cast a petulant glance at the heavens.

'My last day and Thou hast to make it overcast.'

The silence was complete save for the occasional morning bird somewhere out of sight and the quiet pad of his shoes on the spongy ground. Before long his hair and whiskers were glistening wet.

After a steady hour's walk he heard the rhythmic clang of metal on metal ringing faintly through the mist.

Rowan the blacksmith was a massive man who rose every morning long before the other townsfolk and worked steadily through the day, making and mending weapons, fashioning plough-shares and shoeing horses.

When he had first arrived in the town some ten years ago and began to work at first light each day the people of Camelot found it impossible to sleep, but, since he was a youngish man with hands like shovels, only the women dared to complain. He was also a man of few words and had no wife to enforce the women's complaints, so the village learned to sleep through the noise.

The sounds grew louder and gradually the smithy appeared out of the mist. It was little more than a roof on posts with a forge burning beneath. It had only one wall at the back which was covered in shelves stacked with work to be done. On the posts were hooks loaded with horseshoes and bridles. In the midst of this stood the blacksmith, already sweating, his great arm rising and falling upon his anvil.

Merlin was within a few feet of him before he glanced up briefly without breaking his rhythm, then down again, having observed the courtesy of acknowledging the other's presence.

'Good morning, blacksmith.'

The blacksmith nodded without looking up again.

'Busy?'

The blacksmith threw an impassive glance at the sagging shelves. When it became apparent that no further answer was forthcoming Merlin suddenly found it imperative that he flick the wetness from his whiskers and shake his cloak vigorously. Drops of water scattered and arched, sizzling in the fire and tickling the calloused hand holding the tongs. The blacksmith lowered his hammer and let it rest on the anvil. He turned his broad Nordic face patiently to the wizard.

'What can I do for ye, Merlin?'

'I need a horse and . . . a pendant.'

'Of what metal?'

'Iron.'

'Design?'

Merlin reached under his cloak and drew a small piece of parchment from the purse beneath. He held it out. The blacksmith laid down his hammer, took the parchment carefully and examined it. There were two designs, one for each side of the coin-shaped piece which was a thumb's length in diameter.

'I'll have it done in two days,' said the blacksmith.

'I need it by this evening.'

'How much would ye like to pay this evening?'

'Two ducats for the horse and . . . two for the pendant.'

'Two ducats for the horse, five for the pendant and the three that ye's owed me this twelve month.'

'. . . six for the horse and pendant and six later.'

'When?'

'On my return to Camelot.'

'From where?'

'I go in search of an acquaintance.'

'Then I'll have the money now, Merlin. I'll not wait a lifetime for ye to return from London.'

For an instant Merlin was too stunned to react. His face fell before he could catch it and he stared in disbelief at the expressionless eyes holding his own.

In spite of the hot fire crackling between them Merlin felt the cold of the mist sweep through him. He covered his alarm with a snort.

'London! That stench-ridden village. Why would I wish to go there?'

The blacksmith shrugged. 'Sir Griswold has gone there to escape the queen's wrath . . .' He thrust the tongs back into the fire. '. . . who better to seek him out than Merlin the Enchanter?'

So, thought Merlin, relaxing quietly and unnoticed, Lady Fortune has at last favoured me with a smile of sorts. While Camelot and History believe that to be the reason for my disappearance I stand a good chance of reaching this Dimmot without detection.

'Thou art a man of perception,' he chuckled to the blacksmith as he silently offered a word of thanks to Lady Fortune, tempered only by his reservation at her tardiness . . . and her sense of humour.

The blacksmith, ignoring his flattery, came back to the point.

'So ye'll be away for a while.'

'Yes.'

The big man carefully inspected the glowing horseshoe, saying nothing.

Merlin sighed, delved into his purse and handed the man twelve ducats. Ducats and parchment went into a side pocket.

'The horse and pendant will be ready for ye by evening,' said Rowan, picking up his hammer.

Merlin gave a grunt and was about to leave when a thought stopped him in his tracks.

'Er, one more thing, ahm . . . blacksmith.'

The man's hammer, still resting on the anvil, suddenly became of great interest to the magician, who seemed to have difficulty withdrawing his gaze in order to look the blacksmith in the eye.

He coughed.

'Bearing in mind the requirements pertaining to the crafting of magical implements . . . Ahm . . . do I have thine assurance that thou art still . . . er . . .'

A slight pinkness came to his ears for the blacksmith was nothing if not a manly man. With an impassive but definitely mocking smile Rowan offered obligingly, 'Chaste?'

For a second or two he appeared to give this some thought.

'I can assure ye, Merlin,' he said, fingering the ducats in his pocket, 'that our agreement still stands. I have not yet known a woman.'

Had Merlin not had a considerable amount on his mind he might have noticed the slight tremor that occurs whenever the fabric of Truth is stretched a little.

Without further ado he gave a nod, turned on his heel and strode off into the mist towards the castle.

He reached the castle within the hour and crossed the drawbridge. In the courtyard the sergeant-at-arms was addressing a troop of twenty or so soldiers, two or three of whom looked a little the worse for wear.

'Been fighting amongst themselves,' thought Merlin disdainfully. 'No self-discipline.'

The troops were fully armed and had sleeping gear and food supplies at their sides. Sergeant Belkin walked along the ranks inspecting each soldier with a critical eye.

'Belkin,' called the wizard. 'What's this?'

'We leave for London to search for Sir Griswold,' replied the sergeant without taking his eyes from his troops.

'Fruitless,' scoffed Merlin as he swept past. 'Fruitless.'

He crossed the courtyard and went up the steps to the upper floor. Belkin turned to glance at his retreating back and mumbled quietly, 'Indeed.'

Following the familiar corridors Merlin headed towards the

queen's bedroom. On turning the final corner he found the way barred by two young guards.

'Stand aside. I wish to see the queen.'

'The queen sleeps, Master Merlin,' said one. 'Perhaps she had another late night,' he added with a grin. The other guard sniggered.

Merlin glared.

'What?' he growled. 'Dost think to mock thy queen? Dost dare to imply some imperfection therein?' His bony finger pointed at the door as his eyes held theirs.

The older one shrugged, smiling. 'What d'ye want, old man?'

Merlin stiffened, but his eyes remained ice-blue.

'I wish to see the queen,' he repeated quietly.

The guard shook his head, saying nothing.

'It is important that I see Queen Guinevere this morning.'

'Ye'll have to return later.'

'I demand thou let me through,' insisted Merlin, raising a hand threateningly towards them.

The guards grinned easily. 'While we stand between thee and the door, old man, the queen will not be disturbed. Now be gone and return later . . . tomorrow perhaps.'

For a second despair swept across the wizard's face. He turned as if to go.

The soldiers exchanged smiles as they shifted their weight boldly. Then, snapping the fingers of his raised hand, Merlin twizzled full circle and skipped between them as they stood frozen, the smiles fixed foolishly on their faces.

Inside the door he stepped across the room and stared down at the sleeping queen. The bed covers had fallen away to reveal her naked shoulders and breasts. The wizard fondly regarded her familiar face. Gently he pulled the covers up over her shoulders. He allowed himself an amused smile.

'Guinevere,' he whispered softly.

For a moment the queen did not move. Then her eyelids gave a slight flutter and opened. She gave a small, surprised smile.

'Uncle Merlin.'

She pulled a hand from under the covers and held it out towards him. He took it gently in his and sat down beside her.

'Good morning, child. Didst thou sleep well?'

The queen nodded.

'And thee?' she asked.

'Well enough,' he answered.

'But not long enough, Uncle Merlin. Thou lookest so tired.'

'In truth I didn't sleep that well.'

'And in truth my night was a little disturbed.' She went on quickly, 'Oh, Uncle, it's good to see thee again, but what art thou doing here?'

She didn't bother to ask how he got past the guards. Merlin stared down at the woman who was still, to him, a maid, a child, a new-born baby saved from still-birth by his own hand, and he was overcome by a wave of sadness. With eyes that he willed to remain dry he drank in her odd beauty that it might last in his memory throughout the centuries ahead. Then, as her smile turned to a quizzical frown, he pulled himself up quickly and said gruffly, 'Tricks.'

'Tricks?'

'Games. The courtyard is awash with soldiers preparing to leave for London in search of Sir Griswold des Arbres. Thou art up to thy tricks again, assuming the role of monarch.'

'In Arthur's abse . . .'

'Griswold's capture is not for thee to decide.'

At these words Guinevere's mind began to race. She looked closely into Merlin's eyes. 'Perhaps thou hast already decided. Perhaps thou hast already spirited him away out of reach of the king's justice.'

'I do not *spirit* people away,' returned Merlin. 'Griswold has not been spirited away. He has been driven away by a young lady who aspires to rise above her station. And now, to compound thy foolishness, thou hast decided to send a troop of Arthur's best soldiers off on a fruitless errand. With Arthur's return imminent thou wouldst reduce his army by twenty good men, one sergeant worth five and a knight worth another twenty.'

For long seconds the queen held his gaze as if to retain a grip on her authority, but the logic of his words was inescapable except for one small detail. Having admitted that he had laid a false trail towards London the previous evening, Griswold would hardly be likely to run there now. Her gesture of sending Sergeant Belkin and his troops after the knight would be even more fruitless than Merlin himself realized.

Nevertheless she still needed to establish her 'innocence'.

She changed direction and pouted at the wizard.

'Very well, what dost thou suggest?'

'It happens that I am headed for London this evening. 'Tis obvious that, if Griswold is there, then I am best suited to find him. But . . .' He paused for effect.

'Yes?'

'If I return with him the lad is not to be sentenced or harmed in any way until King Arthur decrees it.'

Shortly afterwards Merlin bade the young queen farewell, his heart heavy, and heavier yet because he could not confide that this farewell would almost certainly be their last. That he was forced to indulge in such deceit to ensure Griswold's safety pained him deeply.

If Guinevere's deceit gave her any pain, the relief of knowing that her night of passion, albeit thwarted, remained as yet undiscovered was an effective panacea. What disturbed her most was that, if Griswold hadn't been sucked from her presence by wizardly means, why had the beastly son of a hog's breath walked out on her at such an ill-timed moment?

It would be some time before the truth reached her ears.

Merlin closed the door behind him and edged past the guards. With another snap of his fingers he wandered off down the corridor deep in thought. Their frozen smiles returned to life, their bodies relaxed with renewed swagger.

'Now be gone and return later . . . tomorrow perhaps,' said the taller one.

Merlin nodded absently and disappeared round the corner.

Towards evening he left Rowan the blacksmith and rode noisily through the town, heading east. When he was out of sight of Camelot he turned north, and then west towards the Mendip Hills.

And Goatchurch Cavern.

Chapter 9

1987: The Time of the First Unborn

WISHER: a minor form of wizard whose one talent is the ability to influence events around him by the power of Wishing.

Wishing is a non-hereditary, apparently random talent of uncertain nature and is latent in all men in varying degrees. This talent can cast an influence over many people at once, sometimes thousands.

However, the passive, even negative nature of this talent, i.e. the abandonment of one's responsibilities to real or imagined powers outside oneself, makes it a random and potentially self-destructive force. Because of the extreme difficulty in exercising control and the possible catastrophic effects of uncontrolled and indiscriminate Wishing, it has always been denounced by true wizards as potentially evil and shunned accordingly.

Wizards and witches of a darker persuasion have, of course, attempted either to harness this power or to use it indiscriminately, with little success.

Wishers have appeared at various times throughout Earth's history, often having far-reaching effects on civilization, sometimes for better, sometimes for worse. Apart from sharing a similar power, Wishers have nothing in common. Some use their power to devastating effect. Others do not know that it exists.

A comprehensive list of Wishers, real and mythical, appears in Appendix 758 at the end of this volume.

Encyclopaedia Esoterica,
first edition AD 2706

James Dimmot was in a philosophical mood as he tumbled through the blizzard to the river below.

Down just about sums it up, he thought. Why, when one comes into the world completely helpless, should one end up feeling more helpless than when one started? Why did I so nearly achieve so many things, only to be dumped on my arse at the last moment? I'm intelligent. I went to the right schools, landed the right jobs, married the right girls. Why did I make a mess of everything I touched? Strange.

Almost, he thought, as though a sadistic guardian angel had willed it.

Or an enemy.

Lord knows, he'd had plenty of those in his time. Nothing violent or potentially terminal for he didn't move in those circles, but socially or within the confines of his various careers he seemed to attract enemies with ease, becoming an early victim of their intrigues and political manoeuvres. He was not one of life's manipulators, but one of life's manipulated.

The raincoat flapped up over his face, obscuring from sight the swirling snow and the streetlights ranged along the river bank and exposing his splayed body from ankles to armpits.

Story of my life, he thought. So busy showing everyone that I had the balls, I was unable to see the light.

Dimmot continued his plummet to oblivion, untroubled by the fact that the imperfection of his analogy was itself a fairly perfect analogy of his entire life.

This time, he thought happily, I can't fail. Nothing and nobody can stop me now.

For an infinitely brief instant he wished with all his heart and soul that he could have had one more stab at life, one more chance to succeed, to feel that his life had been worth something.

Then, before this wish could reach the level of his conscious mind, his heart got back to the job of pumping adrenaline and gin into his brain while his soul took the wish off his hands and dutifully dropped it into the depths of Infinity. There, apart from engaging in a brief chat with another soul currently engaged in a pitched battle against lethal odds, it made barely a ripple.

The irony of Dimmot's only chance of success being to commit the ultimate failure would have brought a wry smile to his lips. Only he had no time left to consider it. He was six feet from the ice-studded Thames when a horrendous, shaggy figure burst from the black water, roared, 'Biiitch!' and flung its arms round him.

Chapter 10

It was the first time that Merlin had entered the cavern to find it empty. In the past Uther would always be there waiting but now he was off on his jaunts, ignorant of Merlin's current plans.

The old king alone had shared the secret of Merlin's mission, but now it was best that even he be unaware that Merlin was embarking on a time-spanning journey. Uther, while having his heart in the right place, so to speak, was loose-tongued on occasion. This, together with his tendency to trot around Eternity at will, decreed that he had to be left in ignorance for the time being.

Merlin sat himself down on the ledge and checked all his inner functions while he waited for the pounding in his temples to cease. With relief he found everything to be in order. All that needed to be done was the final assimilation of his morning meal.

The idea of one's breakfast fermenting and eating its way through one's stomach was not to be countenanced, he thought.

He closed his eyes and turned his mind inward, speeding up his bodily functions until every last grain had been broken down and absorbed into his body. This done, he delved into his leather bag and brought out a small earthenware bottle. Without hesitation he pulled out the stopper, drained the contents in one gulp, replaced the stopper carefully and returned the bottle to the bag which he then thrust under his cloak. He pulled the hood over his head, wrapped the cloak firmly round his body and the bag and, lowering himself to the ground, sat on the trailing end of the cloak, ensuring that his legs and ankles were cushioned from the hard rock beneath him.

He sat quietly waiting.

Before long a warm glow began to spread through his body,

filling his head, arms, legs, his whole being with a vibrant, throbbing heat. The heat grew until it radiated from him and seemed to reach the farthest walls of the cavern and bounce back, warming him from outside as well as in. The throbbing became more pronounced, a double beat that echoed that of his own heart, berboomp, berboomp, thudding through his small body and filling his head to the exclusion of all else.

Soon each breath had to be taken bit by bit between beats until his lungs were full and the next beat would send the hard-won air bursting from him, forcing him to fight anew for another breath.

Then, as quickly as it came, the heat died back to the first warm glow, leaving his mind and body floating, basking in an inner sunlight that radiated from the centre of his being. It seemed to shimmer under his eyelids and to nudge gently under the nails of his fingers and toes. It darted playfully beneath the top of his skull and rolled along his thighs and across his back, before settling to a soft, still, comfortable numbness throughout.

Now he knew that the potion had entered every cell of his body, embalming, preserving, ensuring that he would remain intact, completely whole and unchanged.

Ready for his awakening.

Now let's see if the mind within this body is equal to the task, he thought.

Had his body been able to respond to his feelings it might have begun to sweat, to tremble even, but it was as if the shell and the life within it were things apart.

He wondered if this was the way Uther felt in his disembodied freedom.

Pushing all other thoughts aside, he wrote the year 1956, the year of James Dimmot's seventh and most crucial birthday, in square, solid figures of burnished bronze in his mind's eye and stared at it for long seconds. As he did so he recited a spell used by the few magicians who knew the true nature of the local cosmology and who had had the courage to commit themselves, unprotected and totally vulnerable, to its whims.

'*I call upon the golden sun whose fire doth burn without, that I might burn within.*'

The figures took on the colour of the sun, flickering and flashing across the darkness and filling his vision with golden bronze.

'*I call upon the silver moon whose heavenly proximity doth ensure the ebb and flow of my body's life tides.*'

The gold gave way to sparkling silver that flowed over and around the surfaces of the figures, shimmering. Then, in accordance with the wizard's words, other colours took over, flashing, throbbing or merging, changing the bronze into exquisite, indefinable hues.

'*I call upon little, grey Mercury, whose path does spin, quicksilvered, round the sun.*

'*I call upon green Venus, goddess of peace, and Mars, the bloodred warlord, whose paths through the heavens straddle mine own betimes, my she, my he, my love, my hate, my yes, my no, a delicate balance.*

'*I call upon the thundrous blue Jupiter, lord of the skies, whose power commands a dozen worlds and reaches across the heavens to inspire this humble self.*

'*I call upon sad, ponderous Saturn, trudging through the darkness farthest from the sun, beyond my senses' reach, almost.*

'*On the border of death itself.*

'*As am I.*

'*I commit myself to all of thee until the time when I must rise again and stand against the forces of Evil which would overcome Man and which would, in time, seek to rule thee.*'

Deep within his unconscious, senses of which mortal men were only dimly aware stirred. Those senses felt the subtle forces of the sun, the moon and planets with moons of their own maintaining a delicate, ever-changing balance with the world that entombed him. They measured that balance, felt its trends, related it to the glittering and pulsating picture before him of a point fourteen centuries ahead in time.

And they relayed a message down, down to the one part of him that could not feign death because it was beyond death.

They relayed a message to his soul.

The gist of the message was, 'Wake me up when it's time for work.'

This done, he erased the year from his mind, making the figures dissolve into bronze vapour and vanish into nothing.

Unlocking the mental compartment in which the lethal formula had been kept, he allowed it to unfold and expand before him, a vast, incomprehensible organism, each tiny symbol a living nucleus buried in its own cell. The whole thing throbbed and ebbed spasmodically, changing its shape like some obscene malevolence.

But Merlin was uncowed.

He held the formula in front of him, refusing to focus his mind on it, letting thoughts of Camelot, Guinevere and Griswold flow and swirl through his head, thoughts that were terribly, terribly painful. Realizing that they were about to overcome him and destroy his resolve he fought to erase them, only to find that some other part of him was also fighting to retain them.

It was as if some outside force was trying to break his will, but he knew that the force was within himself.

That first step on the journey away from his beloved home in the sixth century was, he now realized, the most difficult step he would ever take. He felt his resolve crumbling and, with a cry that, unable to reach the dormant muscles of his throat, echoed like thunder round his mind, he pulled himself together, driving out his memories and grimly focusing his thoughts on the formula.

He allowed the myriad of individual symbols to find their places in the different parts of his brain, letting them flow along their preordained pathways, to mingle, relate and disperse in accordance with their individual laws of mathematics, creating new and counteractive relationships, effecting closures of open-ended strands of curiosity, balancing and cancelling each other out; countermanding the signals created by other parts, gathering up and steering errant thoughts into areas where opposing thoughts were waiting to bring about a mutual resolution.

Soon the separate parts of the formula had each done their work. A hundred million synapses, relieved of their need to function, ceased to do so. Merlin's mind had been completely closed down.

Total stillness echoed through the halls of the Enchanter's memory.

Chapter 11

Wishers, 20th century.

Dommit, James, circa *1949–?*

Little known early Briton, certainly mythical, discovered recently by historians investigating an unexplained and apparently supernatural manifestation recorded by the main computer system at the World Sperm Bank in AD 2090.

Beliefs regarding Dommit's connection with this event proved to be unfounded – obviously, since he would have had to be approximately 140 years of age. People in that era rarely lived more than sixty years.

Furthermore, legend indicates that James Dommit is meant to have disappeared and/or committed suicide, date and reason unknown, having made no impression on history whatsoever.

Encyclopaedia Esoterica,
revised edition AD 2845,
Appendix 758

As the creature from the Thames rose up to meet him James Dimmot caught a glimpse of dripping black hair and whiskers, glaring eyes and a massive, naked body sporting a purposeful and singularly daunting erection.

'Whatever happened to pink elephants?' he thought. In the next instant the impact of their collision tore the breath from his body and brought both of them to a crashing halt so that for a second they hung suspended above the water, eye to eye in a lewd embrace. Then, locked together, they plunged beneath the surface for what Dimmot imagined would be an Eternity of torment at the hands of a ferocious, horny demon. While Dimmot's body spasmed and sucked desperately at the foul water, his brain, mercifully cushioned from the pain by the alcohol, had in it only one resigned and fast-fading thought:

I just hope Eternity's not as long as it's made out to be.

Eternity lasted some ten seconds, in which he and his companion struggled beneath the Thames. Time seemed to be suspended as Dimmot floated in his own personal eternity in which the only sensations were ones which he least expected. He felt no pain, no cold, only the smooth skin of a heavily muscled arm and a rhythmic jerking as the creature appeared to be dragging him to some unknown lair.

He heard gentle thuds as the blocks of ice juggled together above his head.

Nothing else.

Noise and life rudely returned as they broke through the surface. The creature was roaring as if in pain, the wind was whistling across the ice, Dimmot was coughing, spluttering, and crying out in agony as sobriety coursed through his veins. He felt himself being twisted round. The creature was behind him, its arm about his neck.

It's going to throttle me, he thought and the relief at being reprieved from a fate worse than death was immediately replaced by a frantic indignation.

I don't believe it. I can't even get to die in the way that I want.

He struggled with desperate rage, straining to force his mouth beneath the surface where the filthy water would rob him of the little pocket of breath left in his shuddering lungs. His body arched and stiffened like a child's. It twisted and kicked. Sobs of frustration hissed from his lips. The arm round his neck tightened its grip, but in spite of the demon's terrifying strength, Dimmot almost succeeded in breaking free. Then the creature raised its other arm into the night and brought the great fist down on his temple.

For an instant that unique, uncomprehending shock that comes from an unexpected blow to the head drove out the pain assaulting his body and froze the power in his limbs.

A blinding flash of awareness screamed mockingly at him. 'This is the moment that your whole life has been leading up to. A good smack round the head. And it's not one iota more or less than you sodding well deserve.'

Any thoughts concerning a future which, by all nature's known laws, should have been curtailed some seconds earlier, faded as blackness overcame him and he knew no more.

Chapter 12

Deep, deep below the City of London is a room.

In theory it is impenetrable.

Cosmic radiation cannot enter. Electro-magnetism cannot pierce its shield.

No wave forms of any description can squeeze past its defences. The flow of Time does not pass through but round.

It is designed that way for a purpose.

In the room is a man. He is indescribably old.

Ancient. And as deathly white as the room is deadly black. He is, of course, a prisoner. Has been for . . . a long time.

And he has a secret.

He cannot leave the room. That is impossible, even for him.

And yet.

'Dammit,' he grumbles once every few months.

He doesn't sleep. He doesn't eat. He sits shivering with an inner cold, aware that a tear has been trying to form in the corner of one eye for several years, and unable to remember if its failure to do so is due to a formidable act of will on his part or an almost total lack of fluid within his body.

'Dammit,' he grumbles.

Sometimes he has a visitor. Just one. Very seldom.

The visitor comes to mock. Or to smile. Or sometimes just to stare.

Then he goes.

'Dammit,' says the old man and he tries to coax the tear to swell and fall.

He wonders if his secret isn't a secret after all, but just a dream.

Wishful thinking. Something to hold on to.

'Dammit.'

Chapter 13

Dimmot awoke to pain and cold such as he'd never known. The shock of his near-fatal dip had driven all the alcohol from his system and replaced it with ice. His head throbbed, his muscles cringed, his fingers and elbows ached, his thighs and groin shuddered while his buttocks, for some reason, felt as if they were on fire.

He was less than philosophical.

Dear God Almighty, he thought. I've made the biggest mistake of my stupid life. Whatever happened to Heaven and Blissful Eternity?

Before he could consider an answer to the unanswerable his distraught senses began to register sound ebbing and flowing like waves on a distant shore. He wondered how the tide had managed to carry his corpse as far as the estuary mouth.

I can't have been dead that long. I'm not even stiff yet.

Somehow the logic of this observation was washed away bit by bit with each roll of the tide. The sound of the waves was becoming less wave-like and more disturbingly familiar.

Unwillingly he opened his eyes. The sight that appeared before him both terrified him and threw him into total confusion. Above him, still dripping water, was the face of the creature from the Underworld, although by some reasoning totally beyond Dimmot's grasp, its presence testified to the galling fact that Dimmot was still alive.

His feelings were mixed.

The creature's breathing, heavy from exertion, ebbed and flowed rhythmically as it leaned over him with burning eyes.

'Thou art not Guinevere,' said Griswold accusingly.

'No,' said Dimmot.

'Who then?'

'Dimmot,' whispered Dimmot.

The dark eyes glared menacingly.

'Thou art demon, Dimmot.'

'Demon! Christ, no!'

'Thou camest from out of the sky.'

'I came from off the bridge. You came from out of the water.'

'By thy hand.'

'What?'

'Thou didst spirit me here.'

'Spirit? I don't even know you.'

He stared in disbelief. This is ridiculous, he thought. A loony, swimming around naked in midwinter, leaps out of the Thames and grabs me. Perfectly understandable, 90 per cent proof hallucination. But now I'm sober, why is the crazy bastard talking like Laurence Olivier and blaming *me* for him being here?

He felt his sense of reality wavering before him and he stared fearfully at the maniac, praying that his protest would not incense the man to beat him to pulp.

Surprisingly the ferocious brows relaxed. The man sat back on his haunches, deep in thought, seemingly unaware of either the cold or his nakedness.

Dimmot turned his head carefully and ventured a furtive glance around.

They were in some sort of derelict room, sheltered from the wind, but with boarded windows through which an icy draught and occasional snowflakes swirled. The light from London's streetlamps, enhanced by the all-embracing snow, glimmered through the gaps in the doorframe and windows.

Dimmot heard wind and water dripping from the holes in the roof and more water lapping against the concrete that bordered the deserted Thames. Apparently the man sitting beside him had brought him here. I've got a feeling he's recently saved my life, sod 'im, he thought.

He gave Griswold a sidelong glance, noting with relief that the cold had put paid to the unaccountable erection, although he retained a grudging admiration for the man having achieved it in the first place, considering the circumstances. Warily he cast his gaze over the man's body and was amazed to see the numerous scars that adorned it, some deep and angry, and many criss-crossing his arms and wrists.

Dimmot wondered if the wounds were self-inflicted and a shudder ran through him. With it came a renewed awareness of the bitter cold and the pounding of his bruised temple. A groan escaped his lips and the big man pulled up sharply from his reverie, bringing his eyes back to focus on Dimmot's pained features. To Dimmot's surprise an expression of concern crossed the craggy face and the man stood up quickly as if having reached a decision. 'Can we get food and shelter in this land of ice?'

Dimmot frowned at the strange question, but answered quickly, 'Yes, if you know where.'

'*Dost* thou know where?'

'Well, of course . . . yes, certainly.'

'Is it far?'

Dimmot hesitated. He guessed that they couldn't be far from Tower Bridge, no further than the distance they were carried while swimming for the bank. Probably Butler's Wharf adjacent to the bridge itself, judging by the closeness of the water.

'Just a short walk from here.'

His spirits rose a little. Once we're outside I'll lose this ding-dong and get back to my room and a warm bed, he thought. I don't really fancy another go at the bridge. Not while I'm sober anyway.

'Come,' said Griswold. 'We must start moving or the cold will rob our limbs of the will to move.'

He walked to the door and opened it an inch or two to peer out into the snow.

'Do the thieves and vagabonds of this land come out at night in such weather?'

So matter-of-fact was his tone that, for a second, Dimmot actually gave thought to the question. He pictured dark, vague outlines of horsemen trudging through the snow, intent on mayhem and murder amongst unsuspecting victims who cowered from the weather in their cottages.

Oh my God, Dimmot, what are you doing? he thought. He's the barmy one, not you. Anyway, no mugger in his right mind would be out on a night like this. For a start he'd be hard pushed to find someone to mug.

Squinting up at Griswold he said carefully, 'No thief or vaga-bond in his right mind would be out on a night like this. For a st – '

'Indeed,' replied Griswold. 'I thought the inhabitants might be as hardy as the weather.'

'It isn't always like this,' grumbled Dimmot, feeling oddly defensive, as if the man were some sort of foreigner. Definitely time to leave, he thought and tried to rise to his feet, only to fall back with a cry of pain. To his surprise, the big man caught him in mid-fall and lowered him gently to the floor.

'What ails thee?'

A generally frustrating evening topped off with the relief of knowing that he was not about to suffer grievous bodily harm from the lunatic gave rise to a burst of fearless indignation.

'Just about every bloody thing ails me from the toes up. I can't stand, I'm so cold every bit of me aches, my arse is on fire and my head's bursting from that clout you gave me,' he retorted, raising his fingers gingerly to his temple.

At this the puzzled expression that had come over Griswold's face cleared and he said, 'Ahm, yes. Were it not for that . . . clount?'

'Clout.'

'Clout . . . thou'dst have drowned for certain.'

His voice held no hint of apology as he bent down and hauled Dimmot easily to his feet.

'Come. We must find food and shelter. Then thou canst tell me more about this unGodly land and where I can get a horse, maps and a sword. There are scores to be settled when I get home and a friend who needs my help.'

Griswold stepped out into the blizzard and gazed warily round the deserted alien landscape. Except for the unusually uniform rows of lights bordering the river he saw nothing but snow covering what must be the rocks and hillocks familiar to the terrain. He could see no more than a dozen yards in any direction.

He turned and beckoned.

'Come. Thou must lead us to thy place of safety.'

Reluctantly Dimmot crept out and stood beside him, shivering with the cold and the beginnings of mild shock. Despair was settling about him like a sodden blanket. There was no way that he was going to be able to run away from this nutcase unless the bloke succumbed to the cold. And Dimmot knew with horrible certainly that the man would hold out long after Dimmot had reached rigor mortis.

He must be trained to go through this sort of hell. Not even a maniac could survive in this if he weren't used to it. Then he shuddered as a wild, ludicrous thought occurred to him. Oh, my God. I'll bet he's SAS. A trained killer with homicidal tendencies.

His stomach churned and he stumbled unwillingly against Griswold as nausea and faintness overcame him. Griswold reached down and steadied him with an arm that could break a neck without even straining. Dimmot fought for breath and a vestige of his own sanity.

Staring up at the other man he ventured fearfully, 'Who dares wins?'

A gentle, persuasive hand on his back coaxed him forward.

'Indeed,' said Griswold. 'Lead on.'

Chapter 14

The balance of the cosmos, ever changing, ever shifting, commanding that the greatest stars and the smallest particles yield to its whim, flows throughout all that was and is and ever will be.

And everything that is, is a slave thereof for the balance is all and without it all is lost.

Only two kinds of men exist: those that know this not and ever strive to break bonds of which they know not; and he who accepts his enslavement and so uses it for his own ends.

While they are slaves and are many he becomes his own master.

Encyclopaedia Esoterica,
preface to an early edition

Like the well-oiled components of some celestial alarm clock the nine planets of the solar system and their attendant moons spun into their preordained, vastly distant positions in space. Briefly, they formed the unique matrix of forces for which a sleeping soul had been waiting for fourteen hundred years. Without pause they moved on, unknowing and uncaring.

The soul of Merlin the Enchanter twitched, yawned and stretched into the shape needed to sustain and power the entity known as man. Drawing the force of the Cosmos into itself and dispersing it throughout the cells of his brain, his soul carefully reawakened one function after another. Dormant signals came to life. Familiar symbols sprang unbidden into existence. The dreadful formula that had filled his mind fourteen centuries earlier was beginning to re-form. First the conclusion, then the symbols preceding it, progressively back to the beginning and, as each symbol reappeared, it was confronted and attacked with ruthless deliberation.

The wizard stirred.

His soul worked on, knowing that if any part of the formula were allowed to remain, it could rise up in an unguarded moment and drag him down into the depths where coma, paralysis or madness lay in wait.

Soon, distorted, harshly coloured dreams filled Merlin's brain as realities from his past struggled to come into focus. Faces grew and swirled through his mind, twisted as if seen through buckled mirrors, some recognizable, some new.

Guinevere rose up, cross-eyed and scrawny-necked but still lavishly beautiful, her lascivious smile parting lips that curled back over her face and swallowed it, leaving another new face in view. Griswold appeared, the only living being before whom Merlin could still reveal his full powers. Griswold's furrowed forehead fell in on itself, leaving only a grimace of defiance on a mouth which snapped this way and that at the symbols trying to dissolve it. Then the mouth vanished under a squirming mass of mathematics.

The wizard whimpered.

The ghastly symbols heaved and washed over Griswold, hiding him from view. Then a mighty, calloused hand thrust through the surface and, in an instant, solved a complex hypothesis which was hovering above the knight, trying to twist his mind into an insane, multi-dimensional spiral. Griswold demonstrated his understanding of the immutable interrelationship of the various elements of the hypothesis by crushing them into a mess of indistinguishable gruel.

With a triumphant sneer the knight faded as other faces blossomed and billowed across the embattled terrain of the Enchanter's mental landscape, some to be set upon and dissolved by drooling hieroglyphics, others surrounded, squeezed and crushed into the shape of their Euclidean aggressors that bit at them like multi-legged Jack Russells.

Snatches of the poem given him by the Book became images in his mind. A ghastly figure that was himself, made up only of the parts of him that were reawakened, stood shimmering in the bright sunlight. His outer skin had not yet come to life and his inner organs lay revealed, pulsating and steaming in the sun.

He was eyeless, limbless and without a complete brain, but he was climbing laboriously up a spire of Time's dark castle. Then the spire crumbled beneath him in a swirl of dust and great hewn stones, and he was being dragged down, choking and suffocating, by skinny grasping digits and symbols.

From the song that was the key to the Book's secrets horrendous chords trembled and backed away from the vicious onslaught of snarling demons of temporal trigonometry and the words were choked off in mid-sentence.

'Man is *glulckf*', 'Everyman is MMM!' sank beneath marauding variables and genocidal constants.

Deep in the very core of the Enchanter raged a battle between the essence of life and a lifeless predatory abstract concept.

And the formula was winning.

And, in that zone between the timeless death from which he was struggling to escape and the life that he was trying to return to, hung Merlin's soul, usually content to lie hidden, ticking over just fast enough to keep the wizard alive. Now it was combing around the Infinite, searching desperately for help.

In doing so Merlin's soul came across faces that were only names to the wizard himself, names of people he'd spoken to after a fashion, names of people he'd had cause to practise a certain degree of persuasion on, people who'd been useful, no, vital to his cause.

People like William Wordsworth, Malory, Yeats and Geoffrey of Monmouth (a particularly open-minded and handy chap).

Albert Einstein came briefly into focus, his kindly face reflecting benevolence and love for Mankind before dissolving into some sort of cloudy mushroom that burst into the sunlight and then broke up and blew away, its spores spreading over the little world that was Merlin's home, falling on people who then turned into various forms of misshapen gnomes and dwarves.

Then came the old man.

Older than Merlin himself. As old, in fact, as the wizard and several of his incarnations, before and after, put together. And terribly, terribly white, as if drained of life long since and waiting for his formal application for entry into the Infinite to be stamped by a sadistically pedantic frontier guard.

Which, in a way, he was.

In his equally white and unmoving robes he looked less like an old man and more like something that would sink the *Titanic*. Merlin's soul did not recognize him or have any inkling why he should be within the compass of the wizard's existence but, being Merlin's soul, it recognized irritability when it saw it.

'Dammit,' said the old man in a hoarse croak that promised to be his last, but which, to his apparently intense dissatisfaction, wasn't.

'At last, dammit. Find him, you young fool. He's our only hope.'

With a brief subethereal tremor, much like someone saying, not unkindly, 'Rambling old fart,' Merlin's soul prepared to continue on its way through Infinity when, to its equivalent of astonishment, the old man raised an icy claw, pointed in the soul's direction and wheezed, 'You. I'm talking to you. Dammit, you've got to find him.'

'Who?'

'Dammit.'

'Dammit?'

For a second the old man paused. His face twisted into a glacial grimace with the effort of shifting long-dormant thought processes around.

'Dommit,' he corrected.

'Dommit?'

'James Dommit. He's the only one . . .'

'Where?'

After what would have been an interminable pause, had Merlin's soul been confined within the human body and not at present an integral part of Infinity, the old man concluded frostily, 'Late twentieth century. And hurr – '

But Merlin's soul was already whisking through the nineteen hundreds. In vain he searched for a James Dommit that in any way resembled a force to be reckoned with on a cosmic level. It was only by dint of some inspired guessing and shifty detective work that the battle raging within the Enchanter was able to continue with no more than the briefest nod towards a cardiac arrest.

While Merlin's heart skipped a beat, frantically trying to cope with the overload, his soul, having run through all the Dommits in the phone book, so to speak, reasoned that, if such a Dommit existed and had the sort of power necessary to help a wizard of Merlin's stature, then he would surely qualify for a place in history. More specifically, he would certainly qualify for a place in the *Encyclopaedia Esoterica*, published 2706, revised editions annually thereafter.

Sure enough, there in Appendix 758 of the revised edition of 2845 were details relating to one James Dommit.

Merlin's soul read swiftly through the surprisingly brief details.

'. . . early Briton . . . mythical . . . manifestation . . . World Sperm Bank . . . unfounded . . . suicide.'

With a smug smile of self-satisfaction (no wizard worth his salt would possess a soul without considerable egotistic stature), it shot back to the 1980s, looking for the personal, social, sometimes international and occasionally global carnage that litters the trail of an untrained Wisher.

Chapter 15

'Bum,' said Dimmot in answer to Griswold's question. 'Wastrel. Derelict, scrounger, sponger.'

Griswold continued to frown.

'Vagabond,' explained Dimmot.

'Ah,' said Griswold. His frown disappeared. 'I trust that thou dost not want to steal from *me*, vagabond.'

Dimmot broke into a sickly smile. He glanced at Griswold whose previously naked body was now covered in a thick blanket from Dimmot's bed.

'Steal *what*?' he asked, weakly. To his surprise the big man gave a snort of laughter.

'Jester as well as bom and vagabond,' he chuckled. 'Now, what about food and drink?'

They sat in the strange dwelling of the little native, wrapped in their blankets, their features and surroundings dimly shadowed by a single small candle. While he claimed not to be a demon, this thin-shouldered, spiky-haired little gremlin with the dark, swift eyes had lit the candle from a seemingly dead taper, brought to life with a mumbled incantation that sounded something like, 'Lectrisatee Zorf.'

Not too impressive, thought Griswold. Still he felt that Dimmot would bear watching. There was a strangeness about him and a demeanour that spoke of a certain worldliness. Also, though of a somewhat fragile constitution, Dimmot had displayed a degree of courage not usually associated with the sly creatures of Darkness. However . . .

'Food. Right.' Dimmot's words interrupted his thoughts. 'I can't give you anything cooked, but there's bread and cheese and some odds and sods.'

Griswold waved his hand in agreement, confident from Dimmot's tone that the tumble of strange words would bode their stomachs well. As Dimmot hobbled to an odd-looking chest in one corner, pulled open a door in its side and began to rummage through the contents, Griswold rose to his feet, flexing warmth back into his muscles.

He sniffed the air curiously, trying to identify the strange aromas. The smell of discarded coffee, unwashed clothes bearing a ten-day-old coating of body deodorant, and spilt milk on lino mingled in his nostrils to form an unknown and generally unhealthy odour. Griswold wondered if all the natives of this country lived amidst such odours. He snorted to clear his nostrils and sniffed again, reaffirming his first opinion. The scent of mint and lavender was much preferable to this. Or the lusty female fragrance that had assaulted his senses not two hours since.

He peered through the gloom at the objects about him. Very little of what he saw was familiar to him: a table, some chair-like objects, a fireplace bearing no ashes even though this was obviously a bitterly cold land.

Other objects were very strange. Some, which might have been ornaments or the tools of demonry, stood on shelves and surfaces around the room and, in one corner, a wooden box-like object stood as high as his chest and almost as wide as his arms could span. It was inlaid with patterns of different coloured woods and had a shelf running along its width at waist height. So impressive and out of place did it look in these neglected surroundings that Griswold wondered if it had been acquired by dubious means. Or perhaps its current owner had seen more prosperous days. 'Twould appear to be an altar of sorts, he thought. He wondered what was on the shelf that needed to be hidden under a wooden lid. Possibly the gremlin's weapons, for there was no evidence of them on the walls or at hand. A very stupid strategy, unless, of course, he had no need of mere weapons to defend himself.

It would be well to find out more.

Copious amounts of parchment-like material lay scattered around on the table, shelves and floor. Griswold picked up a sheet from the table and glanced across it briefly. In place of words the page displayed a mass of symbols unlike any he had ever seen before. Crowds of little black dots hung in bunches like dead flies

77

caught in a web, but the threads ran across the page in remarkably straight lines.

Merlin does some sort of wizardry with flies and spiders, thought Griswold.

He was searching the page front and back for spiders when Dimmot pulled his head out of the food chest and came over to the table with an armful of bread, cheese and tomatoes. Dimmot glanced at the parchment.

'I dabble a little,' he explained somewhat deprecatingly.

'This is magic?' asked Griswold mildly.

Dimmot snorted. 'I'd like to think so occasionally. Not that it matters any more.'

Griswold continued to stare at the paper thoughtfully.

'There's not a lot to drink,' said Dimmot. 'Ahmm, lager, couple of cans of bitter or wine.'

'Dost thou have mead?'

'No I doesn't have *mead*, there's lager, a couple of cans of bitter, or wine.'

'I'll have what thou hast,' said Griswold.

He laid down the paper and reached for the food as Dimmot came back with the two cans of bitter. No point in wasting good lager on a loony, Dimmot had decided.

It suddenly occurred to him that giving this bloke alcohol might be the worst thing he could do. Especially if he's on some sort of medication, thought Dimmot with a renewed sinking in the stomach.

Griswold frowned at him, holding up a vegetable.

'Do you *eat* this?' he asked.

'Yes,' whispered Dimmot.

'What is it called?'

'A tomato.'

Griswold nodded. 'And that is the drink?'

Dimmot also nodded, though with more reluctance, and the can of bitter trembled in his hand as he passed it over. He mumbled something and returned to the fridge. For a second the knight stared at the strange cylinder, wondering how to open it. Then he put it to his ear and shook it vigorously. Dimmot arose just in time to see Griswold stop his shaking and tug experimentally at the ring set in the top of the can. He tried to utter a warning as the ring came away in Griswold's hand.

In the dim light a spitting, hissing serpent burst from the can, writhing round the room and smashing itself against the ceiling, where it exploded in a shower of sparkling droplets that fell about his head and shoulders. Flinging the container from him, he threw himself across the table in a roll that brought him to his feet on the other side. Food and drink went flying. The blanket fell from his shoulders and landed in folds upon the table.

'God strike thee, Dimmot! I'll have thy throat for this,' he roared, casting his eyes round for a weapon with which to slay the evil creature.

Dimmot stood rooted to the spot, his eyes wide with terror.

He felt it prudent to explain.

'You shook it. You shook the bloody thing. You shook it up,' he babbled. 'You shook it. You shook it.'

But Griswold's attention was on the serpent. He snatched up the blanket and flung it across the room. It fell across the creature and the hissing dropped to an angry buzz. With a sweep of his arm Griswold grabbed up a chair and leapt after the blanket. His arm rose and the chair crashed down with an ear-splitting crack, sending shards and splinters spinning about them. Dimmot gaped, petrified as Griswold picked up a remaining chair leg and continued to beat at the blanket until he was satisfied the danger was past. Then the knight rose to his full height and threw Dimmot a look that brought terror to his heart.

'Get me water, demon. Much and quickly.'

The power of his command sent Dimmot scurrying into the adjoining bathroom. His hands shook uncontrollably as he fumbled with a plastic bowl under the bath tap, hoping that he'd have the sense to wake up very soon.

Crouching over the bath with his head bowed and his eyelids drooping, he listened to the water from the tap thudding into the bowl. With some surprise he realized that the sound of it was remarkably sharp and fresh as if he'd never really heard it before. There's nothing like being scared to death to bring your senses back to life, he thought bitterly.

Holding the bowl before him, he offered a silent prayer to nobody in particular and glided back to the living room in small,

79

mincing steps, gripping the blanket round him while trying desperately not to spill any of the water. Without a word Griswold grabbed the bowl from him and poured the entire contents over his head and shoulders.

He appeared to be washing himself.

'More,' said Griswold.

Dimmot didn't bother to ask himself why a man should want to beat a can of Ruddles to death and then stand naked in his living room taking a cold shower. There was obviously a logic to it all. It was just that he couldn't quite grasp it. He shambled back to the bathroom. When he returned, the big man was drying himself with a sheet from the bed. He appeared to have calmed down.

Dimmot placed the bowl on the table and stood back quietly. Griswold wrapped the towel round his waist, secured it with a knot and threw Dimmot a glance.

'No need for that now,' he said, nodding at the bowl of water. 'Thy spell was of little worth. The venomous rain of thy serpent was no more than a foul-odoured water. Thou seemst,' he added with an expression that appeared to be an irritating mixture of amusement tempered by sympathy, 'to be a demon of no great consequence.'

Dimmot snorted quietly to himself. Even strangers, crazy ones at that, could sum him up in five minutes flat.

He felt very sick. The adrenaline in his body was beginning to disperse and the pain and cold were starting to overcome him once more. He very much wanted to go to sleep and not to wake up until the nightmare was over. If at all.

'I'm not really a demon,' he whispered miserably.

Griswold pointed with his chin at the crumpled, sodden blanket lying against the wall, then gazed at Dimmot impassively. The big man was very calm, wasting no rage on the creature now lying dead at his feet and, once more, his manner was so matter-of-fact that Dimmot found himself reacting as if the man were perfectly sane, despite the ludicrous horror of the previous minutes.

With a sigh he shuffled round the table, bent down wearily and pulled away the blanket.

The cheese was good, though considerably milder than Griswold was used to, and the white bread a little too bland for his taste, but three cans of lager and most of a litre of wine had brought a certain contentment to his stomach and a slur to his voice. He sat heavily slouched in Dimmot's one armchair, clutching an empty wine bottle to his chest, and clothed in a tightly fitting sweater and tracksuit trousers that usually swamped Dimmot. He was aware that his eyes were having difficulty in focusing, but the reason eluded him. Dimmot lay back on his bed in a similar haphazard fashion, his mind hovering between sleep and wakefulness, between his confused memories and Griswold's strange, rambling words. He was wearing faded cords, thick socks and a shabby dressing gown over an equally shabby pullover. It hadn't occurred to him to ask Griswold's name or where he was from.

Sir Griswold was doing something he never did when sober. He was boasting. While a good deal of what he said was lost in a haze of alcohol and the intervening centuries, the general gist managed to find its way through to Dimmot's weary brain.

'. . .'Twas the time when I did find myself betwixt a maiden fair of face and a dragon of the darkest countenance, with lips afire and eyes that did blaze in crimson and green. While she did lie at my back the creature towered above me, screeching and sending down flames upon my meagre shield. But I did not yield. My sword swung aloft and smote here and smote there while my hair did curl in the heat and my skin did blister. And the dragon's presence was awesome to behold. But I did not yield. And, when it seemed the monster would overwhelm us both, my blade did find its vitals. I struck again and again until the vile being fell before me, screaming and roaring and shaking the ground so that the rocks and trees trembled.'

Griswold belched.

'And with that I did gather up the fair maid and did away with her to a nearby glade, bordered by a lake that did shimmer in the warmth of the sun. And I did put my lips to hers . . .'

'But she did not yield,' mumbled Dimmot sleepily.

'Indeed she did,' retorted Griswold indignantly. 'Oft and plentifully.'

Isn't that bloody typical, thought Dimmot. I flog my cobs off trying to get girls to yield oft and plentifully and this yobbo comes along, beats the balls off poor dumb animals and gets all he wants.

In the borderland between sleep and consciousness he found

himself wishing with all his heart that he could hide away from the world, his lousy past, his failures and most particularly, the man across the room who, despite his craziness, or perhaps because of it, seemed to be the epitome of everything that Dimmot would like to be, but wasn't. With a firm promise that, tomorrow, he'd have another go at the bridge, he mumbled, 'Bleeding Sir Lancelot,' and toppled sideways into a deep, disturbed sleep, open mouth atwist against the pillow.

For a moment or two the room was still.

Then Griswold sat up with a jerk. His face creased into a frown as he tried to grasp the import of Dimmot's words. The reputation of Sir Lancelot du Lac couldn't possibly have reached this distant land. A coldness settled over him as the truth dawned. Dimmot was, after all, in the service of Guinevere! Obviously she'd planned his banishment as her way of wreaking her revenge and, instead of taking his one chance of escape, Griswold had ridden straight back into her clutches in the vain belief that he could charm her into forgiveness. The only puzzle was her choice of timing. He was surprised that she hadn't waited till after . . .

Unless it be that this demon has a particularly sadistic nature, he thought angrily. With his anger he felt a grim hope welling up within him.

If Dimmot had brought him here, then Dimmot would be the one to return him to Camelot. He turned his eyes, with some effort, to the means of his salvation from his dilemma.

But both salvation and dilemma appeared to be taking a turn for the worse. Having passed his taunting jibe Dimmot was making good his escape. As Griswold watched, the dishevelled little imp was rapidly fading into nothing! In the time it took Griswold to leap from his chair and crash drunkenly to the floor Dimmot had completely vanished. Griswold spat out an oath and flung the bottle at the empty space into which Dimmot had disappeared. The bottle seemed to strike nothing and bounced away with a clunk, as if hitting an invisible shield.

It lay on the bed, pointing at him mockingly.

'Hogscobblers,' he grumbled as his head sank wearily on to the carpet. 'Why cannot life be simple? Why cannot men deal honest blows felt with honest venom, instead of resorting to these cowardly magics?'

It occurred to him that, in the space of one day, two men had vanished from his presence for their own reasons.

In a sense he was right.

In the truest sense he was, of course, quite wrong.

Chapter 16

Very little is known about the soul. In fact it can be safely said that the amount actually known about the soul by any single man or, indeed, all the men who ever were, all rolled into one, can be gathered up and placed inside a zero sign of any size with no reduction of breathing space whatsoever.

So, while waiting for the appreciable gaps in their knowledge to be plugged, and in the hope that, once plugged, the secrets of life, the universe and how to succeed with no more than the minimal effort would be revealed, soul owners have relied on simple, crude alternatives to knowledge like believing, dreaming, wishing, hoping and things like that. Believers, dreamers, etc., being abysmally unaware that believing, dreaming, etc. are potent forces at subethereal levels – unlike knowledge which, when it's not busy being an illusion has no inherent force of its own – are apt to underestimate the extent to which their beliefs, dreams, etc. affect the great cosmic plan, which is a fairly loose arrangement anyway.

The truth, for those who wish to plug a gap or two, is that believing and so on are somewhat cumbersome (even vulgar, one might say) methods of communicating directly with one's soul, which distils the messages into intelligible cosmic jargon and passes them on to the cosmos in general. The cosmos, being pretty easy-going and open to suggestion, accepts the messages as facts and alters itself accordingly, and usually imperceptibly, to fit them.

Anything to maintain the balance.

Another truth is that the soul has no sex or vested interest in same for, unlike Mankind, it survives without the constant desire to create more Mankinds in order to ensure their continuing survival. Because of this it is completely faithful unto death where its owner is concerned.

So it is that Merlin's soul, instead of cashing in on its new-found freedom and heading for the hills, is faithfully sniffing out James Dimmot, on the face of it the most unlikely person on Earth to have any lasting effect on history whatsoever.

And find him it does, sitting on the parapet of old Tower Bridge on the verge of abandoning his own soul to a premature fate.

'Oh,' says Merlin's soul, demonstrating the complete range of the average soul's emotional spectrum.

Another truth about souls is that, in return for their own fidelity, they require only that their owner be faithful throughout his/her life which includes allowing that life to run its full course. In this way the soul can be prepared for a new owner when the old one succumbs to natural causes or the whims of Fate which any competent soul can see coming a mile off. If cast out before its time it can wander through Infinity for aeons before finding a new home.

Suicide is, therefore, unforgivable. By the same token, being sold before the allotted span is over is equally disconcerting, especially if the buyer is of the horned, fork-tailed variety, such beings having a tendency to be of an anti-social persuasion and inclined to stunt spiritual growth by means of incarceration, eternal damnation and such.

So, while a soul can be sold it can't be bought.

'Oh,' says Merlin's soul.

'Oh?' responds Dimmot's soul.

'I see that thou art about to be kicked out.'

''Fraid so.'

'This poses a problem. Th'art needed to save Mankind. Both of thee.'

Dimmot's soul ruminates.

'From what?' it asks.

'I know not. Eternal damnation, I should imagine.'

'Things don't change. What do you suggest?'

'Well, first there's my owner to consider,' says Merlin's soul. It outlines the plight even now threatening to overcome and destroy the Enchanter, concluding with, 'So there thou hast it. If thou canst just guide some of thine owner's power in my direction . . .'

'I'll have a word, but I don't hold out much hope. He's almost impossible to reach when he's pissed as a parrot.'

'It *is* important.'

'I'll see what I can do.'

Chapter 17

The soul of Merlin the Enchanter sped back to Goatchurch
Cavern, armed with renewed strength. Despite all odds its erst-
while ally had hacked a sodden path through the alcoholic sponge
that was Dimmot's brain and dropped the seed of a suggestion on
soil thoroughly churned and little more than curdled mud.

But the seed took root.

It grew and blossomed just sufficiently to become a spindly,
short-lived Wish on its owner's part and, before it withered and
died, Dimmot's soul had plucked it from the mud and cast it into
the cosmos where, being basically a good Wish, it thrived and
bore fruit. From the fruit thereof the soul of the Enchanter drew
nourishment and, thus strengthened, returned to its owner to join
in battle.

The heart of Merlin, having just skipped a beat, remember, was
seriously considering whether or not to skip the rest when a surge
of renewed vigour flooded through it. The restored power of his
soul was everywhere, engulfing him in pure, colourless light,
penetrating and dissolving the writhing symbols of the formula.

As the cruel mathematics were systematically destroyed, the
way began to clear. Merlin groaned, his neck strung with tension
while the dreams became sharper, the memories stronger and the
symbols weaker and sparser until the last one faded into nothing.

At last, the terrible formula was no more.

His soul settled down to relax, triumphant and inconspicuous,
beneath the depths of his awareness. His dreams, now wafting
peacefully, parted to allow consciousness to rise to the surface.

Merlin awoke. Eyes still closed, breathing deeply, he savoured
a tranquillity that he'd not felt in himself since his childhood.
Where confusion and doubts had often clouded his brain with the

murk of intrigues, his mind was now clear and calm as a crystal pool. With a flutter, his eyelids opened. He was in darkness.

'So,' he murmured. 'We have arrived.'

He rose slowly to his feet and stood in the blackness of the sealed cavern deep within the heart of the Mendip Hills.

Time for work, thought Merlin, throwing back the hood of his cloak. With a gentle sweep of his hand he drew out the luminosity hidden in the surrounding limestone. A dim glow filled the cavern, giving body and depth to the familiar shapes.

He noted that the lighting was not as bright as it could be.

It seems I might have lost a little of my edge over the years, he thought. Let us see just how much.

He stretched out a hand, pointing a bony finger towards one of the smaller boulders standing against the far wall some ten feet away. The boulder had the weight of about four men. His brow furrowed slightly in concentration and, lifting the outstretched finger, he murmured, 'Rise.'

The boulder rocked for a second and then stopped.

Merlin frowned. He tried again. Lifting the finger more slowly and carefully he intoned, 'I bid thee rise.'

Again the boulder rocked, but refused to leave the ground.

The frown disappeared from Merlin's brow and his face went slack with surprise.

'What foolishness is this? Thou art hardly Stonehenge, thou measly pebble.'

His voice sounded more hurt than angry. With eyebrows that arched high and swept down in a concentrated assault on the bridge of his nose, he splayed out the fingers of his hand, his arm shaking with the effort. In a voice that rumbled round the cavern he said, 'I command thee to rise.'

For a few seconds it appeared that the boulder would defy him for a third time. Then, with a creak, it slid across to an adjacent rock and rose, slightly sideways, a foot or two into the air where it hovered unsteadily under the wizard's threatening gaze.

Merlin sniffed with mild satisfaction.

'Heh, heh! My weaponry is obviously a little rusted from lack of use,' he grunted wryly. 'Though the lessons of youth seem clear enough to me, even these simple tricks seek to present probl—'

With a thud the boulder fell to the ground, hitting an embedded rock and veering alarmingly towards the wizard's legs. Merlin leapt backwards on to the ledge, his cloak swirling around him. As the boulder smashed inches below his toes his head crashed sickeningly against the rock above him. The tranquillity in his face dissolved into fury at the searing pain. The ice-blue of his eyes gave way to flecks of orange and red, flashes of green and purple flickered and bounced off the walls of Goatchurch Cavern, throwing multi-coloured shadows back at him and giving him a look of the daemon that in part he was.

A murderous rage built within him. With a deafening crack, a thunderbolt erupted from his outstretched fingers and flew through the darkness, flooding the cavern in a light so brilliant that it filled every hidden crevice, leaving not a single shadow. Under its force the boulder shattered asunder, sending shards of rock screaming, like blinded hornets. With undiminished force the bolt seared its way into the far wall, leaving a hole the size of a man's girth burrowed deep in the rock. The air was charged with earsplitting crackles and the smell of molten limestone.

Then all was silent.

Gradually the Enchanter's anger subsided and his eyes turned ice-blue. With the smell of burning still in his nostrils Merlin stepped down from the ledge. He sat down, delved into the pouch beneath his cloak and pulled out a small jar, similar to the one which had contained the life-saving potion. He removed the stopper and stuck in his fingertips, scooping out a little of the greasy contents. Replacing the stopper and laying the jar on the ledge he began to rub the grease into the ugly lump that was already forming on top of his head.

With quiet satisfaction he addressed the cavern in general.

'Now that thou knowest who is the master,' he intoned calmly, 'kindly . . . pull thyself together. Yonder pieces, pebbles, dust and smoke, become the formidable rock that thou wert, forged by the power of Time's gentle hammer.'

He swept his arms together in a grand gesture designed, among other things, to rebuild shattered boulders.

But the hornets refused to return to the nest.

Chapter 18

Within the heart of the old man imprisoned deep below the floor of London City a thin and withered vestige of hope stirs like a dried twig touched by the first spring breeze.

He's had a visitor.

No, not the regular one.

Another one.

He didn't stay long.

Long enough, though.

Long enough to be recognized.

They spoke very briefly, refraining from pleasantries, then the visitor left.

But the old man had recognized him.

And now he sits in silence, wondering if he has the nerve to nurture the little dried twig into an oak.

Would that be too much to ask?

Chapter 19

Merlin the Enchanter sat in the darkness of Goatchurch Cavern humming a tune flatly and drumming his fingers in a pattern of dubious rhythmic quality.

He'd long ago realized that when you accept that life is hard, it becomes a lot easier. When you understand that life was never meant to be fair then you know that its malicious humour is nothing personal.

Yet, in the evening of his years, or what now appeared to be their midnight, he'd have been, apparently, quite justified in having some doubts about this.

He snorted.

'How ironic if I, Merlin, creator of kings, adviser of philosophers and seducer of writers and poets not yet born in my own time, but now centuries dead, if I, the arch-manipulator of history, who would do battle with nebulous visions from the future by devious yet wondrous magical means, if I who has spanned the centuries in my quest for Man's salvation, were nothing more than a strutting jester, poked and prodded by some omniscient deity to do lavish tricks with time and space.

'Or perhaps,' he sucked thoughtfully at his teeth, 'nothing more than a pawn wielded by a master player in a tournament of cosmic proportions. Now finally cornered and taken by an opponent of similar ethereal origin.'

His eyes narrowed with grim stubbornness.

'And dismissed as being of no further use while the game goes on without me.'

His hand slid into the leather bag at his side and felt about.

He withdrew the pendant made for him by Rowan the blacksmith.

The words he uttered were one of the few spells in the whole history of magic that would respond to a being not gifted with magical powers. When spoken before the pendant that, in accordance with the laws of magic, must be crafted by a man who has never known a woman, the grimoire would restore to the speaker all the powers he may have lost through such diverse causes as sickness, amnesia, injury, thievery, unconsciousness, grief or unwizardly indulgences.

The words of the spell numbered less than a hundred and were easily remembered, but, needless to say, they were known only to a handful of men.

Merlin hung the pendant solemnly round his neck by its leather thong and waited for a sign that his powers were returning.

He whistled his tuneless tune and drummed his dubious rhythm.

Nothing happened.

His lips pursed and unpursed impatiently. His body began to tremble with anger as the realization dawned that nothing was continuing to happen.

Like a simmering cauldron he came rapidly to the boil, hissing and seething with rage.

'Damn and blast, thou miserable ore,' he spluttered, snatching at the pendant and holding it up before him. 'Dost dare defy the very words for which thou wast created, without which thou wouldst be nothing but a few scribbled words on a lump of iron whose fate would otherwise be but a crude arrowhead or a vulgar rivet on a vulgar warrior's vulgar shield? Hast no sense of thy destiny, no conception of the purpose for which thou wast forged?'

He glared at the pendant, but it refused to meet his gaze. He ripped it from his neck and flung it away in disgust. It flew across the cavern with unintended but unerring accuracy into the tunnel that Merlin had left blasted into the wall, and tinkled to a stop.

A cool draught wafted from the tunnel and touched gently at the folds of the Enchanter's cloak.

Chapter 20

James Dimmot was wild-eyed, frantic and gasping for air.

He had his back to the wall and he was halfway up it.

He stared through rapidly blurring eyes at the hairy apparition below him while his fingers scrabbled lamely at the massive hand encompassing his throat and his dangling feet paddled desperately trying to lift him out of Griswold's reach.

'I din' go anywhere, I haven't *been* anywhere, you stupid, sodding psycho,' he squawked thickly through his constricted windpipe. Remarkably bold words on the face of it, but the truth was that the fear which had been Dimmot's almost constant companion since his plunge into the River Thames, had got thoroughly fed up with the demands he had made on it. So it had ambled off, mumbling vaguely, 'I'll pop back later.'

Griswold's grip tightened. 'If thou wert not elsewhere, then how was it that thou wast not here?'

'Glugglethwirkishgleebugh!' explained Dimmot thickly.

He was finding it a little difficult to understand why an everyday homicidal maniac was behaving so unreasonably towards him when all he'd done was fall asleep. Perhaps the bloke was offended because Dimmot hadn't taken the bit about the dragon seriously. Or maybe he felt that Dimmot doubted his prowess with slightly singed maidens in distress.

'Glugglethwirk,' he said again, adding, 'Oh shit,' as the pounding of blood in his temples focused his senses on the sharp throbbing at the side of his head. Despite the serious shortage of air reaching his lungs and the fact that he was fast approaching unconsciousness, Dimmot jerked up a hand and yelped tearfully when his fingers arrived, earlier than they had expected, at the great blue bump that was standing out there.

Oh, hell, he thought with resignation. That's it. I've had enough. Being alive is just too bloody painful. Let's just hang about here and get it over with. Don't stop now, mate, I'm as ready now as I'll ever be.

Naturally the squeezing stopped.

Dimmot felt himself sliding down the wall as Griswold lowered him gently to the floor. Opening one eye he stared painfully out to see Griswold peering thoughtfully at the throbbing bruise. The knight turned to look at the bottle that he'd thrown lying on the bed, then back again at the lump.

He seemed to be weighing up possibilities.

Which he was.

Is't possible, mused Griswold, that this imp did ply me with such potion as did make mine eyes see that which was not, because in truth he had not the power to magic himself from my presence? Indeed his lack of ability is, perhaps, rivalled only by his guile and devious cunning.

He didn't think to ask himself why Dimmot had returned.

'So be it. I'll believe thee for the present, Dommit . . .'

'Dimmot.'

'. . . in part at least, but, if thou try to play tricks on mine eyes again . . .'

'All right, I promise, I swear, whatever you say [I wish I knew what the hell you *were* saying], OK, OK . . . OK?'

With a nod of agreement Griswold released his grip and pointed to the armchair. 'Sit thee down.'

Dimmot padded over to the chair, slumped gratefully down and yelped again, grabbing his head in both hands.

'Hear me well, Dimmot,' said Griswold, ignoring his discomfort. 'There are things I must have knowledge of and I would get that knowledge from thee.'

Dimmot groaned in pain.

'What knowest thou of Sir Lancelot du Lac?'

'What?' Dimmot stared incredulously.

Griswold cleared his throat. One must of course expect language problems with foreigners. Particularly barbarians.

'What,' he repeated slowly and distinctly, 'knowest thou of Sir Lancelot du Lac?'

'I'm a computer consultant, not a bleeding historian. I don't know anything about him. He was one of King Arthur's knights, that's all I know.'

'How didst thou know of his death?'

'What?' said Dimmot again, tiresomely. Griswold kept his patience.

'Thou hast said, "he was". How didst thou know he was dead?'

'He'd have a hard job not being dead, wouldn't he,' snorted Dimmot, 'after a thousand years or so?'

'Indeed a lance through the vitals may be considered a formidable argument even for so bold a knight as Sir Lan . . . what d'ye mean, a thousand years?'

Dimmot sighed.

'Look,' he said. 'I really am totally knackered, I'm cold, I'm sick-tired and I hurt completely, utterly and all over. Let's reach an agreement.'

Griswold frowned.

'Arrangement,' Dimmot offered.

'. . .?'

'Truce.'

'Agh. What sort of *agreement* . . .?'

Dimmot's head nodded carefully.

'. . . agreement dost thou suggest?'

Beneath its weary surface Dimmot's mind raced, if one could call swimming through a mental mire towing a fleet of reluctant synapses between one's teeth racing. He had to get the loony out of his life somehow. If he could discover who he was, where he came from and a few other things, maybe he could decide a course of action. These convoluted linguistics were slowing everything down.

'I'll tell you all I can to help you get back to your native land. And,' he added generously, 'I'll stop playing tricks on your eyes, on condition that you . . .' He hesitated, choosing his words carefully and speaking carefully as if to a backward child and pointing at Griswold with a long, tapered finger, '. . . talk properly, stop all this fantasizing and tell me who you are and where you come from.'

Griswold said nothing. He appeared to be considering this. Then, 'Phantomizing.'

'Fantasizing.'

'Fantasizing?'

'Yes. You know [bloody hell, he's in a different dimension, this one] . . .' and Dimmot explained slowly and patiently. All the bit about dragons and knights and lances and, wotsername, Guinevere, all that nonsense, just forget all that and Dimmot would tell him anything that he wanted to know.

'Done,' said Griswold.

'Good. First of all, what's your name? . . . Name!'

'I am Griswold.'

'Griswold?'

'For now.'

All right, let it pass, thought Dimmot. Nobody calls their kid Griswold, but don't push it. With a bit of luck this might be a doddle after all. I might even persuade him to give himself up to whoever's responsible for him.

'Uhm – do you have any friends, people who might wonder where you are?'

'I have friends, as much as men can be friends in these troubled times.'

'True, but is there anyone in particular who might be concerned about you?'

'Other than Guinevere?'

'Yes, other than Guinevere,' said Dimmot patiently.

'There is one, perhaps. Old, forgetful, has a somewhat freakish will, but possibly a little concerned.'

Great, thought Dimmot. We're getting somewhere. Dimmot, you might even do something right this time. Now don't balls it up, just get a name and address and grab the phone first chance you get.

'Oh,' he said casually, 'who's that then? Does he live round here?'

The response was not quite what he expected. Nor did it come from the source he expected.

'Round here?' intoned a disbelieving voice that filled the room with resonance, making the walls shudder and the snow-caked windows rattle in their frames. 'I would not be seen within a hundred miles of this stench-filled cesspit.'

Dimmot froze in his chair, his hands gripping the arms. He

96

stared over his shoulder, not knowing what he was looking for and hoping desperately that he wouldn't find it.

Where the voice had been was a tiny wisp of smoke hanging in the air and rapidly becoming larger. As Dimmot gaped over his shoulder into the candle-lit gloom the smoke began to swirl faster and faster, taking on a myriad of changing colours. Sounds vaguely similar to the heave of miniature storm-tossed seas and the roll of tiny thunderclouds came from within the smoke, together with some indefinable noises that could only be described as 'snogck'. Dimmot felt instinctively that these were from soft, unformed bones clicking into place. He swiftly added nausea to his list of things to feel while watching apparitions appear.

For this was apparently what he was doing, as the smoke was definitely taking on the shape of a man-like creature. With his sanity rapidly becoming a thing of the past Dimmot turned to look desperately at Griswold and wondered if he would start hitting the apparition with a chair leg. But Griswold was doing something much more sensible. The most natural thing in the world, of course.

Amidst the rattling crockery and ornaments and the shuddering furniture, Griswold was leaning against Dimmot's table, casually shaking up the last can of lager. As the smoke rapidly condensed into terrifying solidity, he leered contentedly and curled his finger under the tab.

Chapter 21

'Gruntfuttocks!' roared Uther Pendragon, king of all England, deceased. 'Now where's he gone?'

He sat down on the dust-covered stool in Merlin's cottage with a thump, of sorts. The dust, which had begun to gather since Merlin's departure three weeks previously and which would continue to gather until the end of time unless the Enchanter returned, didn't bother to stir. The motes that danced gently in the winter sunlight shining through the window also carried on as if he wasn't there, but they would ignore the tremors of passing armies, hansom cabs and articulated trucks in future years, so one disembodied spirit more or less wasn't about to bother them.

'Buggrit,' said Uther.

He glanced round the room. Merlin had certainly let himself go during the last few months. The place was a tip. Books and instruments lay about everywhere, cupboard doors were left open, bowls of broth crouched in dark corners sprouting dubious life-forms. The bunches of herbs that usually hung from the beams were scattered across the floor. The fossilized toad on the window-sill had toes broken off as if it had been dropped on the stone floor and Merlin had not even bothered to magic them back on.

Uther hoped the toad hadn't taken offence; it could be a tetchy little sod at times.

He gazed about him sadly. The old wizard's favourite chair stood by the window. The air was rich with wizardly aromas. The room was peaceful almost to death.

Uther's gaze turned to the fireplace and, noticing the scrap of parchment lying there, he hauled himself to his feet and wafted across the room. Bending down, he squinted at the words thereon:

Geoffrey of M
11

Malor
d. 1472

Wordswo
1770–18

Einste
1897–195

To name but a few, he thought, for the parchment was no more than a scrap of the original document that Merlin had compiled over the course of ten years or so. A document of names that Uther had sought out for Merlin from books not yet written in his own time. Names that shone like beacons throughout the history yet to come. Names that future men spoke of with awe and quoted in tones of hushed reverence.

'These men are the stuff of greatness,' the wizard had said, 'and, as such, their influence will be felt by thousands. If this be so, then mayhap we can build such strength in men's minds that, when the time of darkness is upon them, they will have enough knowledge, enough strength to resist, enough insight to comprehend the nature of that which would seek to enslave them.'

So saying, the wizard had wandered through the land seeking those ancestors and, on finding them, had wielded his wizardry, leaving them changed, a little stronger, a little more immune to evil. And he'd left them with something else.

To each man and woman whom he visited he secretly gave a gift to be carried down the centuries through their successive seeds until it reached those descendants whose greatness would make best use of it and whose names were in the document.

The gift was the gift of words.

'With that gift,' said Merlin, 'men whose minds embrace the depths of their souls and who can see through the mundane and the meaningless to recognize both the nature of Evil and the true destiny of Mankind, would pass on their visions to the multitude. With luck the terror of the Eternal Dark Age might be averted.'

But it was not enough.

Later, when Uther had brought the news that nothing had changed in that distant future and Merlin had realized how ridiculously short of the mark he'd been, he'd cried out, 'How could I have been so stupid? To hope that the peoples of an entire world would respond to the words of a godly few and rise in revolt when the time decreed.'

And he had wept with despair behind the locked door of his bedroom.

He'd emerged three days later, tossed the parchment on to the logs in the grate and set it ablaze with a vicious stab of his finger.

'What art thou still doing here?' he'd snapped.

And Uther Pendragon, monarch by name, peasant by nature, sitting slumped in the Enchanter's favourite chair, had revealed simply and comprehensively to the greatest magician of the age the vital flaws in his methodology and the approach needed to attack the problem in a logical and sequentially constructive manner to achieve optimum effectiveness.

'Make the buggers do as they're told,' he'd bawled. 'Tell 'em what they're up against and make 'em face it like a man.'

Then he'd spat across the room with enviable accuracy on to the fire, wherein lay the burning remains of ten years' labour. A cloud of sparks leapt from the wood and swirled up the chimney.

'That's what I'd do,' he added by way of explanation. 'Your trouble is that you're too much of an idealist. You expect great things from all men as you expect great things from yourself. You ask great things of all men just as you demand great things of yourself. You see a greatness in all men just as you are aware of the greatness in yourself. You forget that all men aren't Merlin.'

'Why didst thou not speak up before?'

Merlin's eyes narrowed questioningly. Uther gave a shrug.

'You're not the world's best listener.'

After a pause which was very long, and which crackled slightly, the Enchanter spoke.

'Make them do as they're told?'

'Yes.'

'What dost thou suggest?'

Uther crossed his legs and planted his feet on nothing two feet above the ground.

'You're at loggerheads and on the verge of defeat.'

Merlin nodded.

'Therefore, your troops, your riders, your archers, your foot-soldiers must be exhorted to turn defeat into victory.'

'A spell!'

'No! Not a spell,' spluttered Uther, slapping his forehead in exasperation. 'What use are spells if your troops' victory is not of their making? Where will be their strength, their will to win the next battle? It must be *their* courage that wins the war, not *your* magic. The tales they tell round the camp fires must be of their victory, not yours. The feel of the wind across the strewn battlefield and the smell of the enemies' blood will only be sweet to those whose will has been tested fully and who rose to the test.

'Your job is to inspire that courage, to dredge up the will of your fighting men so that, when the day seems lost as it surely will, they will find strength in their weakness and summon willpower from their despair.'

'Hmm. A speech. Yes, a speech to inspire. Let me see. How does this sound? . . . "Once more unto the" . . .'

'You've already done that one,' said Uther.

'Oh, yes.'

They talked and planned anew, discarding and amending until they'd agreed on a first draft of the message to the masses. It began, 'In thy darkness there is darkness still,' and with its creation the Enchanter began to regain his confidence. He was back on home ground.

'Now all that is required is an orator,' he'd announced confidently.

Chapter 22

Merlin quickly realized that explaining things to the native Dimmot was going to be exceptionally difficult for the wrong reasons. It wasn't that Dimmot was lacking in intelligence. Quite the opposite. He was, according to Uther's information, a man of singular insight with an understanding of the power of numbers which was indeed remarkable, being by trade a mathematician versed in the use of a type of abacus advanced far beyond anything that Merlin could comfortably conceive.

He had a profound grasp of the numeracy of the ancient Greeks, Egyptians and Arabs and he spoke of different mathematical languages which the wizard had never even encountered. The people of Cobol and Fortran must be wondrously adept at wizardry if their languages could achieve as much with a few symbols as Dimmot's lectures would have Uther believe.

No, it wasn't that Dimmot was a fool. A fool had, among his other dubious attributes, the ability to believe implicitly in the common aspects of Man's everyday existence. Things that stared him in the face. Dimmot just couldn't find it in him to believe that such things as wizardry, dragons, demons, levitation or time travelling existed.

So when Merlin materialized in his living room, out of breath and sighing with relief as old bones and organs nestled into place, and announced that he was Merlin the Enchanter and was delighted to meet Dimmot who, Dimmot might like to know, had led him a merry chase through the centuries, Dimmot said as much.

'No, no, no, no, no, no i's not possible, ohGodi'sa nighmare, Idon'believe it, oh Jesus why me, why me, why me?' he said.

'A hymn of homage to a master magician,' explained Merlin to Griswold by way of interpretation.

Griswold noted the droop in the old wizard's shoulders and the tiredness in his eyes.

'Of course,' he said, reluctantly placing the bulging lager can back on the table.

He squinted round Merlin's small frame at the native.

'Although he appears not to be too deeply convinced that thou art who thou art,' he observed.

'He is a fool, then. So is his Lord and Master, Ibiem, of whom I have never heard and who, therefore, must be either one of men's fairly recent deities or one of little consequence, which is no great surprise if he entertains such disbelieving heathens as this in his flock.'

He glared at Dimmot trembling before him. Can this really be the one who will aid me in my quest? he wondered to himself. By the gods, Uther Pendragon, I'll have words with thee when next we meet.

'Get off thy knees, Dimmot, and cease thy snivelling,' he snapped.

Dimmot got reluctantly to his feet and stared mutely. The old man shook off the last wisps of smoke clinging to his cloak and whiskers and gave a curt nod to the grinning Griswold. Griswold glanced briefly towards the window where the gradual lightening of the sky was squeezing in through the curtains.

'Thou didst take thy time getting here,' he said mildly. ''Tis nearly morning.'

'I rested on the way.'

And, as Dimmot stared dully from one to the other, first the big loony one went on about how he knew the white-haired one would come looking for him and the white-haired one said the big loony one knew nothing of the sort.

Then the big loony one shrugged and said, however, he was grateful and were they going home to Camelot now? Then the white-haired one said he hadn't come to rescue the big loony one at all, but that he'd got here first and had had to drag Griswold away from whatever it was that he'd been doing to stop this dreary excuse for a hero from dashing the hopes of Mankind by his selfish, thoughtless attempt to drown himself.

103

Then they started squabbling.

'Didst thou stop to consider the nature of my activities before thou so thoughtfully dragged me away?'

'I had but seconds in which to act, not the benefit of idle hours like thee, thou insolent whelp. I asked only that thou be without the armour that would have sealed both thy miserable fates in the river.'

Dimmot wondered who the hero was.

'Asked?' growled Griswold. 'Asked who?'

The old fellow started gabbling about employing the services of an inhabitant of the nether regions, some miserable sod called Botham who kept grumbling about the snow and the cold and why couldn't Merlin do his own body-snatching and all right, he'd do it, but just remember Merlin was in his debt and one day he'd come to collect . . .

'Who's this hero you're talking about?' inquired Dimmot.

Ignoring Dimmot, Griswold rose to his feet with his fists clenched like boulders.

'And thou didst magic me away from my home to this desolate land just to save this miserable wretch who wished not to be saved?'

'There are things at stake of far greater import than the wishes of one man.'

'Two,' snapped Griswold.

'Excuse me. Who's this . . .'

Then the white-haired one was off again, grubbing away about Mankind being enslaved in what he called the Eternal Dark Age by deceit and subterfuge and Man's only hope of freedom lay within Man himself.

Then he said something about planting a seed of rebellion.

Griswold's eyes narrowed. 'Against the king?' he whispered.

'Queen,' mumbled Dimmot.

'The king?' snapped Merlin. 'Dost thou not understand a word of what I say? The king is dead centuries since. We are many hundreds of years away from Camelot, from Arthur, from Guinevere . . . from home.'

And while Griswold listened intently the white-haired one finally explained how and why he, Merlin, was here in the year nineteen hundred and eighty-seven, albeit some thirty years later than he'd planned and how James Dimmot was the only one who could ensure that his plan to save Mankind had at least a ghost of a chance. And why Merlin now needed Griswold's help.

When Merlin had finished Griswold stood, unmoving, staring long and hard at nothing in particular. Merlin waited uneasily for him to speak while Dimmot sank into the armchair mumbling incoherently to himself.

'When this is finished,' said Griswold so suddenly that Merlin jumped with surprise, 'and thy mission is completed . . .'

'Yes?'

'Then will we be able to return to Camelot?'

'We will,' said Merlin looking away.

'And all will be as it was when we left?'

The wizard nodded. Griswold pursed his lips in thought.

'And thou sayest thou hast lost some of thy powers?'

Merlin nodded again. 'For which reason I did need have recourse to thee, to do, by physical means, that which by magical means I could not.'

'I am hardly enamoured of such comforts as bathing naked in icy rivers,' growled Griswold. 'If I agree to protect this wretch from himself . . .'

'I swear to thee that I'll not visit any more magical assaults on thy being.'

'Tell me, Master Merlin,' demanded Griswold softly. 'If I decline to help thee and request that thou return me to Camelot now, wouldst thou agree?'

With a sigh the old man turned his attention to James Dimmot who sat mumbling to himself, his head lolling loosely like a rag doll's. Merlin gazed at the native intently. Nothing a little hypnosis and subconscious persuasion couldn't cure, he thought.

If needs be he would fight his fight without Griswold by his side. The fact that it would break his heart was irrelevant, of course.

Without turning he addressed himself to Griswold's question.

'Aye, of course I'll send thee back to the soft life, lad, if thou hast not the stomach for adventure. I've no time for arse-wiping. I have only to summon the demon Bathym and he will return thee to the very place and time from which he did snatch thee.'

'The very place?'

'And the very same time.'

'And if I should die on this mission? What of my return to Camelot then?'

'If thou diest, thou diest. Whatever thou wast doing at the time of thy departure will remain undone for all time. A small part of history may have to be rewritten, of course, for the lives of those around thee will take a slightly different turn as a result of thy going.'

When, after some seconds, no reply was forthcoming, the wizard turned and squinted over one shoulder. Griswold was staring into space with an expression quite indescribable.

'Well, speak up, lad. Art thou staying or not?'

Sir Griswold gave a small shrug, a slow nod and an ill-concealed smirk.

'Oak hay,' he said.

Chapter 23

Uther Pendragon sat in Merlin's armchair and stared moodily across the valley to where Camelot castle stood basking in the sunlight.

Having access to Infinity certainly has its drawbacks, he thought.

When he was monarch he'd had no problems finding people. He'd stand on those same battlements and yell, 'Get me so-and-so,' and troops of soldiers would scour the countryside and get so-and-so. *And* they wouldn't even have to look upwards (unless their quarry was hiding in the branches of a forest, in which case they'd just surround it, set it alight and wait for him to come out).

When I was king, thought Uther, no one hid in mid-air, let alone any other dimensions. One had only two to contend with, forwards and sideways. Life was quite straightf . . . simple.

Then all at once, buffet!

You take your last gasp, and there's Eternity stretching away from you, every combination you can think of, forsideways backupacrossways, downabitand vroomp fifty years ahead, over y'shoulder and . . . every direction and dimension imaginable.

And without even a breaking-in period to cope with a mere three dimensions like the twentieth-century bunch. What with learning to fly and Einstein and such, at least they'd got a glimpse of what Infinity was all about.

He slid a finger up his nostril and rummaged thoughtfully.

Merlin could have done more good teaching ordinary men how to cope with such intangibles, thought Uther the philosopher, instead of wasting his time, sending messages to Wordsworth and Keats and Malory and the like. All they had done was turn them into poems.

The spectre scratched his nose and pondered his problem.

It had been some three weeks ago, local time, when Uther had first told the wizard of James Dimmot's existence, and watched those old shoulders sag with despair and heard the words, 'Too far, too far.'

On his travels, some three thousand years later he'd come upon a new and drastic sequence of events that had turned his ectoplasm to jelly and which had sent him scuttling back down the aeons to find the Enchanter.

And two days ago, twentieth-century time, on 13 February 1956, James Dimmot's seventh birthday, Uther, bearing the news that time was literally about to run out for Mankind, had arrived at the Dimmot residence expecting to find Merlin, in the one place he should definitely have been if his journey via the long way round had succeeded.

Only to find that the wizard hadn't turned up.

Furthermore, it seemed, Merlin had never got to meet James Dimmot, which could well explain why the Eternal Dark Age suddenly seemed about to live up to its name.

The Dimmot house was empty, save for a woman who came in and 'did'. She was, in fact, 'doing' when King Uther Pendragon wandered through a nearby wall.

'Oh, good morning, sir,' she said. 'I don't think I know you.'

On the face of it this was a fairly innocuous statement. Bearing in mind, however, that Uther was generally invisible and also that he was attired in typical spiritual garb, i.e. nothing, one can appreciate his surprise at her unexpected and somewhat remarkable composure.

With an effort of will he brought his attention to bear on the matter in hand and said, perceptively, 'You can see me.'

The lady looked him up and down with no attempt to hide her admiration and remarked with a smile, 'As clearly as if you were here in body.'

'Then you are a witch woman,' said Uther warily for, though he was privy to Infinity, he was not beyond the reach of men's magic.

'No. Just clairvoyant. Always have been.'

Uther thought for a moment, weighing up the odds. She looked harmless and fairly friendly. If she started waving her hands and chanting he could always take to his heels and whip off to another dimension.

He straightened up and pulled his shoulders back.

'I am Uther Pendragon, king of all England.' (He couldn't quite bring himself to add 'deceased'.) 'I come looking for Merlin the Enchanter. Tell me, do you have the power to detect his presence in the vicinity?'

'*The* Merlin?' Her eyes lit up with interest.

'Yes.'

'No.'

'Damn!'

The trouble with trying to find someone else capable of trotting around Infinity was that it could take for ever.

'What of the young master, James Dimmot? Is he here?'

'Away at boarding school.'

'His mother and father then?'

'Away on holiday.'

'Damn,' said Uther again.

There were two possibilities, one which gave rise to hope and one which he didn't care to contemplate.

He raised a hand to his chin and scratched his stubble.

Only two people in all of space and time knew of the significance of this moment, he thought. If I start blabbing to strangers, especially women, it could be all over the countryside and into the enemy camp within the hour.

Although the 'countryside' covered an area approximately thirty centuries of Time by a thousand light years of Space, and 'hour' was somewhat short of the mark, he was, of course, right in principle.

He cast another glance at the woman. She was full-bodied with a slight cast in one eye, giving her a marked, albeit podgy, resemblance to his daughter-in-law, Guinevere, for whom he'd had more than a passing fancy. She also had a way of looking at him . . .

The old king felt his attention wandering again.

'Have you the power to tell the future?' he mumbled.

'Some,' she replied.

Uther hesitated and gave a sigh. He thought he'd finished making historical decisions on the day he died.

He hoped he was doing the right thing.

'Merlin the Enchanter was due to meet your young master today, the day of his seventh birthday. It's possible he might have been held up. D'ye think you could have a nose round the next few years and try to find them for me?'

'How far would you like me to look?'

Uther frowned.

'Well, up to the time of James Dimmot's demise, I suppose. Not much point in looking any further than that.'

The lady eyed Uther up and down thoughtfully.

'I'm not sure I fancy the idea of that, watching the young master pop off and such . . .'

'It might not come to that,' murmured Uther uneasily. Under her steady gaze he began to feel an urge that he'd not known for some years.

He felt that he ought to cover himself up.

'. . . but I think I might be able to bring myself to accommodate your majesty,' she added, tossing her duster on to the table and sidling towards him. 'If the price is right . . .'

Chapter 24

The month that it took for Merlin to convince Dimmot that his destiny was to be more than just another blob of fish-nibbled effluent, was an eventful one all round.

The snow cleared almost as quickly as it had come and the world was revealed to the two time-travellers in all its harsh reality.

Dimmot caused minor havoc to the environment about him by attempting several times to escape and/or commit suicide. Twice he tried to have the old man and his barbaric minder arrested for abduction, and once made an abortive attempt to get either them or himself committed to an asylum. It wasn't clear which of them he tried to have committed, but then it wasn't particularly clear to Dimmot which of them was sane and which was not, for he found himself actually beginning to believe Merlin and Griswold to be who they claimed, though he couldn't imagine why.

The doctors, to whom he carefully and patiently explained about talking smoke-clouds and chaps suffering from dragon burns, were not wholly convinced. They explained this to Mr Dimmot's two companions who, while possibly bearing a vague resemblance to something from *King Lear*, were obviously no stranger than the doctors themselves.

He also managed once again to disappear, which astounded Merlin and finally explained why the Enchanter had made no progress whatever with him.

Not that Dimmot made a conscious effort to disappear. The truth, as one might guess, is that he didn't actually know he was doing it. He did nothing more than fall asleep, Wishing (with a capital W) that he could hide from the world as he'd done that first night when Griswold had burst into his life.

Besides, Merlin's and Griswold's eyes were shut.

It was, again, the middle of the night some three weeks into the month in question. They were all asleep. Griswold and Dimmot were lying side by side, their wrists bound firmly at either end of a four-foot rope. Dimmot had this inclination to creep out into the night and run away, giving Merlin the irksome job of finding him and enticing him back, Svengali-style. While it was not difficult for Merlin to locate Dimmot's presence, the business of dragging him back telepathically was a drain on the wizard's resources which were still well under par.

It was much easier just to tie him up.

The first that Griswold was aware of Dimmot's disappearance was when he was woken up by a sharp cuff on the ear.

'Fool,' hissed Merlin. 'Thou'st let him go again.'

Griswold shook the sleep from his head and glanced at the place where Dimmot should have been. A growl rumbled deep in his throat and he reached towards the other end of the rope. After groping about in the air for a second, he gave a grunt of satisfaction and, getting a firm grip on nothing in particular, shook it vigorously.

'Enough of your tricks, Dimmot,' he said sternly. 'You gave me your word.'

From out of nowhere came the strangled reply, '*Glurk!*' and Dimmot appeared, his throat gripped in Griswold's hand and looking as though he'd just been rudely awakened, which he had.

Seeing Merlin's frown of dismay Griswold explained about the native's irritating trick of pulling a cloak over the eyes so that he appeared not to be where, in fact, he was. He added lightly, 'It surprises me that the mighty Merlin is confused by so simple a trick.'

'Simple for me,' snapped Merlin. 'For ordinary men impossible. Hence my surprise.'

'Thy surprise is disturbing,' mumbled Griswold casually. 'We have travelled over fourteen hundred years in search of one who would save Mankind, only to find that he is an ordinary man.'

Griswold had a knack of making innocuous questions sound like statements that reeked of scepticism.

'It's not as simple as that,' grumbled Merlin.

'*Glurk??*' said Dimmot.

112

But Merlin had a chilling feeling that Griswold was right. In spite of this singular and remarkable hint that Dimmot might be more than just an ordinary human being and an abject failure, all the wizard's skills and efforts had done little more than convince Dimmot of their true identities and even in this his conviction was somewhat transitory. So far the Enchanter had failed to find any hidden powers in the depths of Dimmot's mind, much less bring them to the surface.

If only he'd arrived on time instead of thirty years late.

'It's not as simple as that. In truth I cannot be certain whether my failure to find the source of Dimmot's power is because that power no longer exists or because my own powers are not equal to the task. Indeed they are but a shadow of what they were prior to my departure from Camelot, in spite of Rowan's pendant.'

Griswold looked up with mild interest. 'The blacksmith?'

'No less. And certainly no more than a common artisan for all that he purports to be a crafter of wizardly paraphernalia. It appears that he has lost his touch, for this pendant that I wear, and which was made by him, steadfastly refuses to fulfil its destiny and return the most formidable set of powers in magical history to their rightful master.'

'One wonders if thy powers were already in decline when thou sought to approach Rowan the blacksmith for such a service. Thy powers of perception, for instance.'

Merlin's eyebrows furrowed. 'What sayest thou?'

Griswold dumped Dimmot absently on the bed beside him and revealed a few indications as to why the pendant had failed. When he had finished Merlin sat aghast.

'*Rowan?*' he uttered in disbelief.

Griswold nodded gravely.

''Tis plain,' he said, 'that thou hadst much on thy mind during those past few months. What was common knowledge to all Camelot appears to have escaped thine omniscient eyes.'

Merlin could only shake his head.

'He was such a manly man,' he said as if by way of explanation.

'And restoration of thy powers by this manly man's pendant is beyond hope,' concluded Griswold.

'Indeed. It seems that the salvation of Mankind has been thwarted by that same urge as has toppled monarchs from their thrones, divested priests of their vestments and reduced ordinary men to little more than animals all through the thousands of years since first they crawled across the Earth.'

'This being . . .?' began Griswold.

'The urge to get their end away,' mumbled Dimmot. The meaning of his words was lost on them, but there was little mistaking the lascivious twentieth-century gesture that went with them.

'Indeed,' they nodded in unison.

'You need all the help you can get, mate,' Dimmot observed, 'especially if you were daft enough to trust a bloke who humps sheep.'

Three days later Dimmot saw the first glimmer of how much trust was being placed in him and of the frighteningly far-reaching power of his own innate gift.

It was on the day that Griswold got into a fight.

Chapter 25

Griswold was not an easy man to annoy.

As with many men of his physical power and experience of death at first hand, he could be very patient. He had been known to go for days without getting into trouble with vagabonds, irate husbands or other knights.

He sometimes wondered if, with all his patience and understanding, he should be a man of peace. A priest perhaps.

However, since the priesthood required one's belief in God and the Ten Commandments to be fairly adaptable, in order to accommodate the ecclesiastical lust for power, virgins and choirboys, Griswold knew that his qualifications fell short of the mark. He would settle for being what he was good at: a fighter, a protector of monarch and realm, a Knight of the Round Table. He was a warrior.

And now he was annoyed.

Except for the storming of high castles or the occasional trek over a mountain range, life in his own time was lived on a single level, two-dimensional, so to speak. By the same token the only harsh sounds to be heard in that distant age, other than those of Nature venting her rage through storm, flood or forest fire, were the sounds of violence, the thunder of hooves, the clash of swords on shields, the screams of men dismembered, the crack of earthenware on drunken skulls.

For a while the snow had served to hide a different reality from the bold knight. Now he could see this reality, the harshness was unexplainable to him; a host of meaningless sounds from sources unknown, sights that bore no relation to anything his senses had encountered. Voices from the air. Gleaming castles that towered into the sky, shining with a light of their own, like those in the tales that Merlin had told him during their first years together; sparkling winged dragons roaring through the skies above, a legion of ghastly horseless carriages, screaming with an internal life, tumbling before his confused gaze as though carried along by invisible torrents. He witnessed more sorcery in each and every day than he would normally have seen in a lifetime.

The world rose high above him, constantly alive with the swirl of barbaric loudness.

But with very little sign of any worthwhile barbarians.

These people wander the city streets without weapons, he thought, while all around the sounds of danger and death assault their ears. The air crackled constantly with sorcery, the sights were ever changing before their eyes and yet these people were either deaf, blind or uncaring. Perhaps this sorcery was their protection from marauding invaders.

He studied the men closely on his infrequent trips round the city, noting with surprise that long-haired Vikings walked and talked with African slaves as equals and many of the Mongol races wandered freely about as if they were allies.

Gangs of young men with their hair cropped even shorter than Sergeant Belkin's strutted cockily through the streets in groups, laughing and jostling, cutting a ragged swathe of hostility through the townsfolk around them. Griswold thought at first that they must be the occupying troops, but they wore no armour and what few weapons they carried were concealed from sight instead of worn at their belts within easy reach. They were not the stuff of battle.

Men playing at warriors, neither allies nor enemies of any worth, he thought sadly. But even they showed more vestiges of manliness than his pathetic companion. He glanced down at Dimmot trotting along beside him, wrapped in sweaters, scarf and overcoat with his head bowed.

The snow had all but gone and they were able to walk briskly through the streets, weaving in and out of the crowds unnoticed. Griswold was dressed in sweaters, tracksuit trousers and a large pair of trainers that Dimmot had found for him. Apart from a couple of facial scars, the constant wariness in his eyes and his walk, he was quite inconspicuous in a population that reflected every type of race and strangeness.

They were heading for the market to get food and had left Merlin back at the flat, deep in meditation and searching for the source of his lost powers. This task had occupied almost all his waking hours over the past weeks and, while it left Griswold often at a loose end, the knight knew that to drag Merlin out of his trance would bring an almighty wrath upon any heads within striking distance.

His job of nursemaiding James Dimmot had become more tedious by the day and, while Dimmot's flat held wonders and mysteries beyond Griswold's comprehension, the little man rarely managed to satisfy Griswold's curiosity in spite of the knight's continual questioning and probing.

'It's just a plastic cylinder full of coloured wax. Heats up when you switch on the light, oil or air bubbles or something float to the top. Christ, I don't know how it works!'

'It has a life of its own. It is most wondrous.'

'It's diabolical! My first wife bought it. *I* only keep it to remind me what lousy taste she had.'

'You ate her?'

'Oh, good grief!'

'Are they in pain?'

'You'd think so, wouldn't you? No, they're just dancing.'

'That is not like any dancing I have ever seen. What is this story called?'

'It's called *Top of the Pops*. Why, do you like it?'

'It's diabolical.'

After two weeks Griswold had taken to prowling round the rooms restlessly and with growing impatience.

He was in dire need of action.

So when he and Dimmot were forced into a confrontation at a subway entrance with eight gentlemen of mixed origin and degrees of overt aggression, the feeling of satisfaction that spread through his large frame was so powerful that it could safely be classified as pure relief.

And when the one the others called 'Arny', after some chap whose name they couldn't pronounce properly and who'd won

117

more Mr Universe contests than he had fingers, announced that, if Griswold didn't look where he was friggin' goin', he, Arny, was going to suck his friggin' eyeballs out, the smile that spread over Griswold's features was one of unashamed bliss.

''Twould appear that you and I wish to stand on the same piece of . . .'

He gave Dimmot a nudge. Dimmot looked up at two behemoths towering above him and knew that nothing he was going to say could avert what was about to happen.

'Pavement,' he said.

'. . . pavement,' grinned Griswold.

'*********,' said Arny.

A slight look of doubt flitted across Griswold's face. He glanced at Dimmot.

Dimmot shook his head.

'Pavement,' he whispered.

'And what was the meaning of his first words to us?'

'To *you*,' said Dimmot, and he explained briefly the nature of Arny's proposal.

Merlin sat on James Dimmot's beer- and coffee-stained carpet, cross-legged and deep in trance.

While a tiny exploratory cursor searched through his mind, seeking his lost powers for the umpteenth time, the rest of him languished in the peace of meditation, thinking nothing, feeling nothing, content to dwell on nothing at all.

The search progressed through the familiar halls and well-trodden corridors of his memory to the place where lay his first lesson in magic. Over the weeks he had constantly striven to reach that particular place where he might be able to pick up the threads that wove the first crude, stringy pictures of Merlin the child flexing his puny magical muscles.

Gradually he had worked his way back, further and further until he knew he was nearing his goal. Once there, he hoped that he would be able to rebuild those muscles up to their former strength. The strength necessary to grasp the power of the cosmos and bend it to his will.

The cursor skittered hither and yon, peeping through the ancient iron keyholes and nosing into dark stony passageways.

Now he knew it was getting near. Down one more corridor, round a corner, between twin pillars of stone and before it lay the heavy oak door that had been built in his child's mind by his teacher so many hundreds of years ago. Behind this door lay his first and most crucial lesson in magic. Behind this door was where he was given the First Power.

All that remained was to open the door.

A small crowd had gathered to watch.

It was an odd sort of argument. First the big, greasy-haired bloke would growl something in perfectly intelligible English at the shaggy-haired bloke with the beard and scars. The shaggy bloke would look at the little scruffy bloke who'd translate the greasy-haired bloke's words into perfectly intelligible English. Then the shaggy one would smile and the other two would snap at him with comments like 'Wotcher gonna doboudit!' and 'For God's sake, Griswold . . .'

It was difficult to decide who was arguing with whom.

The crowd watched attentively.

Now the greasy one, known to the more volatile part of the crowd as Arny, turned to the little one and offered him the option of keeping out of it or losing his nuts.

'What sayeth he?' asked Griswold.

'Nothing,' Dimmot shrugged.

'Don't lie to me, Dommit. He threatened you.'

'Can we go now?'

'He threatened you and you do nothing. Where is your sense of honour? What sad sort of creature art you?'

'"*Are* you". Look, just say sorry and let's go.'

'Oy!' bellowed Arny, feeling that his control of the situation might be slipping. 'Nobody's going anywhere 'til I say so.'

He thrust out his chin.

His colleagues shuffled menacingly.

Griswold smiled happily.

Then Arny held his fist under Griswold's nose and the crowd stepped back expectantly.

The door to Merlin's innermost self was firmly shut. The source of his power was beyond his reach.

What kind of door is this that has neither lock nor keyhole, yet cannot be opened? he thought. Doth need a spell to open it? Why should it be sealed?

Metaphorically he gritted his teeth and shook his head in frustration.

I have not the faintest notion of how to reach that inner sanctum. Why have I not been prepared for this? Why did my teacher not foresee such an obstacle and forewarn me? Why is every step of the way so damnably and accursedly difficult!

Frustration gave way to anger and anger to fury and with that fury his will gathered strength. He glared at the door with a boiling venom and prepared to unleash the full force of his power at the despicable barrier, not knowing if that power was equal to the task or even what form it would take. But, before he could bring it to bear, another force commanded his attention.

James Dimmot was calling him.

The crowd was very understanding.

When it became clear that the resolution of the argument would require more than just the immediate vicinity, it disbanded peacefully and merged into the larger picture of inner city existence, leaving Griswold and James Dimmot to reach some sort of amicable agreement with the eight gentlemen who had begun laying into them from all sides.

With roars of delight, Griswold swung his great fists to left and to right, sending men tumbling, while blows rained upon him and kicks bounced off his battle-hardened body. Behind him, squealing with terror, Dimmot hopped around with his arms wrapped about his head, managing somehow to avoid all but the occasional glancing blow.

For a while it seemed as if the odds were fairly even. No more than two or three of the men could reach Griswold at a time and, though there were eight of them, he was a fighter and survivor by profession, stronger than any two of them and with more years' experience than all of them put together.

Then the men were stepping back out of reach and scrabbling in their pockets for weapons, as they realized this was no ordinary man they were fighting.

'I see your law regarding weapons applies only to the law-abiding, Dommit,' Griswold called over his shoulder as he leapt forward.

His great fists felled two of them before their hands left their pockets, then he turned to face the others, the blood ice-cool in his veins and his eyes narrowed.

A cry and a thud behind him said that Dimmot had fallen. For a second his attention wavered as he glanced round to see if the little man was badly hurt. At that moment his opponents leapt in, one flailing at his head with a strange weapon made of two wooden handles joined end to end by a short metal chain, which made it very light and very fast.

Before Griswold could avoid it, a blow from one of the handles caught him on the side of the head and, with lights flashing across his vision, he staggered and went down on one knee. Pain lanced through him and he tried to rise, but the blows came more viciously from all sides as the other men closed in. His body flinched in anticipation of a blade slicing through his skin at any moment.

Behind him Dimmot, curled up on the ground and now largely ignored, scrambled to his feet and threw himself in blind fury on to the backs of the attackers, pounding with unskilled fists into heads and bodies and grasping hair, ears, noses, anything that stuck out and served as a lever in order to wrench them away from the stricken knight.

'Get your hands off him, you bastards,' he screamed. His fingers fortuitously found an eye socket and dug in relentlessly. For a short and glorious moment he was a tornado, noble, indignant and unstoppable, roaring, thrashing and kicking. Street-hardened men were scrambling out of his path as Griswold rose painfully to stand by his side.

Then his brief strength drained away and he was Dimmot again.

As Arny and his bullies moved in and the two allies fell beneath their weight, Griswold caught sight of Dimmot and for an instant he wondered what the brave little man was thinking.

As for Dimmot, looking out at the London traffic sweeping past uncaring and the people watching from a safe distance, his bitterness was complete.

I wish to God that you were here right now, Merlin, he thought,

121

just so that I could say, 'See, you old fool. You were wrong. I was right. I was always right. Mankind's not worth fighting for.'

There was nothing else for it. The door would have to wait. Whatever Dimmot wanted, he wanted it badly and he wanted it now, so it didn't occur to Merlin to question or challenge the thought any more than it occurred to him to curb his fury. He turned away from the door and sped back to the surface of his mind where he would no doubt find the little native slopping around with some mundane request or inane suggestion regarding 'lunch'.

The Enchanter sped on until he burst through into full wakefulness with a shudder, a jerk and a cry of pain.

He glanced round the room, but Dimmot was not there. Yet his presence was still ringing in Merlin's mind and the wizard realized that Dimmot hadn't been calling him at all. Not in so many words.

He'd been Wishing. So earnestly and with such force that he'd created a different reality in the local area of the cosmos. A reality so designed as to ensure that his Wish would come true. A reality that required Merlin the Enchanter to *be* Merlin the Enchanter.

With triumphant relish Merlin felt his powers flooding in as if the cosmos were tumbling back into its rightful design.

He would have offered a silent, if reluctant, prayer of thanks to the little man who'd achieved with apparent ease what he had personally failed to do with over a century's experience behind him, but a change in circumstances made it rather difficult.

For, suddenly, he wasn't there to offer a prayer. Instead he was flashing through . . . Infinity, presumably? Neither here, nor there, nowhere and everywhere, unable to stop, guide or control his flight.

An instant later he was somewhere. Men were all around him, angry, aggressive men with knives and chains, threatening and snarling, while Griswold and Dimmot lay at their feet.

His rage was blind and all-embracing.

'What power is this that plays with Merlin and tosses him about like a squealing rat in a dog's jaws?' he thundered. 'What creatures are these that dare to threaten him with snarls and puny weapons?'

His arm swept in a broad curve across his body.

A bolt of fire burst from his fingertips.

Chapter 26

It was an unusual request, Uther had to admit, and it didn't seem to make a lot of sense.

'You want me to *what*?' he roared in disbelief.

The lady who came in and 'did' outlined the details of the bargain again.

'I'll chase up young Jamie and Merlin the Enchanter for you, Uther love, if you promise to make love to me as soon as I'm dead.'

'By the hair o' my bum, madam, d'ye have no taste? That's necripholly . . . negrofil . . . that's disgusting. Besides, I cannot copulate with material bodies. Doesn't work.'

'Not my body, you old silly. My spirit.'

'Oh,' said Uther as understanding dawned.

'Oh,' he said again.

She moved close to him and ran her fingers up his chest, unperturbed that they sank in up to the knuckles.

'One thing I can't see too clearly is my future after I've died,' she explained. 'I'm just lounging around for about half an hour and then the picture fades and I can never get further than that.'

She looked up at him with a petulant air. In spite of her years, which must have been all of fifty-five or so, it worked on Uther quite well.

'If I had something to look forward to, I'd be ever so grateful.'

She was a full-lipped, big-breasted woman and Uther could not help feeling that he was the one who should be grateful.

His eyes sparkled and, with a slap of hand on thigh (his), he chuckled, 'It's a bargain. Start looking.'

'Uh, uh. You first, your majesty.'

Uther stared. 'But you're not dead yet!'

'Well, find out when I will be.' She patted him on the buttock, more or less. 'And, when you're done, come straight back and you'll get your reward.'

Uther paused, caught by the thought that an old familiar tapestry had just been unravelled and rewoven back to front.

With a shrug he faded into nothing and followed the lady's life through the next eight years to the moment when a mercifully swift heart attack left her lounging about, waiting on his arrival.

On his return, several hours later, Uther sat on the edge of the settee in the house of young James Dimmot, feeling a curious mixture of smugness and acute embarrassment.

'Was I really that good?' he asked for the third time.

'The best it's ever been,' said the lady (whose name he had discovered was Rose Falworthy). She turned to give him a wide grin. 'I'm really looking forward to my demise now.'

'You should be heartily ashamed, madam. If I'd known you were spying on me . . . us . . .'

'If you'd known I was spying on us, you'd have made a right pig's ear of it.'

'Indeed,' conceded the monarch of medieval England.

And not for the first time, he added silently. Had he been better versed in such ways in his own era, history, including his own, might have taken a different turn.

Possibly several.

He sighed. He was not given to regrets and, anyway, life, which had been good to him since he died, was apparently about to get even better.

'I trust, madam . . .'

'Rose.'

'I trust, madam Rose, that this will be the first of many such liaisons between us.'

'So do I, dear. Shall we get on?'

Tucking the duster into her apron, she beckoned Uther to join her at the table.

Although James Dimmot's life was a tangled shambles, seemingly impossible to predict at times, his life-line was not difficult to trace, primarily because of the areas of chaos and destruction that littered its path.

Just as Dimmot threatened to sink out of sight into an obscure and mundane existence, a catastrophe would strike, lighting up his presence like a beacon shining through the mists of Time.

It was clear to Rose and the old king that each catastrophe was self-induced. James Dimmot was a walking (when sober) disaster.

'Poor little love,' sighed Rose through moistened eyes, as they threaded their way through his ill-fated affairs, ruined careers and marital break-ups.

'Ribwash!' replied Uther who knew a loser when he saw one. 'The fool's got no one to blame but himself.'

In Uther's world, where one swung one's sword and one's enemies fell dead, cause and effect were easily recognizable as such.

'Your lad's a self-appointed failure,' he sniggered as they stared down at Dimmot's second wife walking out on him late one autumn morning in 1985. 'What Earthly use can he be to Merlin the Enchanter?'

'We shall soon see,' intoned the lady gravely.

'When?'

'Don't know. But I feel the presence of a great and awesome power bearing down on him. Follow me.'

She wafted mentally through Dimmot's personal ether with Uther at her heels. They watched his three-week bender following the departure of his second wife, followed by three days of rambling, discordant worship at the wooden altar which stood in the living room of his flat not far from Tower Bridge.

'He always was fond of music, even as a child,' smiled Rose as Dimmot sat over the altar, his fingers numb and his mind stupefied from three days' lack of sleep.

There followed a week of harsh, clean-shaven satiating of the senses in the arms of women following a profession that Uther had heard of, though one which he had never had cause to resort to himself, being a monarch who took full advantage of the perks of the job.

Then Dimmot, obtaining apparently little satisfaction from his indulgences, returned to bottled solace and staggered along the downward path for two more bleak and cynical years until the winter of '87 when he could live with himself no longer.

Oblivious of any great and awesome powers that might be

converging on him, Dimmot wove a purposeful course to the parapet of the bridge, speculated for a sad, brief instant, drained both his bottle and the last grains of sand from his hour-glass and slid towards the Thames.

With a choked gasp Rose turned away and buried her face in Uther's chest up to her ears.

The old king slipped his arms round her and stared at the tumbling figure with rage.

'Damn,' he snapped. 'Mankind is lost. Stupid little bugger!'

He was just wondering if he still had time to return to Camelot and warn Merlin that all was lost when, to his amazement, the tiny figure that was James Dimmot suddenly snapped to a stop in mid-air as a horrendous, shaggy figure leapt out of the Thames with a roar and flung its arms round him.

Uther pressed Rose's face to his chest, but not before she had caught a glimpse of the terrible, black-bearded beast. As the demon dragged James Dimmot under the surface, Uther thought that it looked remarkably like a young and naked Griswold des Arbres.

Which was ridiculous.

Griswold was a strapping lad, but by no stretch could he be called a man of 'awesome powers'.

Besides, this was the twentieth century.

Uther would have given ten years of his eternal life to have Merlin around right then.

The motes of dust rolled through the sunlight, signalling their contempt for Uther Pendragon by drifting through his personal space with a total lack of regard for the fact that he was still in it.

He cast a glance at the stone toad.

He pursed his lips and gazed for a second through the cottage window.

The castle languished in the hot afternoon.

There was nothing he could do here. Mankind's future looked bleak.

Young Dimmot was dead, his part in Merlin's plan unfulfilled. The Enchanter had disappeared and the lady Rose had told Uther that they could not go on with the shadow of young Jamie's death looming between them.

'Everybody dies,' Uther had grumbled at her.

'But he's not due to for another thirty rotten, miserable years,' Rose reminded him. 'And I've got to live with the vision of that awful creature for the rest of my life.'

When Uther, who prided himself on his sensitivity, gently informed her that she had less than ten years herself and, anyway, she'd get over it, being good, buxom peasant stock, her reply had been surprisingly terse.

The old king turned his gaze from the cottage window, sighed, grunted and hauled himself to his feet.

He whistled philosophically to himself.

He was at a loose end. All eternity at his feet. He could go anywhere, anywhen.

He was completely free to do what he wanted.

And yet.

When he was king he had borne great responsibilities, ruling, protecting, taxing his subjects, fighting off invaders, making top-level decisions – it was all very demanding. Even though he had revelled in it, when he died, the relief was like having a boil lanced. It had surprised even him.

When he died he had relished his compulsory retirement as much as he'd relished his monarchy.

Now he wasn't so sure that freedom was all that sweet.

'A man ought to have a purpose,' he grumbled at the sunlight. 'Something to exercise his will, his . . . manliness.'

In his head a voice whispered.

Men will always need leaders.

'Men will always need leaders,' mumbled Uther thoughtfully.

Fighters.

'And fighters.'

Heroes.

'And her . . . who said that?'

It is my voice you hear, Uther Pendragon. The voice of all knowledge, of all wisdom, of all purpose.

Uther spun round gaping.

'Where are you? *What* are you? Are you a demon? By the gods, demon, come out and face me like a . . .'

No, King Uther Pendragon. You come and face me.

'And where, pray, do I find you?'

I reside in the nexus of multidimensional forces of which time, space and mind are but a part and before which pale to insignificance the magics and sorceries of all save that which created me.

'What?'

I'm in the back room, sighed the Book.

Chapter 27

'Earlier today fighting broke out between rival gangs in the Borough Market area of London, outside the entrance to London Bridge Underground Station. Several members of one gang and two spectators were admitted to hospital with superficial burns and one man suffered a severe eye injury. Conflicting eye-witness reports spoke of knives, chains and a home-made flame thro—'

Dimmot made the beautiful dark-skinned woman with her big, moist lips vanish with the flick of a button and turned to Merlin with confusion and anger on his face.

'You should have thrashed 'em. Why didn't you finish the bastards? They would have killed us if you hadn't turned up.'

'I am not a killer of slaves,' said Merlin.

'They weren't slaves. They were a bunch of sadistic animals, who enjoy kicking people into mush.'

'All men are slaves, Dimmot. All but a few. They are slaves of their needs, their desires, their whims. Your picture box testifies to that.'

'Yeah, well, some of them have bloody strange whims.'

'Such whims are spawned in their minds, and their minds are what the world has made them.'

In the corner Griswold was sitting quietly tinkering at the piano, on top of which lay a recently honed and lethally sharp breadknife.

He was unimpressed by Dimmot's amateur hypnotisms.

Merlin could make faces appear from woodsmoke and waterfalls, just as beautiful as the dark woman and more spectacular *and* they spoke intelligible English. Why the Enchanter bothered to humour Dimmot by pretending that the images in the box were anything other than Dimmot's meagre magics, Griswold couldn't understand.

He ignored the box.

Staring fixedly at the parchment with the flies, he tinkered with the strange sounds to see if he could make the flies fly.

'It's the sounds that bring all those flies to life,' Dimmot had explained to him. 'Without the sounds they are dead, meaningless.'

And Dimmot had sat at the altar, his fingers dancing over the keys, making sounds that flitted and darted like the woodland insects, soared and sparkled like starlings, clashed and jarred like grit-jawed warriors in battle.

Insects, starlings, warriors had all failed to disturb the flies.

Griswold wasn't surprised.

'So you admit that Mankind is an abysmal failure?' said Dimmot, flopping down in the armchair.

Merlin sat cross-legged on the floor with his back to Dimmot's bed, waiting for the pains of his uncontrolled journey to subside.

'Mankind is but a child, yet to become the Man he thinks he is,' he said quietly. 'And, because he is a child, he is prey to his impulses and cannot help but be governed and enslaved by them.'

'A child normally has parents to guide him,' said Dimmot. 'If they happen to care, that is.'

'He has parents. His mother is the cosmos, all that was, is and ever will be. The sun that gives him life, the moon without whose rhythms he could not have been conceived, the planets and the stars whose guidance he generally ignores as being of little consequence to his childish games.'

'And his father?'

'The need to survive.'

'That all?'

'It is all. From this one need all others grow. The crudest physical actions, the subtlest thoughts, the wildest emotions all have their roots in this one instinct. Men cheat, kill and destroy in response to this need.

'They build their religions and beliefs and fight for them as they build and fight for their vast empires and their sky-touching castles from this one need. They create their works of art from this same need. They explore the heights, the depths, the very boundaries of their experience, fired by this same need.'

Dimmot curbed his impatience.

'How wonderful,' he said. 'The world is full of spoilt kids, running around, doing the most god-awful things to each other in the name of their religions, meditating themselves silly and spraying graffiti on public buildings out of a "need to survive". That's a bit naive, isn't? What about alcoholics and masochists and . . . suicides?'

''Tis the fate of most men to see things as they are not. Then their distorted visions lead them to believe in dreams, nightmares, fantasies. From those fantasies come men's personal truths and 'tis these "truths" that give men their own purpose or lack thereof. 'Tis these "truths" that they yearn to experience or strive to escape from.'

Merlin screwed up his eyes in pain and took a long deep breath, then went on.

'Men need a purpose, something to make their lives have meaning. When a man's yearning or striving becomes his purpose, he will pursue that purpose with all his heart and all his will and therein lies his true glory.'

'What! In wallowing in the depths of degradation and self-pity, out of touch with reality, living in a personal hell. That's what you call glory? I'm sorry, Merlin, you've lost me.'

The Enchanter gazed at the floor. If only he'd arrived on time and caught Dimmot in his childhood as planned. So much could have been achieved. The awesome gift he possessed could have been harnessed and trained to a devastating power instead of being allowed to run riot, in a way that used only a fraction of its potential. As it was, Merlin had virtually to start from scratch.

So be it.

He spoke quietly. 'The glory lies not in the degradation. It lies not in a man's personal hell. It lies in the strength with which he pursues good and bad alike, for it is the need to survive that gives him the means to such glory.'

'What has his need to surv—?'

'Not "his" need,' smiled the wizard. '*The* need.'

'What's the difference?'

'The difference,' said Merlin matter-of-factly, 'is that the need to survive belongs to all creation. Now the survival of creation is in jeopardy and Man has been created to ensure that survival. The means he has been given for this titanic task is his will.'

He talked about the universe entering a state of Darkness because the forces of Evil had begun to dominate all and the balance between Good and Evil was being disturbed.

Then he talked about Man being created by the cosmos and Man's purpose being to try to redress the balance of Good in the universe before the forces of Evil reduced all of creation to a state of chaos.

He talked of Evil as a disease ravaging the body of creation and of Mankind growing in power, driven by the ailing cosmos, and expanding throughout the stars and galaxies, throughout the very body of the universe over many millions of years to fight the disease.

'Like little antibodies,' intoned Dimmot.

'Like antibodies,' agreed Merlin.

He talked of the raging battle between the disease and the cure and, if his diagnosis, gleaned from his visions, was correct, the disease was winning.

He talked about the desperate need for the cure to be purged of impurities, to be cleansed and strengthened over the next centuries, so that it might flourish and fight off the disease. Then it would go on the attack and, with luck and faith, it would become strong enough to strike back and destroy the ravaging sickness.

He stared deep into Dimmot's eyes to drive his point home.

'So you see, James Dimmot, the future of all creation lies with Mankind. The purpose that eludes his limited perceptions is the greatest purpose of all. Victory is his goal and his weapon is his will without which both he and all creation are lost.'

His voice, which had grown in volume and intensity as he spoke, dropped to a whisper.

'Man's greatest glory lies in the strength of his will.'

Dimmot stared back at the eyes boring into his.

He had the distinct impression that he was standing on the edge of a vast black precipice, beneath an equally vast black sky, unable to see the ground or the stars and on the verge of being asked to throw himself into the abyss.

In the interest of Mankind of course.

Unable to take his eyes from Merlin's face, he stared back.

The paleness of the small, porcelain face spoke of great age.

The lines and the creases told of an immense amount of living, striving, pain conquered, temptation overcome, friends lost, loves remembered. The eyes glowed with strength, ruthless, yes, but noble and of an intense, unbending will. They gazed rheumily at him, not without warmth, and certainly with deep understanding.

With some effort Dimmot tore his gaze away and focused it on Griswold's great muscled back hunched over the piano. He knew that if the knight turned round, a similar intensity would be there, a similar strength, a similar vibrance. Dimmot realized that, in all his life, he had never encountered anyone as profoundly alive as these two people who came from a past long dead.

He felt their presence dominating the room and, in doing so, felt an awareness of himself that was more vital than anything he'd ever experienced.

They were truly the most real people he had ever met. He suddenly felt a burning desire to gain their approval and to be worthy of their trust and friendship.

He didn't know what they were aiming to do. He didn't know if they were under a delusion.

To tell the truth he didn't really know what the old man was talking about.

He did know that they would behave with courage and nobility whatever their tasks.

He remembered his burst of courage earlier that day when he'd given Griswold a few precious seconds and possibly saved him from death. He felt somehow very contented and very frightened. He also realized that for the first time in months he didn't feel the need for a drink.

'What do you want of me?' he asked.

'Somewhere near here live the First Unborn. 'Tis they whose help we must enlist. Now where can we find them?'

'The First Unborn.'

'Yes.'

'Never heard of them.'

Chapter 28

In the prison beneath the City the old man sits, immobile down to his very soul, hardly daring to exist.

A little ray of hope is held in fearful suspense before his inner eye.

His regular visitor has just left and the manner of his going was . . . different. Reflective.

As was the way he looked at the old man.

For the first time the visitor's eyes had held a hint of suspicion.

The old man stares at the ray of hope.

His plan of action, formed many years ago, might allow that hope to become a flame, or it might snuff out in the fragile light and leave him even deeper in darkness and cold than before.

He wonders if he has any courage left to take the risk.

Chapter 29

And there you have it, Uther Pendragon, concluded the Book.

'Guinea pigs? Rats in a maze?' Uther shook his head in disbelief. 'Is that all Man is?'

At the moment, yes. In time . . .

'What of Merlin?' growled Uther. 'What of Griswold and Dim . . .'

Pawns.

'. . . mot. What of men, women and children?'

Puppets, Uther Pendragon, but puppets who may, one day, become . . .

'No more! No more!' snapped Uther.

He turned away from the shelf, and stood in the almost lightless gloom of Merlin's bedroom with anger in his eyes.

'And what of you?' he asked over his shoulder. 'What is your place in this scheme of things?'

My task is to record.

'Is that all?'

And to advise.

'And Merlin? Did you advise him?'

Indeed.

'Well, for all your powers, your advice was clearly short of the mark. The Enchanter is lost, his plan has failed and Mankind is doomed. Go and tell *that* to your . . .'

Uther Pendragon, your lack of respect is, understandably, a result of your concern and is thus forgiven, said the Book casually.

The Enchanter, it went on, *was victim of the common ignorance of his times. For this reason he arrived late at his destination.*

'What ignorance?' said Uther with a frown.

The Book talked briefly of celestial balance and forces, of

temporal coordination and Man's inner rhythms reflecting those of his environment, and of going off half-cocked, concluding with, *. . . if you get my drift.*

'I see,' said Uther weakly. 'How late?'

Thirty years, give or take.

The old king did a quick calculation and his heart sank.

'Thirty years. Too late, dammit. He arrived too late.'

Mmm? mumbled the Book absently.

Uther got the impression that it was, metaphorically, inspecting its fingernails.

Chapter 30

At first Dimmot declined Merlin's offer of a trip into the twenty-first century.

'Not in a million years,' he said.

On finding that Dimmot had never heard of the race that was meant to inhabit this particular era, Merlin spent half an hour raging around the flat, growling about some stupid old monarch who didn't know his past from his future.

Then he disappeared in a puff of smoke and was gone for three days.

Griswold patiently played the piano and Dimmot rapidly lost his nerve.

On his return Merlin explained that, according to his probings, the First Unborn, residing in a sleep close to death on different parts of the planet, were of insufficient numbers and too scattered to be a discernible force at the present time.

If the lessons of history were to be believed, he said, this force would expand and become organized, centralized and concentrated in the interests of . . . er . . .

'Optimum efficiency,' said Dimmot the computer consultant.

'Indeed,' said Merlin. And therefore, he explained, in the space of one hundred years or so, the beings known as the First Unborn would no doubt be a force powerful enough to fulfil their part in Merlin's plan.

The journey to AD 2090 would be as simple as a twopenny bus-ride.

'Sorry,' said Dimmot.

'Man's future depends on thee.'

'You didn't say anything about *going* there!'

137

'Thou'dst rather go to thy grave with Man's demise on thy conscience?'

'Yes.'

Merlin sighed. 'I hoped thou'dst have a little more compassion. But if a man is neither born great nor becomes great it is not for such as I to thrust greatness upon him. The choice must, of course, be thine. If thou choosest to turn thy back on Mankind,' his shoulders sagged and he turned away with a helpless snap of his fingers, '. . . so be it.'

'One hundred million sperm donations are housed in these sealed containers in liquid nitrogen at a constant temperature of minus one hundred and ninety-five degrees centigrade. Each of the donations is catalogued and cross-referenced on computer under nearly eighty different categories, according to parental status, character, medical history, physical fitness, IQ, emotional stability, etc.'

The blonde girl wore a skin-tight, one-piece, micro-thin silver suit that reflected both the majestic technology of the World Sperm Bank and the rivet-eyed stares of the thirty-odd tourists and potential donors trailing happily behind her.

'Most of the donations are at the request of the donors themselves, of course, and the reasons vary enormously. They may be intending to have a vasectomy, they may be preparing to undergo radiotherapy. They may have some dreams of immortality or they may wish their offspring to be born in a future where "the world has become a better place for kids to live in".'

She embraced the all-male group with a warm, subtly sensual smile.

All but three of the men grinned back at her, nodding eagerly.

Switching smoothly to second person singular she continued, 'If you so wish, you may specify the year of birth, the type, race and religion of the mother. You may pick the mother according to emotional stability, esoteric inclinations, engram compatibility or potential telepathic powers.

'There is no limit to the permutations you can apply to your children,' she smiled an intimate, but slightly stern smile, 'provided they are socially acceptable and within the law, of course.'

The group nodded and grinned again, most of them wondering if she would be present, should they choose to submit a donation.

'We even have a system whereby you may choose a mate according to the signs of the Zodiac, Chinese astrology, social peerage in previous incarnations or . . .'

'Where does that door lead to?' demanded Merlin.

'Er . . . Control Centre,' she replied a mite peevishly, and went on, '. . . or Yin/Yang compatibility. You might want to insist that no mother is involved . . .'

Turning to Dimmot, Merlin whispered, 'That's the door we want. Come.'

'. . . but that your children are conceived and produced artificially. In the next section we pass through you will be able to see the artificial wombs functioning . . .'

Merlin caught Griswold's eye and nodded towards the girl. Griswold sidled towards her, blocking her view of Merlin and Dimmot. Taking Dimmot's arm, Merlin waited while the group flowed past them.

Then he turned to the door they'd just passed and they moved off quietly, while Griswold smiled a winsome smile at the girl and she forgot her lines.

The door was six-inch-thick beryllium steel. Dimmot grabbed the handle and gave it a yank.

'*You are not authorized to enter. Please insert your pass card, bearing finger and retina pattern, into the appropriate slot and place your palm against the screen for verification.*'

Merlin looked round. 'Who spake?'

'The door spake,' said Dimmot.

'And what sayeth it?'

'It said we can't go in.'

Merlin looked at the door. 'It defies us?'

Dimmot nodded. 'Can we go home now?'

'Home! May your tongue rot if you dare to speak thus before our task is finished.'

Dimmot blanched and stepped back quickly. 'That's not a spell, is it?'

'*Personnel are not authorized to enter unless . . .*'

'Quiet, scurrilous servant,' hissed the Enchanter.

Then he spoke a few words to the door, most of which were unintelligible to Dimmot, but which sounded quite poetic.

With a series of deep, ponderous clicks the door swung open.

139

'That,' said Merlin, 'is a spell.'

'Could I learn to do that?' said Dimmot as they trod cautiously into the next room.

'No.'

'I thought I was meant to be a wizard.'

'Thy wizardry consists of manipulating minds, hearts and, betimes, the odd soul or two. No more.'

'If I'm so skilful, how come I'm such a failure?'

But Merlin was not listening. He stood in the doorway gazing at row upon row of metal box-like containers stretching along the walkway and rising to the ceiling high above them. Each box was no more than six inches across. A little six-inch coffin that contained the beginnings of life.

Far ahead the walkway ended and disappeared out of sight to left and right.

No doubt there would be others just like it with further identical rows of boxes.

The First Unborn.

Dimmot looked briefly up and down the rows.

'Hardly worth writing home about. There's nobody here.'

Except for his eyes wandering quietly over the scene the wizard was motionless. Even his breathing appeared to have stopped.

Dimmot waited uneasily. He knew better than to speak, but turned to peer nervously through the door. He returned his gaze to Merlin's face. The wizard's expression was strange, quite indescribable. Dimmot thought of the pictures he'd seen of saints staring up at the sky in wonderment. With considerable willpower he remained silent.

'Dost feel it?' whispered Merlin.

'Feel what?'

Merlin's face had softened and his eyes were glowing with a childlike wonder as if the mask of an old man had been taken away to reveal the face of childhood beneath.

'The peace. The infinite quietness.'

Dimmot felt the cold and shivered. He'd have felt happier with Griswold close at hand and the blonde with the long legs to look at.

He turned to go, but Merlin's hand reached out and clamped his arm in a frighteningly strong grip.

140

'Be still, James Dimmot. It is time for thee to meet thy destiny.'

And, as Merlin turned his face towards him, Dimmot felt the icy fear of knowing that whatever the wizard was about to do was totally inevitable.

Merlin passed his hand across Dimmot's face as if drawing aside a curtain. As he did so, the deathly stillness was broken and the room burst into life. Sensations poured into Dimmot's senses like brilliant colours and sounds flowing through a man who has been blind and deaf since birth.

Vibrancy pulsated about him, making his skin and eyelids tingle, sweeping up his spine and round his ears and scalp, like the featherlight touch of a woman's caress.

He inhaled and with the cool air came the essence of a million lives filling his lungs with their presence until it felt that they were an integral part of him. He was expanding, filling the vast room, reaching out, here, there to embrace them and become one with them.

The room about him sang with life, recalling with breath-taking vividness his first orgasm when he knew that something beautiful was happening, but did not know what it was. A strange beauty overwhelmed his body and mind. Something he couldn't hope to stop was flooding his senses.

Merlin waved his hand and the sensations ceased abruptly, leaving Dimmot shaking from the intensity of his emotions.

His eyes darted about the room, searching for any remaining wisps of whatever had happened.

The room was bare.

'What did you do to me?'

'Merely drew aside the shield that divides a man from the rest of humanity.'

'My God, it was beautiful . . . inexplicable. I want it back.'

'That would be inadvisable.'

'But I felt so alive. I felt part of something purposeful. Godly. Aren't I entitled to feel that?'

'Thou art entitled to beauty. Thou art entitled to purpose. Godliness is something else, however.'

'Why?'

'Because the price is too high.'

'What price?'

141

'Come,' said the wizard. 'We have work to do.'

He strode off towards the far end of the walkway. He seemed to know just where he was going.

Dimmot followed, his head spinning with aftervisions, his mind struggling to grasp what he'd experienced. Something, some specific thing that had shone through all the emotions he'd felt, was eluding him. He knew instinctively that it must be peculiar to this one place.

On reaching the far end of the walkway Merlin turned to his right, guided by an unerring intuition.

Ahead was another turning, round which streamed lights of various colours and intensities, reflecting off the metal containers.

A soft buzz of activity reached their ears.

Merlin halted and raised his hand to indicate silence. He gazed towards the turning and Dimmot noticed that the wizard's eyes seemed to be reflecting the colours ahead. They danced with flecks of red and green, violet and orange, which was odd because the lights were blue and pink.

'At last,' whispered the Enchanter. 'We are all here. Despite all adversity, against all odds.'

His voice trembled with triumph.

'We are all together. Now the task begins.'

He turned to Dimmot.

'The feeling that eludes thy grasp.'

'Yes?'

'A quality unique to such as the First Unborn. It is called innocence.'

'It was beautiful,' said Dimmot again. 'So . . . pure.'

'Indeed. A pure, virgin-like parchment on which no vile word has yet been writ.'

'A brand new computer disc,' murmured Dimmot half to himself. 'Clean and . . .' A small tendril of understanding was deciding whether or not to crawl across the terrain of Dimmot's awareness. '. . . blank?'

The Enchanter smiled gravely.

'A blank disc,' he nodded.

Chapter 31

The door to the old man's prison opens, but the glaring light of the outside world doesn't stream in because it's not allowed to.

His prison never sees the light.

He sits, white against the infinite black, in a room of no walls, no ceiling, no floor, no ordinary boundaries.

Stark-outlined against the light in the doorway his regular visitor stands.

For the first time ever the visitor's stance is wary and he hesitates before entering and the old man, staring down at his feet, knows that it is time to act.

He raises his head slowly and squints in a slightly wrong direction as if the centuries of incarceration have finally taken their toll on his ancient eyes.

'Merlin?' he whispers.

Chapter 32

The control room of the World Sperm Bank was vast, awesome and alive with activity. Banks of consoles flickered and flashed signals of light to each other along translucent tubes hundreds of yards long.

As Merlin and Dimmot crossed the floor, the reflections of a million messages being processed by the wall-to-wall computers danced beneath their feet. The only sounds were the quiet hum of electrical power and the loud slurp of the Control Centre security man draining his Stero-Protein Superpower Shake from its High Carb Digestible Carton through a Multi-Vit-Min Chewable Straw.

They approached as he crushed the carton in a hand roughly the size of a baseball glove and took a bite out of it.

'My God,' whispered Dimmot. 'He's like Hercules and King Kong rolled into one.'

'I have seen larger men, though not often,' admitted Merlin.

He strode over to where the man sprawled in a reclining chair at the console in the very centre of the room. The console had a dozen screens and one large red button.

Catching sight of the wizard from the corner of his eye the giant turned. His face split into an amiable grin. He tossed his *Bulkbuilder* magazine on to the console.

'Hi, how you doin'?' he managed through a mouthful of carton.

'Morrow,' nodded Merlin.

'Me too.' He glanced past the wizard at Dimmot and raised a hand in greeting.

'Hi, how yo' doin'?'

'Morrow,' mumbled Dimmot.

'Me too. Wo' can I do fyuh?'

Merlin sighed. He had adopted simple telepathy to interpret

144

Dimmot's mode of speech and translate his own words into Dimmot's mind since their first meeting. Much simpler than trying to learn another language at his age.

Three-way telepathy was not that simple. He wasn't in the mood for straddling the space between two minds of such vastly different intellectual and emotional make-ups with one foot in each.

He glanced at the identity disc on the man's shirt.

'Simple tour of inspection, Arthur Shultz,' he said.

'Oh. Sho', help yoself.'

'Don't get up.'

'OK.'

They wandered off. Arthur Shultz put his feet up on the desk, picked up his spring-loaded power grip developer and thumbed through his magazine until he came to the centrefold which depicted a naked couple. Somehow they were manipulating the bars of the 'Couples' Computerized Pneumatic Double Training Machine, while in the act of doing something very personal.

Dimmot was confused.

'Is that great twit all that stands between a hundred million potential lives and the ravages of the outside world? What sort of security is that?'

'The sort that does not recognize the power of wizardry. History is rife with them. We came through the door that allows in only . . . "authorized personnel"?'

Dimmot nodded.

'To Arthur Shultz we are, therefore, authorized personnel.'

'He's a moron.'

'Indeed.'

'And he controls all this?'

'No! *This* controls all this. He merely guards it.'

'Against who?'

'Against what thou callest "malfunction".'

'But he's a moron,' said Dimmot again.

'He is better qualified than thee. He is perfect.'

Merlin wandered the length of the room, staring up at the machinery with a narrow, faraway expression.

'Do you know what you're looking for?' asked Dimmot.

'Oh, I've *found* what I'm seeking,' answered Merlin.

'Then how about we do what we came for and go home?'

'Come with me,' said the wizard and strode off to the far end of the room with his cloak flapping purposefully behind him. Dimmot scampered after him. They rounded a corner and came to a small door.

This door opened at a touch and they found themselves in a tiny utility room with what looked remarkably like vacuum cleaners, mops and buckets.

'Are we here?' said Dimmot.

'We are here.'

Dimmot glanced around the room. I might have guessed my destiny would be fulfilled in a broom cupboard, he thought.

The wizard closed the door behind him and swept a hand across his body. A warm glow lit the room.

'Sit thee down and make thyself comfortable. We will be here some while.'

'Where's Griswold?'

'He is engaged. Worry not about him.'

I'm not worried about him, thought Dimmot. I'm worried about me.

'Nor about thyself,' hissed Merlin. 'There are far greater things at stake than thy safety or mine. Now, shut thine eyes and listen to my words.'

Before he could object Dimmot found himself doing as he was bid and realized that Merlin had not simply ordered him, he'd willed him to obey. And Dimmot was powerless to resist. But then willpower was never his strong point.

'I have enough willpower for both of us,' whispered the Enchanter, 'but 'tis thee, Dimmot, that must speak for me now, for I lack the wild skill that is thy birthright and which, for want of such will, has brought nothing but chaos to thy life. Now hear my words.'

The Enchanter began to intone a poem. The words formed in Dimmot's head as if written there. Each line seemed to hover before him before exploding silently into a thousand colours to make way for the next. The colours, needless to say, were wondrous and memorable. More so than the words.

'In the darkness there is darkness still,
    Layer on layer is builded there until

146

Sunlight cannot reach thee where thou lie,
  Thus the sight is stolen from thine eye.

'The hum of life's too faint for thee to hear,
  Thus is hearing stolen from thine ear.
  Numbness keeps thee and thy soul apart,
  Thus is feeling stolen from thine heart.

'Comes the time when all these words are true,
When the darkness fills thee through and through,
  And the cold and silence are complete,
  And thy heart knows bitterest defeat,

'Then from darkness there will come a burning light,
From the silence there will rise the word to fight,
From the cold will blaze the fire of hope and love,
Each builded from the other, as below, so above.'

'Now,' said Merlin, 'repeat it to me.'

'I can't remember all that,' said Dimmot.

'On the contrary, Dimmot, thou canst not forget until I decree it. Repeat the poem.'

Dimmot repeated the poem.

'What do you think?' asked the wizard.

'Very metaphorical. Bit Wordsworth, perhaps?'

'Hardly. You haven't answered my question.'

Dimmot ran the poem through once more. 'I think it's a load of pretentious crap.'

'You didn't understand it?'

'Oh, I got the gist. It's your seed of rebellion, isn't it?'

'Pity. I did hope it would be a little less obvious. I suppose I must be grateful that it has the guise of "pretentious crap" and hope that is sufficient for it to pass unnoticed through the millennia to come. Poetry was never one of my strengths.'

'You wrote this?'

'I did.'

'You dragged me all this way through time to give a poetry recital?'

'It is more than that. It is the only course left for me to take. It

147

is what those in my profession would call "magic". In thy trade 'tis known as "programming".'

'People can't be programmed just like that,' said Dimmot. 'Not by poetry, anyway.'

'People cannot help but be programmed. It is the essence of their survival. Without it they would flounder helplessly with no purpose, no direction and little hope of survival. They are programmed by the cosmos.' The wizard smiled. 'By their father and mother.'

'So what are we doing here then? Why not leave it up to Man's parents? They're not perfect, but they seem to be coping.'

'They are not coping. They are succumbing.'

Merlin looked deep into Dimmot's mind, searching for the words that Dimmot used in his trade that would bring home the impact of what he was trying to convey. He also looked for a key that would turn Dimmot's reluctance into the bitter fury needed to drive his Wishes into the ether where their power could be embraced and turned into reality.

At last he had it.

'The source of all men's powers, strengths and weaknesses lies within themselves, whether these be wizardry, religious zeal, a sense of purpose or blind slavery.

'It is all down to programming. Man's destiny will finally be controlled by that which can control the Mind of Man by such programming. Even now the fight for supreme control over the Mind of Man has begun, and that Mind is the goal, the prize . . . and the battleground.'

The smell of disinfectant drifted into Dimmot's nostrils. It was remarkably like the stuff he frequently used on his carpet the morning after.

'And doesn't Man have a say in this?' he whispered.

'Man goes about the business of playing his little games, quite unaware that his parents are unable to save him from drowning in his own ignorance . . . for all their caring.'

'Isn't that always the way?' said Dimmot, and his eyes brimmed with tears.

Merlin laid a hand on the trembling shoulder.

'So often. So often.'

The warmth of the little man's hand was strong and comforting. Dimmot brushed a hand across his eyes.

'What do you want me to do?' he said.

'The Forces of Darkness have hacked into Man's programme and infected it with a virus. The way to destroy the virus is to attack it with something that will thrive on the virus itself.'

'So?'

'So we will plant a bug in Man's programme.'

'Oh, my God,' gasped Dimmot quietly as understanding finally dawned on him. 'A hundred million little blank discs!'

'Close thine eyes,' said Merlin.

As soon as his eyes were closed Dimmot felt himself to be totally alone. He knew that this would be Merlin's doing just as he knew that, in fact, he was surrounded by millions of lives. Little half-people waiting to be matched with other little half-people to make people. He wondered if sperms had half a soul and could only be complete when they found another half. He wondered if sperms had a whole soul that couldn't thrive until it found an egg to live in. Perhaps female eggs didn't have souls. Perhaps females didn't have souls. His first wife didn't, he was sure of that. His second . . .

A voice called out to him.

'James. Jamie. Here I am, darling.'

A woman was walking towards him, treading on the nothing that filled his vision, an isolated figure in the distance, coming nearer.

He knew who it was even before he recognized her.

'Oh, no. Don't do this, Merlin. I don't want this,' he whispered, but he knew his words would be ignored and he thought he knew why and, right now, he wasn't convinced that he wanted to suffer this much even for the whole of Mankind.

The woman came closer. He could see her clearly now, the long auburn hair, the full figure, the slightly excessive make-up. She held out her hands.

'Come on, Jamie. Come to me. There's just time for a cuddle before your train leaves.'

'No, Mother. I don't want to. It makes it worse. Merlin, for God's sake stop this, will you?'

The woman's hands held him and pulled him towards her. He tried to dig his heels into the void, but he was powerless. She hugged him to her and he felt the warmth of her body and the motherly smell that always struck him afresh because he rarely had a chance to smell it.

He tugged and pulled, but the warmth and the smell and the softness were too much for him, so he clung on with all his might, his little body shaking.

His school cap fell from his head.

Then he was being pulled off by firm hands and made to stand back, away from the warmth, silent, with eyes aflame.

'Come on, Jamie,' his father was saying. 'Time to go. If you miss the train, we'll miss the plane.'

It was his parents' standing joke. They always said it when he went back to boarding school and they went on holiday.

Then, still smiling with their arms entwined, they began to recede into the distance, growing smaller and somehow changing. They drifted apart and Dimmot realized, to his horror, that they were becoming younger and younger, changing into children, unaware of each other's existence or his. They began to behave as if there were other people around them though Dimmot could see no one else. He realized that they were going through their own childhoods.

And through their own little hells.

He saw them suffering, isolated and lonely, buffeted by fate and at the mercy of the cosmos, no more able to govern their feelings or faults or weaknesses than he was.

And while he watched and saw them as children he sobbed, because he'd never had the chance to know them as parents, or to forgive them for being what they were, or to say sorry for what he was.

And he'd never be able to tell them that he now understood why they were the way they were; like so many others, himself included, unaware of the reason for their existence and oblivious of their destinies, or of the glory that lay beyond their reach.

Because Evil had already got to them.

James Dimmot didn't know too much about good and evil on a cosmic scale, or about destiny or any wondrous cosmic plan. He didn't and never would comprehend the vastness of space, time, life, the universe and everything, nor could he begin to grasp the idea of titanic struggles for supremacy spanning thousands of centuries or encompassing galaxies and dimensions unknown.

But one thing he did know.

The Forces of Darkness were out of bloody order.

'Balance,' Merlin corrected him.

Dimmot woke up sobbing, glared at Merlin the Enchanter and snarled, 'Thanks a lot, you little medieval sod.'

'Art thou ready now?'

'You're damn right I am. Let's screw the bastards back into Hell where they belong.'

'How wouldst thou fare in addressing the masses?'

'What, public speaking? I've done the odd lecture or two. Why?'

'Thou art about to address a hundred million souls.'

'Bit like God, eh?'

'Or like Satan. But thou art not God. Thou art not Satan. Thou art Dimmot.'

Thankyou, thought Dimmot. Your confidence is touching.

'Can we get on with it?' he said impatiently.

'Indeed. Thy task is now simple. I can do little to help thee further. The desire that now burns within thee must be used before it loses its edge. Close thine eyes, repeat the verse and make a Wish. Wish that thy words be heeded by those to whom thou speakest, for, if thy words fall on deaf ears, the suffering that thou hast had will be as nothing compared with that of the children in the Eternal Dark Age. Thy loneliness will be a joyous tumult of warmth compared to their isolation, thy despair a burning beacon of hope compared to their bleak greyness,' said Merlin. 'And those of thy tribe who helped thee to all but destroy thyself will seem like Godly benefactors beside the forces that would seek to condemn Man to eternal darkness.'

Merlin's voice trembled with a quiet and terrible fury, but it was not that which made Dimmot realize the extent to which Man would be made to suffer before he was finally destroyed. It was the desperate frustration in the Enchanter's voice.

'For all my wizardry, in this, I am powerless to help. I feel as though I'm at the edge of a dark lake watching a child drowning and I'm unable to reach him because I'm shackled to the ground. Thou art the only one who can reach the water and swim.'

Dimmot gaped. 'Merlin, I can't begin to grasp the sort of concepts you're talking about. It's just too big for me to get into focus. I don't know where to start.'

'Think of the child,' said the Enchanter.

And Dimmot knew exactly what he had to do.

He closed his eyes and began to recite the poem. As he did so, he pictured a child in black water, pulling with its little hands at a surface that parted cruelly under their touch. He saw its eyes begging for help and its lips clamped tight, letting neither water nor life-giving oxygen into the little lungs until the brain forced the body to gasp for air that was just out of reach.

He saw himself scrambling into the water, splashing clumsily towards the child, shouting for it to swim to him. The words of the poem floated before him and he knew they were still pouring from his lips, though he could hear nothing but the child choking and himself shouting.

Then it disappeared beneath the surface. His own fury and frustration overwhelmed him. He saw himself swimming faster, screaming for it to try for God's sake and Wishing, Wishing with every cell of his body that the child would hear him and respond.

For seconds the words of the poem obscured his vision and time seemed to stand still around his thrashing body. Then one flailing hand broke the surface, then another, and then the little face, thrown back and puckered with concentration as the child swam in Dimmot's direction with that near-useless technique that small children have.

He reached for the hand, felt it elude his grasp and reached out again, grabbing the wrist in his fingers and pulling the child to him. As he reached the shore the poem ended. Merlin the Enchanter stood before him, smiling. He looked round for the child but it was not there.

'We did it, didn't we?' he asked anxiously. 'We got through?'

Merlin nodded. '*Thou* didst get through,' he corrected.

'And *I* saved the child . . . little Mankind?'

His eyes glowed with pride.

'It is too soon to tell,' said Merlin gently, reluctant to spoil Dimmot's moment.

'And when will you know? When will it happen?'

'If our plan has worked it has already happened many centuries hence, in the year of our Lord three thousand seven hundred and ninety-seven. Give or take a year. My old friend Uther will tell us before too long.'

'What now?'

The Enchanter pulled him to his feet and dispersed the magical glow from the walls. He opened the door into the brightly lit control room.

'Now,' he said, 'we must duck out of sight and run like hell.'

Chapter 33

They stepped out into the control room just as the alarm bells rang out all over the complex. Arthur Shultz lifted his great fist from the smashed remains of the red button.

'We gotta . . . massive . . . power . . . surge,' he said, adding, 'I just put everyone on red alert.'

Dimmot glanced at the screens ranged along the control console.

'He's right, Merlin,' he gasped. 'Look.'

Every screen but one was going berserk, flashing messages and mathematical codes at unreadable speeds, blowing images up larger and larger in order to locate the source of the malfunction, searching and discarding each location in the heart of the computer. The one screen unaffected by the mass epilepsy displayed in flashing red capitals the words 'MASSIVE POWER SURGE. SECURITY FORCES AND DIRECTOR TO CONTROL ROOM'.

'See,' shouted Dimmot above the clanging, 'there'll be monitors like that all over the area. We'd better get out of here or they'll think we had something to do with it.'

The Enchanter stood unmoving, his eyes narrowed with concentration as if listening.

He sighed with resignation.

'In truth I fear that we *are* the cause of the disturbance, though the turmoil therein has been created by another. This being so, wherever we hide, we will be found. Indeed we *have* been found.'

'What do you mean?'

Before Merlin could answer, the sounds of shouted command and frantic activity told them that the security door had been opened and the corridors outside were alive with authorities doing authorized things. They heard the untidy clatter of numerous feet running towards them and a trail of official looking people streamed round the corner. Some of them carried guns. Dimmot began to babble.

'Oh my God, Merlin. Don't just stand there. Zap them or turn them into something.'

He scuttled behind the wizard.

'Make us invisible or get us out of here, I don't care which, but do it quick.'

The crowd skidded to an untidy halt before Merlin's calm and steady gaze.

'Who the devil are you?' asked the one who was obviously the director, for he wore neither the long, white cloak of the alchemist nor the helmet of the soldier-at-arms.

'It matters not who I am,' said Merlin. 'What matters is that thou attend to thy duties. The First Unborn within these walls will have been stricken a mortal blow if thou dost not bring thy machines back to life.'

The director waved the soldiers forward. 'Restrain them . . .'

'Hold!' roared the Enchanter, raising his hand in a gesture guaranteed to freeze advancing adversaries in their tracks.

Everyone froze. Their eyes glazed.

'I have no fight with thee and I wish thee no harm. My battle is with another who will be here very soon. As for thee, there are duties to perform and millions of souls to be saved.'

His voice took on a soft, compelling quality.

'I command thee to go about thy duties without further ado. Thou wilt tackle thy tasks with clarity of mind and strength of heart for the lives of the First Unborn are in thy hands.'

He took Dimmot by the arm and led him quietly to one side.

'As for my companion and myself, we no longer have a place in thine eyes or thy thoughts. We do not exist.'

His raised hand gave an obscure sort of wave and the room burst into activity. The men in white coats set about examining the information on the screens and making phone calls. The guards left, scratching their helmets. Arthur Shultz wandered over to an unused chair with his magazine.

For a second Dimmot stared with his mouth agape. If only he had that sort of power.

'Thou hast it. But thou knowest not how to use it,' said Merlin absently.

'I wish you'd keep out of my head,' grumbled Dimmot. 'I'd like to keep *some* thoughts to myself.'

''Tis difficult to ignore thee when thy mind constantly shouts its thoughts all over the ether like a screeching jackdaw. I envy mortal men their deafness when thou art abroad . . .'

'If I had that sort of power,' Dimmot said, 'I'd learn to shout more quietly.' He squinted at the wizard. 'Could you teach me to use my powers? Properly, I mean.'

'There is no time left to us. I warned thee. Somehow we have been discovered.'

Dimmot looked around. A tiny worm of suspicion crawled across his mind. He jerked a thumb towards the crowd behind him.

'I thought you meant them,' he said weakly.

'No. I mean him,' said Merlin thickly.

His trembling finger pointed past Dimmot to the far wall. The wall was beginning to waver as if it were a mirage and the banks of lights covering the wall shimmered.

Something was materializing out of the air. As Dimmot watched in horror, an eye formed before them. Red blood vessels crawled across it as it became more solid, obscuring from sight the lights behind it. A black iris appeared, contracting and dilating, then the pupil, responding to the contractions by opening and closing in rhythm.

Apart from the pupil, which, instead of being round, was the shape of a cat's, and the size of the eyeball, which was more than eight feet across, there was something horribly, obscenely wrong with it.

Dimmot shuddered and turned to the Enchanter beseechingly. He was about to say, 'Do something,' or, 'Oh, God, I don't want to die,' when the look in Merlin's eyes pulled him up short.

Merlin was standing quietly with his hands folded before him, his face totally calm, his fury inexplicably abated. For the second time in an hour Dimmot had that feeling of inevitability, irrevocable and final.

But somehow he doubted that the subsequent experience would be even remotely Godly.

He felt his knees weaken and start to buckle. A wave of darkness swept over him and his stomach heaved.

The voice of Merlin spoke quietly to him.

'Be of strong will, Dimmot, for thy strength of will is all that thou hast left. There is nothing else.'

And James Dimmot then knew hopelessness and with hopelessness came resignation. With that came a strange calm.

Another eyeball appeared beside the first.

Dimmot stared at it passively, still wondering what was wrong about it and why no one else in the room was taking any notice of it.

The technicians juggled with control keyboards, fingers flashing, bringing up messages on their screens to override those already there, thrusting instructions into the system to damp down, to divert, to control the power and to drain off the electrical surplus. They barked orders down the phones to engineers in the bowels of the building to shut down and hold steady until advised. They looked at clipboards and manuals and wondered 'What in hell?', not knowing how close that question was to the truth.

Beneath the eyes a mouth full of needle-sharp teeth appeared. Then a long, aquiline nose.

Dimmot had just realized what was wrong with the eyeballs when Griswold thundered into view, clutching Dimmot's bread-knife in his hand. With a quick glance to assess the danger he sprinted towards them, prepared for battle.

As soon as he saw the knight Merlin's calm fell from him like a cloak and his old face contorted with anguish.

'No,' he screamed. 'Turn back, lad. Enter not, I command thee.'

But Griswold ignored him and skidded to a halt at their side, turning outwards with his knife held before him.

'What is occurring?' he asked over his shoulder.

'Damn thee, fool and thrice fool,' snarled Merlin. 'Canst thou never do as thou art bid? Our fate is sealed and there is nothing thou canst do to save us. Were there a chance I would have offered it to thee if only for Dimmot's sake, but there is not, and thy presence is wasted.'

'Then the choice is to stand by and watch thee destroyed or to go down fighting by thy side. A simple choice. Now where is the enemy?'

'I am here, Sir Griswold des Arbres,' said the deepest, most resonant voice they had ever heard. It was a voice that filled the vast room and seemed to come from everywhere at once. It was a cultured voice, beautifully modulated, and it rang with limitless power.

'You are welcome to join your colleagues in their hour of need,' it said, 'though "hour" is, in truth, a mild approximation.'

'Thou art a brave and noble adversary that sends his voice to do the fighting instead of his body,' smiled Griswold. 'My blade will feel a sad lack of purpose when it opens up thy miserable throat.'

Dimmot couldn't find it in him to appreciate the courage of Griswold's words. Apart from the fear that was simply the habit of a lifetime, the thought of a throat the size of the face pouring with blood was not too comforting.

There was something else that he found disquieting. As the voice was speaking, the eyes were twinkling with a friendly sort of malice and the mouth, lips and tongue were dancing in time to the words. And Dimmot understood why the rapidly solidifying features had looked so odd. The face wasn't turned towards them, it was turned away. When he noticed the ears appearing on either side of Merlin and himself and the small, horn-like stumps sprouting up through the sleek, black hair high above them, Dimmot felt compelled to voice his opinion.

'Ah,' he said. 'I see what's happening. What's happening is that we're inside, aren't we? We're inside. Inside his head. He's all round us and we're inside. Well, well.'

To his right Sir Griswold growled deep in his throat.

'In a manner of speaking you are right, James Dimmot,' said the voice.

'How do you know my name?' said Dimmot.

'An acquaintance mentioned you to me. Now be silent while I concentrate.'

The room had all but disappeared from sight. Everyone was going about their work oblivious to the presence of the three men and the entity in their midst. The great head around them was almost complete, obscuring all the lights, although somehow it was not becoming any darker. The last glimpse that Dimmot had of the outside world was of Arthur Shultz engrossed in his magazine while scratching reflectively at his crotch and the main monitor screen displaying the words 'POWER LEVEL NORMAL'.

The alarm bells became silent. The face and head were complete, filling their vision all round. From the eyeballs nerves and blood vessels had sprung and were snaking along their natural paths while skull and jaw, cheek and forehead formed. Brain tissue began to appear in little, grey convoluted islands around and above the three men, growing and joining together, approaching them from all sides and filling the skull.

Soon they stood in a tiny pocket of space surrounded by brain. Merlin and Dimmot stood motionless, each unable, for his own reasons, to offer resistance.

But Griswold, with a roar of rage, threw himself at the approaching mass and drove his knife into it up to his fist. Withdrawing the blade he swept it from side to side, up, down, slashing, thrusting, twisting it into the tissue. Then he stepped back, grimly staring from tissue to blade and back. The tissue was unharmed, blade unbloodied as if it had passed right through without any effect.

Griswold dropped his arm and returned to the Enchanter's side.

'What becomes of us now, Master Merlin?' he said in a strong and steady voice.

'Are we going to die?' whispered Dimmot.

'Die?' The entity's voiced trembled with amusement. 'Not yet. That would be no fun. There is much for you to see. Much for you to learn. Much suffering. Then you will die. Now you are coming with me.'

And the brain snapped into completeness with an unpleasant plop, engulfing them and holding them suspended in its midst.

Instead of choking, they stood quite still, breathing normally and still able to see and hear although, oddly, they could not smell or feel anything. Then their bodies began to tingle.

At first Dimmot thought that it was a tremble of fear, but when he realized that he wasn't feeling it but simply registering it in parts of his body that don't normally feel such feelings, he knew it was something else.

The tingle became a series of wave-like vibrations of different lengths, longer and shorter until the three men could feel every part of their bodies undulating at different speeds like piano strings registering notes and their harmonics simultaneously. The vibrations filled their awareness, driving out all other thoughts and feelings until they became one with their vibrations, until they were the vibrations. Their bodies no longer existed as they had known them.

Then the mind of the creature took charge, absorbing them into his own thoughts and commanding them to obey the dictates of his own will. And dutifully they did as they were ordered.

You don't have much choice when you've just been transformed into a figment of someone else's imagination.

The mind and face of the entity left as it had come, transcending the barrier of Time easily because there is no barrier to such as he and leaving nothing to show that Merlin and his friends had existed in 2090, except an old-fashioned, razor-sharp kitchen knife glittering on the control-room floor of the World Sperm Bank.

Chapter 34

Rose Falworthy had many passions and, being a woman who believed in doing rather than watching, she always took active steps to satisfy them. Being passionately concerned about right and wrong, she had joined the Women's Institute, served tea and cakes to old folks and wiped their chins. Being passionately concerned about the good of the nation she had refused to vote for Mrs Thatcher. Being passionately involved in the arts, albeit transiently, and hopelessly out of her depth, she had taken in penniless artists and musicians. They had eaten her food, slept in the spare room and then left, usually to return to their parents' estates, and almost invariably stealing at least one item of value on their way out.

But Rose was undaunted. Despite having contacts in the ethereal world, she was a down-to-earth lady who did not speculate about her place in the cosmos and who spelt Mankind with a small 'm'. Nevertheless, she had a passionate belief in the basic goodness of human beings and, when bad people were hurting good people, in harsh justice.

She identified strongly with other women who felt as she did and who went about righting wrongs and visiting such justice on the unjust.

Rose Falworthy had avidly watched every episode of *The Avengers*, and read every book about two-fisted heroines that she could find. In her dreams she saw herself as Emma Peel or Modesty Blaise, high-kicking, zapping and powing the arch villains of crime.

But, when one is over fifty, on the wrong side of twelve stone, and one's physical activities are confined to the twice-weekly manhandling of a crippled Meals on Wheels wagon, the notion of engaging arch villains in mortal combat seems an unlikely prospect.

She flicked her duster disdainfully over the vase on the Dimmots' dining table. The vase rocked gently.

A week had passed since she had said a bitter thanks to King Uther for making her delve into little Jamie's future, only to find it unbearably miserable. She had sent Uther packing and, with his departure, she now realized that a golden opportunity to fulfil her dreams had gone with him.

If only she could be free of mortal limitations, like Uther. She'd go and save little Jamie's life for a start, *and* show that black-bearded creature the back of her hand into the bargain.

She swept the duster grimly across the top of the piano, catching the glass ashtray a glancing blow. The ashtray spun lazily across the smooth surface, stopping just short of the edge.

Oh, she thought coldly, how she would love to fulfil those dreams.

So, when Uther suddenly appeared, shuffling his feet and looking generally embarrassed, Rose's face lit up with a welcoming smile, tempered only by an imperceptible narrowing of the eyes and an accurate flick of her duster. Throwing her arms about him, she hugged him energetically to her chest until they had almost merged into one, as the sand-filled Isle of Wight hourglass leapt into the air and hit the floor with a crash.

'Uther, my love,' she crooned. 'Where've you been? I've missed you.'

Uther, whose recollection of their parting appeared to differ slightly from Rose's, felt it necessary to say as much.

'Err . . . ?' he said.

Red. All. Everything. Rich red. Sun red, blood orange, plasma, mahogany.

As far as the mind could see. Across the very galaxy.

The black of 'nothing' has become red.

In an instant. And I'm alive.

The red fills all as far as the . . .

It fills me!

Me!

I'm alive!

162

Nothing has become . . . me.

I stare into the red and see nothing but red, yet I live.

Dimmot wondered if there should be a sound of some sort, a hum perhaps. A scene of such an indeterminate, ethereal nature usually had an indeterminate, ethereal hum to go with it. Or a choir weaving Holst-like harmonies in the background. It was all very red and ominous and sort of misty but not quite.

He felt warm and comfortable, which he considered strange, for he was not in any physical condition, being merely a memory.

Still, warm was warm and one should be grateful, especially after the agonizing cold of the Thames . . .

. . . in winter. But this is not the sort of warmth that I want. I yearn for the hills and woodlands of my Englande. I wish to lie in the sun and gaze across the valley at the castle and listen to the sounds of the townsfolk floating up the hillside, the lowing of the cattle, the bleating of the lambs.

The thought pattern that was Sir Griswold des Arbres smiled a thought pattern sort of smile.

There's many a maid I've had squinting up at the sun on those lush hills. And many a foe on a distant shore has stared sightless and blood-limbed into the eye of that fire because he dared to challenge my blade. The sun and I have been through much together.

Griswold was not in the habit of waxing poetic and he was surprised that such thoughts were singing through his brain.

He stared through narrowed eyes into the redness for signs of danger and wondered if Merlin was . . .

. . . anywhere about. I'll bet the little sod's running round exploring and not giving a toss about me, or danger . . . or me in danger. The trouble with him and Griswold is that they can't seem to recognize danger when it pokes 'em in the eye. They're totally blind . . .

. . . how could I have been so blind! Not to recognize the stench even across the centuries. Of all the evils to contend with why was I chosen to confront Nemestis?

'Why indeed, old man?'

The voice of the being boomed quietly about them. Their patterns stirred in his mind in the way that tiny oil slicks might on the surface of a pond as the ripples of his words passed beneath them.

'I know not why fortune conspired to reveal your presence to me, but it is an unexpected and delightful bonus. Now I will enjoy the sweetness of my imminent victory even more.'

There was a pause as if he was waiting for Merlin to reply, but it was Griswold who spoke.

Do something, Merlin. Conjure me a weapon.

Preferably a bazooka, thought Dimmot.

'Weapons?' chuckled Nemestis, and he burst into laughter, delighted and deep throated, like the cracking of thunder in a vast hollow ball. It exploded around them, sending them tumbling and tossing as the ripples rose higher and fell like crashing waves. The helpless oil slicks shimmered, multi-coloured beneath the pervading redness, stretching and distorting, threatening to tear into a hundred separate patches.

In their eyes the landscape veered and wheeled about them like a vast, distorted video film in which they were the central figures.

'I am beyond anything that you can do. Your weapons, like your magics, are as candles in a storm. You are totally at my mercy,' he concluded quietly and lapsed into silence.

All became still. The patterns of the three men returned to their rightful shapes, once again reflecting the redness about them.

Amid the stillness Dimmot's mind reeled with fear and nausea. *For God's sake, Merlin, save us from this maniac.*

He got no reply, for Merlin the Enchanter lay spread across the pathways of Nemestis' mind, face down and unmoving save for a slight tremor that ran through his little body like the sobbing of an abandoned child.

Deep in his throat Sir Griswold des Arbres growled a thought pattern sort of growl.

'I see that you still retain many of your animal instincts, young Griswold. Perhaps we may see more of them if we are in need of entertainment in the days to come.'

What know you of my instincts? snarled Griswold. *I know not of you.*

'Oh, you will, sir knight. Given time. Given *enough* time, that is.'

Nemestis chuckled, sending reverberations rumbling through

164

the three prisoners' patterns and rattling their teeth in their heads. So to speak.

'But, enough of this. It is time for you to be reborn, to leave my imagination and spew forth into a world from which you should, strictly speaking, have disappeared many centuries since. Come, my little ones.'

Through the vagueness that filled their perceptions came a high whistle, barely audible, pulsing very slowly and pregnant with suspense.

It grew, keening, cutting through them, the pulses becoming faster until they were jagged vibrations that seemed to be attacking the three from all sides, swirling them in a giant blender and beating them into solid, cohesive shapes.

Somehow there was no pain, but Dimmot screamed and Griswold was roaring in anticipation of the agony that seemed bound to come.

The whole universe became a mass of sound in their ears.

Then, with the impression of an explosion happening back-to-front, they snapped into existence.

They were in a vast hall of bare, shining walls and floor, with hidden lights and a high-arched ceiling. Save for two great iron doors at the far end, the walls were unbroken and, like the floor and ceiling, were made totally of pink, red-veined marble.

Not unlike the inside of that sod's brains, thought Dimmot gravely.

He turned to see Griswold crouching over the old man who lay with eyes closed at their feet.

With a pang of alarm Dimmot gasped, 'He's not dead, is he?'

'He's alive,' replied Griswold. 'And while he lives all men have cause to tremble.'

The knight rose to his feet, glaring about him.

'Where is the coward who abuses his powers to visit grief upon mortal men?' he roared, making Dimmot jump with fright.

The hall echoed to his words, then there was silence.

'Come out and face me,' yelled Griswold, sending another shot of adrenaline into Dimmot's overworked nervous system.

'I wish you wouldn't do that,' mumbled Dimmot.

He glanced down at Merlin and opened his mouth to speak.

'COWARD,' thundered Griswold. 'Coward and thrice coward. Come forth and . . .'

'Oh, for crying out loud, come and get us before this loony scares me to death!' Dimmot screamed. He glared at Griswold. 'God, you're a noisy bastard,' he snapped.

The doors opened and light poured through.

Framed in the doorway like a squat, black fly against a sunlit window was a very little man.

From his sparse-haired head to his thick bandy legs and naked feet that closely resembled two ancient cow pats with toes, he was grotesquely ugly. The massive, protruding ears, bulbous nose and thick lips each reflected an aspect of ugliness raised to an art form.

The enormous grey eyes spoke of eager cruelty.

Dimmot stared at him in horror.

'Are you Nemestis?' he gurgled.

'No,' said Griswold, casting a look of contempt at the creature. 'He has neither the demeanour of a leader nor the air of cowardice about him that Nemestis exhibits. He is a lackey.'

The gnome growled deep in his throat and shambled towards them with all the appearance of one wishing to sink his shark-like teeth into anything fleshy. Then he turned aside and stood by the door, waiting.

Through the doorway came four figures, more or less identical, carrying swords and more weight in solid muscle than the average horse. Having a distinctly Neanderthal appearance, they would have made Arthur Shultz look like an underfed pixie. They towered over Griswold and Dimmot, looking very cold and very hard, while the little man looked on with interest.

Griswold weighed up the guards with narrowed eyes.

Then another came through the doors and it was clear at a glance that this man was Nemestis.

The power that emanated from him could be felt in one's bones, resonating languidly and generating unease in all those around him.

As he approached, Griswold placed his weight imperceptibly on to his toes.

'Don't bother, sir knight,' murmured Nemestis, 'unless you think you can reach me in less than four pieces. Who's this?'

166

Griswold relaxed, while Dimmot raised himself to his full height.

'*This*,' he said, trying to keep his voice steady, 'is Dimmot.'

'And what are you, Dimmot? Wizard or warrior?'

'Vagabond,' said Dimmot.

'A self-confessed nothing, eh?' Nemestis smiled.

Dimmot said nothing.

'What do you intend to do with us?' asked Griswold, who still hadn't given up the idea of making a leap at Nemestis. He might be able to take out an eye or even shatter the demon's windpipe before he was cut down.

Nemestis was unconcerned.

'Well,' he said expansively, 'the first thing I think we'll do is dice you into one-inch cubes if that old fool doesn't stop pretending to be totally harmless.'

He waved a finger and one of the guards gave Merlin a sharp nudge with his foot.

Griswold gave a deep growl and moved forward, his fists balled tight, while Dimmot went weak at the knees. The guards whipped up their swords, pinning the knight's throat between the points.

Four beads of blood welled up and trickled down Griswold's neck.

'Fool.'

The word floated up from the floor followed by the face of the Enchanter as he rose to his feet.

'If thou wouldst once do as thou art told thou might survive to middle age.'

Griswold grinned, coming dangerously close to slicing through his own jugular. Dimmot gave a gasp of relief.

'I'd thought you were a goner,' he said.

'A thought I would have had thee retain were it not for this stupid pup and his rebellious ways.'

He glared at Griswold from beneath his high-arched brows, hissed, 'Fool,' again and turned to stare up into the face of the demon.

'I take it,' said Nemestis, 'that this lad is the bane of your life.'

'A jumped-up, would-be knight from Arthur's court. We were thrown together by circumstance.'

The Enchanter waved his hand dismissively.

Nemestis eyed him with an amused smile.

'Then you won't object if I remove him from your presence. As a precautionary measure, you understand.'

He nodded to the guards who turned and marched Griswold towards the door, keeping his throat pinned between their swords.

As they reached the door Griswold called over his shoulder, very carefully and through gritted teeth, 'Your loyalty to a fellow being is touching, Enchanter. I trust that I'll be able to repay it before too long.'

The doors slammed shut behind him.

From somewhere deep down Dimmot dredged up a faint wisp of courage.

'What are you going to do with him, you bastard?' he whispered.

Nemestis' eyes glinted for an instant and Dimmot thought that he'd possibly made his last mistake, but the demon merely smiled and said, 'He will be unharmed for the time being, as long as Merlin here acquits himself as befits a man of wisdom and compassion.'

Dimmot saw Merlin's face harden.

'What do you mean?' he asked.

'Griswold is my insurance against any little tricks that Merlin may try to play. Isn't that so, Enchanter?'

Merlin looked back at him steadily.

'Thou thinkest that I am still a force to be reckoned with, then?' he asked.

For a split second Dimmot saw the demon's eyes go cold as he looked down at the tiny Merlin. Then the amused smile returned.

'Merely a nuisance, old man. As well you know.'

Merlin gave him a thoughtful nod.

'Clearly not worth reaching back two thousand years to pluck me from my harmless meanderings,' he murmured. 'Might one ask how thou camest to find me . . . and why?'

Nemestis raised his hand, ushering the two men towards the door.

'As to your first question: a mutual acquaintance pointed you out to me. As to your second . . .'

He placed a long, spider-thin arm round Merlin's shoulders and gave him a smile as black as space.

'I am about to realize a very old dream. Your presence will give that dream a downright heavenly aspect.'

The Enchanter looked down at the demon's hand about his shoulder and then into Nemestis' dark eyes.

'And what *hast* thou dreamed of for so very long?'

The demon shrugged.

'The destruction of Mankind. What else?'

He nodded towards the door.

'Come. I'll show you around.'

They walked out into a wide, red-carpeted, pink-marbled corridor. Dimmot followed with the gnome at his side.

After a few minutes' walk in silence, seeing no one else, they turned a corner into a great hall some thirty feet wide by one hundred long. Here there were signs of life of sorts. At regular intervals forty great alcoves were set in the marble walls and in each one stood a red statue, apparently carved from marble. Some were up to twenty feet in height.

They were the stuff of nightmares. They were the sort of things one sees when one gets home at midnight, half-legless, and switches on the horror movie.

Most of them bore a vague similarity to familiar creatures, though some of their poses left a lot of propriety to be desired. Though they were unable to uproot their feet from the floor they all moved restlessly in their open prisons and stared down with interest as demon, gnome and humans passed beneath them.

Dimmot stood for a moment, staring back in wonder. He scampered after the gnome, grabbed his shoulder and said, breathlessly, 'These are incredible! Everything moves. The mouths, the eyes, they even seem to be breathing. Who made them?'

The creature didn't answer immediately.

Turning his head very, very slowly he stared at Dimmot's hand with a mixture of horror and revulsion. Then his eyes rose to meet Dimmot's and the pupils contracted to pin-pricks leaving two great expanses of pulsating greyness astride the bulbous nose.

Dimmot lowered his hand and stepped back.

After some very long seconds the pupils dilated and the look on the creature's face changed from fury into simple hatred. Then the lips parted in a grin. He sniggered and his body began to

169

shake with silent laughter. Casting his gaze along the alcoves he cocked a thumb at Dimmot.

Something snuffled.

It was the sort of amused snuffle that spoke of the enjoyment gained from pulling the legs off things. It was joined by assorted titters of mirth, and the hall filled with the sounds of the things that weren't really statues laughing nastily.

Up ahead Nemestis turned and took in the scene.

'I think you're probably safest out of the way, Mr Dimmot, where you can't get hurt. You can come back in time for the Last Trump.'

He waved a hand vaguely in Dimmot's direction. What he did next Dimmot wasn't able to see, because Dimmot wasn't there. He'd vanished without a sound.

Chapter 35

Sir Griswold would always acknowledge an enemy's merits, even in the heat of battle.

'You are very impressive,' he said cheerfully as the four guards marched him steadily down the winding stone stairs to what was clearly a dungeon area. The points of their swords moved gracefully with each step, barely touching the skin of his neck. The blades were held low, angled upwards so that any adventurous prisoner trying to duck beneath the points would guarantee instant and terminal perforation.

'Your skill invokes my admiration.'

No one replied.

'I expect that your blades have seen much blood and glory in their time,' said Griswold. 'Not being a warrior myself, I'd find it difficult to imagine what fearsome adversaries you've encountered, what mighty enemies you've slain. Dragons, perhaps,' he murmured dreamily.

The merest tremor ran through each blade, sending a tickle through Griswold's neck as the guards' pace almost faltered.

'I knew a man who fought dragons for a living,' he went on.

The largest guard spoke.

'The old man was right. You are a fool. No man fights dragons and lives to tell.'

Griswold shrugged. 'This one did. Mind you, he had the intelligence to start on small dragons and work his way up.'

'Small dragons!'

The guard snorted. The others sniggered. Their alert steps relaxed to a saunter.

'Since when were the fiery beasts ever born less than full grown?' said one.

'And spread their wings and took to the skies . . .' said another.

'And filled their bellies with men's charred remains within the hour?'

Griswold rolled his eyes and gave them an imbecile grin.

'I've seen little dragons,' he said confidentially. 'I've seen them as small as this.'

He squinted myopically as he held his hands out and raised them up between the blades for the guards to see.

Sitting in a darkness so black that it seemed solid, Dimmot stretched out a hand and felt around him. Finding nothing within reach he whimpered, stood up and carefully placed one foot in front of him, his hands outstretched. He had no idea what his prison was like or what dangers it held. If there was a bottomless pit or jagged rocks around he was unable to judge. He had no idea where the door was or when it might open next.

He wished for a second that he could be sitting on the parapet of London Bridge, gave another whimper and sank to the floor.

Then he got to his feet.

He didn't actully remember getting to his feet. One second he was sitting hunched with despair and in the next instant, with no apparent time lapse, he was on his feet, giving out a long, blood-curdling cry of terror.

As the cry came to an end for want of air, he looked round for the cause of his fear and saw a faint glow, roughly man-sized, several feet off. The glow shifted three-dimensionally.

'Well,' it snapped, 'are you or aren't you?'

Something in its tone said that it could be sheer hell to live with, what with its bunions and all, but that it wasn't actually something to fear.

'Aren't I what?' said Dimmot.

After what felt simultaneously like an instant and several thousand years, the glow gave a snort.

'Good grief! Do I have to repeat myself, man? Are you going to sit there all day or are you going to get us out of here?'

'Out? How?'

'How! I don't know how. You're the magician, I'm not.' The glow solidified into the shape of an incredibly old man with a

172

beard down to his knees, dressed in white robes and sitting on nothing in particular. 'Not any more,' he added glumly.

'I'm not a magician,' said Dimmot.

Some kind of eternity followed while the old man gazed into space.

'You're not?'

'No.'

'But you *are* Merlin the Enchanter?'

'No.'

'Who then?'

'Dimmot,' sighed Dimmot.

'Dommit?'

'Dimmot!'

'Dammit.'

Griswold trod stealthily up the stairs from the dungeons with a sword in each hand. They were much lighter than the two-handed broadsword he was used to, hardly more than rapiers with only one cutting edge, but they'd do.

Down below, four guards were contemplating possible changes to their strategy.

They had come to realize that the weakness in adopting four identical methods of restraint was that often only one method was needed to counter them. They understood this when Griswold had raised his hands up to their swords, spun full circle, flipping all four swords aside in one action, and had dropped to the floor, driving fists and elbows into four unsuspecting groins.

They consolidated their understanding as the two fists and a bullet head rose up and connected with three jaws, followed by a great and fearsome hand wrapping itself round the one remaining throat.

They confirmed their basic agreement, that their methods might need some updating, on their arrival in a tangled heap at the bottom of the stairs.

They also considered the possibility of a career move.

'When Nemestis hears about this we're dead.'

'If we're lucky.'

'Nevertheless, if we want to live, we'd better get out of here and catch a boat.'

'Wherever we go, he'll find us.'

'Perhaps he won't bother. He's got enough on his plate at the moment.'

'He'll probably send that little grunt Scarbald after us.'

A collective shudder ran through their massive frames.

They discussed the wisdom of raising the alarm, then, very quietly, they applied their combined strength to uncurling the two swords that pinned the chains around their necks to the cell bars behind them.

Reaching the top of the stairs Griswold peered cautiously into the corridor.

It was deserted.

He didn't know what he intended to do apart from keep alive and find Merlin and Dimmot, but he knew that they had come this way because Merlin had left a trail.

It was nothing one could see or smell but, with training, one could feel it.

It was a slight tingle in the air that said someone was deliberately shedding minute quantities of magic.

It was something that Merlin had taught only to him.

Griswold noted with satisfaction that his perceptions had not diminished with the centuries.

He followed the tingle.

At the end of the corridor a sharp turn led to a great hall.

Padding quietly towards the turning Griswold heard what sounded vaguely like laughter.

Chapter 36

Nemestis, Merlin and Scarbald were halfway along the corridor leading from the great hall when the walls and ceiling faded into nothing and the landscape became breathtakingly beautiful.

And very green.

Grassland stretched away in all directions over the hills and meadows, while trees patiently littered the countryside as far as the eye could see. The sounds of sheep crept over the hills and caressed the ears.

Merlin gazed out across the green, and a pang of longing for his home and his friends cut through his heart like a knife.

'Familiar country, Merlin,' said Nemestis at his side. 'Not the man-made cacophony of the mechanical era from which you've not long come. Not the science-ridden, pleasure-minded world of Mr Dimmot's twentieth century, but,' he waved a hand airily, 'a reminder of a world long ago, when powers such as yours and mine were recognized and revered. Do you remember how beings like you and me were respected and feared throughout the land? A beautiful . . . innocent land.'

'What knowest thou of innocence, Lord of Darkness?' snapped the Enchanter. 'Thy presence on my world is an affront to beauty and innocence.'

Nemestis stared at Merlin, then burst into laughter.

'So! *Your* world, little wizard. You are the owner of the planet Earth.'

'Merely its guardian.'

Nemestis burst into renewed laughter while Scarbald's face split into a horrific grin and he snuffled in lieu of laughter.

'Then perhaps you'd better see what it is you guard so assiduously,' chortled the demon.

He snapped his fingers. The landscape vanished. The silence of the green meadows exploded into the thundering and clattering of a thousand vast machines and the babbling of a million beings ebbing and flowing about them, between harsh, grey buildings and beneath a thousand flashing signs.

'Here is reality, Merlin. The world you once knew has come to this. No more nebulous chivalry, no more high-minded concepts of honour and loyalty. The Arthurian dream that you devoted your life to creating is long dead. The ideals of your naive monarch have been buried so deeply in the past that even the faintest memories of them and of him have long since ceased to exist. Look upon your world and grieve.'

Merlin stared about him and shuddered at what he saw. He had known sadism and hate and evil of all kinds in his own era and he knew that Man had more capacity for cruelty than all the animals on Earth.

But there had always been other qualities in evidence. The qualities of which King Arthur was a symbol, a beacon to shine through the centuries and light Man's way through the forests of Evil.

Looking into the faces of the people milling around and past him, the Enchanter saw bleak despair in the eyes and lifeless cruelty in the set of the mouths. Deep down in the region of his soul, where no other being could reach, he allowed himself a wisp of thought.

Am I too late? he wondered.

He glanced up at the demon.

'Man was always a fool to himself,' he sneered. 'Clearly my time was wasted on him. What, may I ask, has beset him over the centuries during my absence that would bring him to this sorry state?'

'Why, me, of course,' said Nemestis. 'The emissary of Darkness, sent from the nether regions to destroy the miserable attempts of the cosmos to recreate the Balance.'

He gave Merlin a sideways glance.

'You are familiar with the laws of Balance, of course.'

'Of course,' said Merlin, rubbing his eyes tiredly with his fingers. 'It appears that thou'st all but succeeded, though I cannot for my

176

life's worth see how thou couldst break Man's spirit without first breaking his bones.'

'You always were somewhat less than worldly, Merlin. One does not break the spirit of a species such as Man. One destroys it by planting seeds which Man matures and brings to fruition by use of his own greeds and fears. Thus fed, such seeds blossom into weeds which choke and kill. Look around and see the living dead.'

Nemestis grinned and gave the gnome a wink.

'Soon to be the dead dead,' he said.

'All that I know,' said Uther, 'is that there is going to be one hell of a fight and that I'll need all the leaders, fighters and heroes I can get. I don't even know if we'll be able to get there in time.'

He was dressed in an ethereal version of a leather tunic and leggings and he was wearing boots of animal hide secured with thongs. If the monarch of all England, deceased, was going to step on to the field of battle, he was going to cover up his aged limbs in the interests of both piety and dignity, not to mention credibility.

Besides, it gave him somewhere to put things.

He dug his hand into his tunic, pulled out a folded sheet of paper and handed it to Rose. The paper seemed to be doing several odd things all at once. She took it gingerly from him between her finger and thumb.

'What's this?' she asked suspiciously.

'It's a list. People I need you to contact for me. Leaders, fighters and . . .'

'And heroes. Why is it glowing and crackling like this?'

Uther hesitated.

'It's angry,' he murmured. 'Wants to go back to where it belongs.'

'Which is where?'

'It belongs in a book. Now kindly look at it and tell me, can you contact these men or not?'

'No need to snap, love,' said Rose gently.

She unfolded the paper, ignoring the fact that, while one hazy version of it remained open, another even hazier version was trying to refold itself like a sulking child.

'And you can behave yourself as well,' she told it firmly. 'You're not getting your own way, so you might as well make up your mind.'

Holding the parchment down on the table she read it through, then looked up at Uther.

'And you want me to put you in contact with these men?'

'That's right.'

'And then what will you do?'

'Together we'll gather our armies and set forth into the future. The battle to end all battles awaits us.'

'But all these men are dead,' said Rose.

'Of course they're dead, woman!' spluttered Uther. 'If they were alive they'd be no more use than flies on a cow pat. Well?'

She glanced down the list again.

'Well,' said Rose, 'I know him for a start. And him I met once. Doris introduced us.'

'Doris?'

'Stokes, dear. Don't know any of the others, I'm afraid. Know the names, of course.'

The names numbered only ten, but, as Uther explained, each one was a leader of men and would have a small army of his old troops at his command. They were names which had made their mark on history. They were known throughout the land. In some cases, throughout the world.

'Except for him. I've never heard of him,' said Rose.

'I can vouch for him,' grinned Uther. 'Owed my life to him more than once *and* he was only a lad at the time. Miserable sod, young Belkin, but the best sergeant I ever had.'

'All right, dear,' said Rose without hesitation. 'Let's see what we can do.'

Sitting herself at the table, she spread the list and weighted it down with ashtrays and a vase. She beckoned Uther to sit opposite her and took his hands in her own.

'Oh, there's just one thing before we start.'

She smiled sweetly.

Uther had seen that smile once before.

'Oh?' he said hopefully.

'You can take *that* look off your face, Uther Pendragon,' she said. 'Just how long have I got?'

'For what?'

'To live, silly.'

'Oh. You *really* want to know?'

'Oh, yes.'

'Little under eight years. Why?'

Rose closed her eyes contentedly and prepared to slip into her spirit-finding trance.

'Because I'm coming with you,' she said. 'Pick me up at eight.'

The old man seemed to be spending Eternity deciding what to say next.

Which he was, but that's another infinitely long and convoluted story.

When he finally spoke, startling Dimmot out of his skin for a second time, his first words overlapped with the last words he'd spoken seemingly hours ago. The jumble reverberated dully about them.

'I Dom . . . know . . . mit? . . . who you . . . Dam . . . are . . . mit . . . it . . . it. You're that Wisher chappie from the thirtieth? . . . twentieth century, wot's his name?'

'Dimmot?'

'That's the one. Wrote about him in my book, y'know.'

'Book?' said Dimmot.

He felt that, if he stayed perfectly still and spoke as little and as quietly as possible, he might just prevent reality from entirely deserting him.

'*Encyclopaedia Esoterica*. First published 2706, your time, revised edition 2845. Did all the research m'self, you know,' he added with a creak of satisfaction.

Reality was getting decidedly slippery. Dimmot sat down and began to hum.

'Oh yes,' continued the ancient creature dreamily. 'Spent a few thousand eventful years on Earth foraging through the human race, digging out the gifted, the talented, the truly magical ones. Got 'em all down in my book.'

Dimmot punctuated his hum with a brief burst of curiosity.

'Mmmmmm mmmm . . . why . . . mmm?'

He rocked gently to and fro.

'Why?' said the old man, frowning as if wondering what the word meant.

'Why? Oh . . . records. Had to keep records. All the people who might be able to help Mankind win his "age-old battle against the Forces of Darkness".'

He appeared to say the last part in inverted commas as if reading from a very old and well-used manual.

'And those who might help him lose it,' he added.

'Mmmmmm . . . mmm . . . why . . . mmm?' said Dimmot again, only louder.

A small eternity elapsed.

'Had to know who we could call on if we needed help. Sort of reference book. Directory.'

'Mmmmmm . . . Yellow Pages . . . mmm.'

'Probably.'

The old man stared at Dimmot vaguely.

'I expect you're wondering why I'm here,' he said at last.

Dimmot nodded. His hum was becoming more determined, and more desperate by the second.

'I'm here because I stuck my head up and was seen, albeit briefly, by the wrong people. Metaphorically, that is. That was my one mistake.'

He paused for ever.

'My one mistake,' he said again with a very faraway look in his eyes.

'Part of the job, you see,' he went on. 'The Forces of Evil had already had the planet in their grip for many centuries when I got here.

'They'd got at Man's instincts. Watered 'em down with intellectual anomalies, philosophical red-herrings, conflicting beliefs, all the sort of stuff that makes him lose sight of reality. Long before I had completed the records, I'd discovered that, of all the beings on Earth, not even the few with singular strength and insight had the power to help save the world.'

He frowned and shook his head slowly. Just when it seemed as though he would go on doing it for ever, he cocked an eye at Dimmot.

'Where was I?'

'Pardothejob mmmmm.'

'Oh, yes.' The old man gave a grunt. 'I had, therefore, to seek out some of those men and women of merit, and enlighten them. Guide them along the path of rightness, y'might say.

'Then an event occurred, oh, round about the sixth century as I remember, which made me want to go one better and I overstepped my authority! Tried to justify it, of course, as one does. Tried to say I'd given Mankind a helping hand by creating one of his kind with my own magical powers in him. Sort of guardian. I really believed it at the time, but truth was I was a lonely old man far from home in a different galaxy. Different dimension actually. And she really was a very beautiful young lady.'

He gave a sigh and seemed to fade slightly for a second.

'She was English. Just like you.'

Dimmot's response was, naturally, righteous indignation heavily tinged with envy.

'Mmmm you dirdy ol'man mmm.'

'Quite,' agreed the old man without heat. 'But it *did* provide Mankind with the hero he badly needed.'

Dimmot's hum faltered momentarily. Two pieces of a vaguely remembered jigsaw slid towards each other, but, guided by disbelief, wouldn't quite slot into place.

'Anyway, a few centuries later my misdoing caught up with me. History gave me away. What with stories of the most powerful, half-human, half-alien magician on Earth and all that sort of thing. Naturally the creatures of Darkness came to hear of him. They nosed around, discovered from whence he came and traced him back to his father . . . me. Oh, dear,' he sniggered. 'Did *they* get a surprise!'

The two pieces of the jigsaw stubbornly refused to lock into place in Dimmot's head, primarily because he wouldn't let them. He just knew that, if he did, he'd finally have to let go his hold on his present reality and accept a totally new one, which would be as painful as having one's old skin stripped from one's bones and replaced with another one three sizes too large.

He'd never grow into it.

He sank back into the depths of his hum and began to wish that he was somewhere else.

Griswold would have liked to be somewhere else, but he wasn't, and, rather than waste energy on idle wishes, he put his mind to resolving his present dilemma.

Driving the points of his swords into the marble-covered scrotum had left him with two buckled swords, and the ever-tightening grip of marble claws on his throat told him that alternative action was required very soon. He dropped the swords, reached up and, grasping a long, bony pinky in both hands, gave a wrench. With a calciferous crack the finger snapped and hung at an obscene angle, but Griswold didn't have to be a mathematician to work out that twelve fingers times the number of seconds it takes to break enough of them was greater than the time he had left before things started to go very black.

The statue gave a roar and tightened its grip, while the others applauded noisily from their alcoves.

Through a pink haze Griswold cursed himself for his lack of vigilance in wandering too close to the monsters. He grabbed another finger. As he struggled in vain to free himself, he felt his head beginning to pound. Nausea rose up in his throat as the creature lifted him off his feet and raised him up towards its gaping jaws.

The voice that rose above the din was very feminine, very loud and dripping with authority.

'Craggus! Put him down at once, you dis-*gust*-ing little wretch.'

Griswold hit the floor with a crash and lay gasping for air. As he tried to focus, the owner of the voice appeared at the farthest edge of his vision. She seemed to waft hazily as though drifting between different dimensions in time, though this wouldn't be the description given by a sixth-century knight whose experience was limited to the normal run of wizardries, vanishing tricks, fireballs and the like.

To Griswold she looked as if she were a spirit of the nether regions, of gossamer wings and timeless demeanour.

In fact, her appearance was due to inspired tailoring.

'Are you all right, sir knight?' she asked in a voice that impossibly combined womanly warmth with arctic coldness.

She stood over Griswold as his eyes focused and he shook his head to clear the pounding in his temples.

Between gasps he informed her that he was fine and asked what manner of creatures were the statues.

'These are my . . . pets. Nemestis allows this one indulgence.' She gave a sniff. 'By way of compensation,' she added sourly.

Griswold filed her tone of voice away in his memory, climbed to his feet and moving out of reach of the marbled statues, gave the woman a flashing smile and a bow without taking his eyes off her.

'I'm Sir Griswold des . . .'

'I know. I am Amanda.'

'You know me?' frowned Griswold.

'Amanda,' she whispered huskily.

'Amanda,' said Griswold dutifully.

'And that is Craggus,' she said ignoring his question.

'A formidable opponent,' said Griswold, giving the statue a nod.

Craggus was only eight feet in height and apart from the sabre-tooth fangs and the claws on his heels, he was one of the more human-looking creatures.

He snarled a snarl with a degree of dark promise in it.

'That's Diophine,' went on Amanda, pointing vaguely. 'Ptyus, Agramium . . .'

Griswold acknowledged each one in turn, taking in their obvious strengths and weaknesses as he did so.

'And *this* is my latest acquisition,' murmured Amanda gazing up at Griswold with deep green eyes. 'The demon Bathym.'

Griswold returned the gaze steadily.

'You have clearly searched far and wide for such a fine and diverse collection of ornaments,' he said lightly. 'They must give you much satisfaction.'

'On the contrary,' said Amanda, her lips trembling.

Chapter 37

The air flickered as Nemestis snapped his fingers and the world of AD 3797 vanished, leaving them standing in the corridor. With a gentle but firm push Scarbald urged Merlin forward. Giving the gnome a look of disdain and his cloak a slight shake, as if to rid it of any unwelcome foreign bodies, the Enchanter strolled on.

'May I ask how thou intend to bring about Man's demise?' he asked the demon.

'Oh, simple genocidal procedure, all the latest methods. One, undermine the species' natural predilection for social interdependence. Two, isolate every individual's psyche from the global consciousness by mass-programming. Then three, throw the switch that sets the isolated components to remass and function in a coordinated and mutually self-destructive mode. Oh, and four, mop up the tiny portion that slip through the net. Standard practice nowadays. Never fails.'

His sleek, black cloak drifted lightly about him, reflecting dully the lights spaced along the corridor and the red of the carpet. His teeth were white, large and mostly pointed.

Merlin held his feelings in a grip of iron.

'I take it this momentous occasion is fairly imminent?'

'This evening, actually. Which is why I'm so glad you were able to come.'

'And Mankind's demise is all down to thyself?'

'Indeed.'

An ominous snuffle came from behind them.

'With the help of the little cretin behind us,' said the demon. 'He takes care of the technical side of things.'

'Just the two of thee?'

'No, no, of course not. I have an unlimited army of creatures at

184

my command when the situation demands, and I always recruit local help. Caligulas, Attilas, Hitlers, Saddams, every world has them, as you know. So what do you think?'

'I'm sure thy methods will be as crude as they are vile. Thou didst never have any class.'

'On the contrary, old man,' Nemestis gave a jovial laugh, but it was noticeably gritty at the edges. 'I take great pride in my work. We both do. But one tailors one's methods to suit the situation. One uses the enemy's weaknesses to destroy him in his own camp. Earth is my greatest challenge yet. Also my last. Did you know that this world is the last on the list? The final hope of the galaxy. All the others, all the little outposts of humanity, sought out, discovered, destroyed. By me.'

Snuffle.

'Us. No, there will be no "crude genocides", no "vulgar holocausts".'

His lips compressed to thin cruelty.

'No heroic last stands, no martyrs, no memorable battles to the death. Nothing to serve as a shining example to the cosmos that the wisdom and audacity of its choice in creating Mankind would be worth another chance . . .'

He gave the wizard a cold leer.

'Mankind, the spawn of the cosmos, must be seen to succumb to his fate with ignominy,' said the ancient creature in the timeless prison. 'It is Nemestis' job to see that he does. So far he has succeeded admirably. But then he hasn't had to contend with the powers of my offspring, Merlin the Enchanter.'

All at once, James Dimmot felt that his rapidly dwindling quota of marbles had reached critical level.

Death he could live with, but to give in to insanity was sheer madness.

'Can I raise a point of order?' he said at last.

'Of course.'

'You, together with me, are imprisoned by a genocidal maniac, an arch enemy of Mankind, namely Nemestis, who is a demon.'

'Correct.'

'If my scant knowledge of English history serves, the father of Merlin was a demon.'

'Daemon.'

'You?'

'Correct.'

'Well, if you are both demons, are *you* one of the good guys or one of the bad guys?'

After one of his eternally long pauses, the old man gave Dimmot a rheumy squint. 'Neither,' he croaked. 'My name is Asmethyum. I'm one of the other guys.'

Chapter 38

In a forest clearing in a dimension not normally accessible to mortal man, nine spectral leaders, fighters and heroes stood around jabbing their swords irritably at the ground and generally fidgeting with impatience.

Of the ten on Uther's list, only one had still to be called up.

Rose had left Sergeant Belkin to last and the others were beginning to envy him, for the row, which had been brewing for several days, was about to come to the boil.

'You are a woman!' roared Uther Pendragon. 'And women do not go around waggling swords and screaming, "Up and at 'em, you scurvy *bastards*!"'

'Listen, your royal, chauvinist, pig-headed majesty! I've spent the last eight years of my life preparing for this,' snarled the spirit of Rose Falworthy. 'Jogging, swimming, aerobics, self-def—'

'And what did you get for your pains, woman? Your heart packed up. Hardly surprising,' said Uther. 'At your age,' he finished, rather bravely.

The leaders, fighters and heroes nodded and growled quietly in their throats.

'That was on the cards anyway,' retorted Rose. 'We both knew that.'

'You were meant to breathe your last at the local annual flower show, not while learning how to break a rear stranglehold!' said Uther.

The leaders, fighters and heroes scuffed their feet and glanced at one another under their eyebrows. If this row followed the general pattern of the last few days, it would be the petulant bit next, then the implied promise, then the smug smile of womanly victory.

You never had this trouble with chaps. They either did as they were told or had their heads split open. The woman had been a problem right from the start, with her wilful ways and her silly ideas about demolishing screaming hordes with a broadsword.

Damn good spanking would sort her out. Trouble was that, when it came to women, Uther was too soft. He'd been renowned for it in life, and he hadn't improved since.

Rose plumped herself down on a fallen treetrunk, somehow managing to maintain both her air of petulance and her dignity, despite sinking into the peeling bark and nearly toppling backwards. She hadn't yet learned to judge the delicate relationship between the ethereal and the material worlds that the dead have to master if they want to survive in spiritual comfort.

'Oh, Uther, you old silly,' she purred. 'There's no need for us to quarrel.'

The leaders, fighters, etc., were, in the main, heavily muscled, well scarred and the genuine article. The one exception was athletic but lightly built. He wore a green tunic and a hat with a silly feather, and therefore had a reputation with the ladies.

It was clearly time for him to intervene. The leaders, etc., urged him forward.

'Go on, Robin.'

'Sort her out, Robin.'

He strolled over to where she sat, patted Uther on the shoulder and said, 'Leave this to me, old chap.'

Uther nodded thankfully and strode away to discuss the frustrating hog-headedness of women with his troops.

Robin gave his pencil-thin moustache a delicate brush, leaned towards Rose and treated her to a smile that had weakened the knees of women throughout the world.

'Dear lady . . .' he began.

Having failed to find the original hero on Uther's list, Rose, in a moment of inspired cunning, had called upon the perfect substitute. When he was alive he had averaged more battles in a month than the original hero would have fought in a lifetime. Such battles, so legend has it, were often against seamen and, though they never required the use of the blade with which he was so adept, he always found them thoroughly enjoyable.

Choosing a moment when Uther wasn't around, Rose had

located the bogus Robin and had made a simple agreement with him. If they both kept their mouths shut, he would have enough adventure to last him a lifetime and Uther would have his full complement, courtesy of Rose Falworthy. Being none the wiser, Uther would have to honour his word to Rose.

She was beginning to realize that she had made a mistake on two counts. Uther's word was open to interpretation, particularly by Uther.

She gazed up at the limpid pools and the tempting lips.

'Errol,' she hissed. 'Shut it!'

Enough was enough. She'd played fair up to now, with the petulance and the implied promise and such.

It was time to fight dirty.

She pushed past the hero in green and the forest rang to her strident screech.

'Uther Pendragon, if I don't have a sword in my hands in ten seconds from now, you can kiss your precious Belkin goodbye!'

Sir Griswold des Arbres found himself in the very last place he'd have expected to be, doing the very last thing he'd have imagined right now, but then, allies were always worth cultivating.

'Oh, Griswold,' sighed his latest ally. 'Where did you learn a trick like that?'

'Oh, one of the warmer countries where body oils are very popular,' murmured Griswold.

He'd cast his eyes round the room over an hour ago, taking in the ways of escape and any ornaments or furniture that might serve as weapons. Finding neither, he'd applied himself to persuading his jailer that his freedom was a small price to pay for services rendered.

'I haven't felt this wonderful in centuries,' whispered Amanda.

Beneath the languid gaze of her eyes flickered two sparks of disbelief.

'You *are* only human, aren't you?'

Griswold ran his fingers over her body, careful not to touch parts that had just transcended the bounds of ecstasy and were now hovering on the borders of hypersensitivity.

'I am but a man. Why?'

'There is something truly heavenly about the way you ply your skills.'

She shuddered and curled herself about him, seeking his lips with her own.

'If they came not from heaven, then whence?'

'Practice,' mumbled Griswold.

'In common with most of your race,' said Asmethyum, 'your "scant" knowledge of history is more scant than you think. I am no more demon than angel. I am a *daemon*. There's a significant difference.'

'You're not trying to tell me you're a disinterested party?'

'Heh, heh, heh!' cackled Asmethyum for the first time in many years, fading slightly before returning to fragile solidity. 'No, I'm very interested. Heh, heh. Very. I'm simply not disposed to evil and not inclined to piety. None of my race is. My only commitment is to maintain the balance of the cosmos.'

'Balance?'

'Between Good and Evil.'

'Cobblers,' said Dimmot. 'How can you talk about a balance between things as . . . nebulous as that?'

'Nebulous to you, James Dimmot, because your race was only allowed to see through eyes of limited vision. Of course it's nebulous to you. That's why you invented credible entities to make the nebulous into something concrete and acceptable.'

'Entities?'

The old man raised his arms and made little inverted commas with his fingers.

'Good and Evil . . .' His elbows creaked and his fingers clicked. 'Equals God and Devil.'

Creak.

Click.

'QED,' he said.

His arms fell to his sides and he gave Dimmot a piercing stare.

'Only you always go to extremes. That's the trouble with a race that has to justify everything it does. Everything's either totally good or thoroughly evil. Your minds and your religions can't encompass the idea of something in between. That's how I got

190

such a bad name. In all the tales of yore, I'm an unknown entity. Therefore I must be "one of the bad guys".'

He gave the sigh of one patiently resigned to an eternity of being misunderstood.

'I take it my son was with you when you arrived?' he wheezed.

'Yes.'

'Then get us out of here and we'll see if we can't tie this smutty business up once and for all. Heaven knows,' he murmured quietly to himself, 'it's been going on long enough.'

'But . . .'

'Oh, come on, man, concentrate. We really haven't got much time.'

The old man seemed to be growing both in strength and solidity.

'How?'

'How! How! How do you think, you fool? Do what you do best. Bend the forces of the cosmos to your will.'

'But I'm a failure,' whined James Dimmot. 'I've got degrees in it. If I had the power to change things, do you think I'd have been sitting on Tower Bridge when I first got dragged into this mess?'

Asmethyum gave a sigh of resignation, and explained.

He gave Dimmot a potted history of Mankind.

'I've heard all that before, from Merlin,' grumbled Dimmot.

'And did my son explain how he came to choose you of all the world's failures to become instrumental in averting the demise of both Mankind and the entire cosmos as we know it?'

'He made me recite a poem,' said Dimmot flatly.

Asmethyum smiled a watery smile.

'Ah,' he said. 'The lad has learnt well.'

'Which is more than I'm doing,' replied Dimmot. 'You haven't told me a thing. What am I – "one of Earth's most powerful forces in the etc., etc." according to you – doing . . .' he pointed a finger emphatically at his feet, '. . . here?'

In a disturbingly measured tone, Asmethyum said, 'Well, there's a good reason for that.'

When Nemestis had thrown him into that timeless cell, said the old man, over three thousand years ago, he had tried in vain to find a way out. Finally he accepted that there *was* no escape and he realized that another course of action was necessary. So he had passed the information concerning Man's impending destruction out through the bars, so to speak. He had tossed the seeds of Merlin's visions into the ether. The seeds had blossomed and spread throughout Time until they'd reached back through the centuries, touching, as they did so, the minds of a few visionaries on the way.

'Nostradamus was one,' he told Dimmot. 'He saw many and much of the visions that I created, but he was neither wizard nor diplomat. He could not help, neither could he keep his mouth shut. I was often afraid he'd give the game away. His predictions were so close to the mark I was certain Nemestis would become suspicious when he heard of them. And the time wasn't right for that.'

'Didn't he predict World War Two, stuff like that?' said Dimmot.

'He did. Very smart young man, but he could only foresee what was there at the time. My visions had not reached full bloom, nor were they meant to. It wasn't until they'd reached back to the sixth century that they blossomed in all their gory glory.'

'The age of Merlin the Enchanter!'

'The age of my son the Enchanter,' nodded Asmethyum proudly.

'Then what?'

'Then, with luck, Merlin would grasp the enormity of Man's plight and apply his skills to overcoming it.'

'Well, it wasn't skill that landed us *here*. It was luck,' said Dimmot. Bad luck, he added to himself.

'You were caught. By the demon.'

'How did you know?'

'Another seed,' said the old man with a chuckle. 'A seed planted when the time is right can achieve more than any form of coercion.'

For a moment Dimmot strove to understand what the old fool was driving at. When he did his comment was perceptive and to the point.

'You bastard. You set us up.'

'I merely planted the seed of suspicion in Nemestis' mind. He husbanded it into a reality, just as mortal men do, and the "reality" became a threat that he had to eliminate.'

'How did he find us?'

192

'He simply scoured through history and the tales of yore for some hint of long dead mechanist skills coming to light to touch the minds of Man.'

'And he traced them to the World Sperm Bank!'

'Is that where he found you? Reciting poetry, I trust.'

'As it happens, yes. But, why *me*? Why was I . . . ?'

'Do you know why you never achieved greatness?' said the old man.

'Yes. I was a born failure right from the start. My parents always said . . .'

'You never achieved greatness because you weren't prepared to pay the price.'

'What price?'

'Responsibility. You weren't prepared to take responsibility for anything or anyone, which is why you wished chaos and failure on yourself whenever the threat of responsibility loomed. But now the choice is no longer yours. You will pay the price and your reward, if we succeed . . .'

'Yes?'

'. . . will be the obscurity you deserve.'

'That's no reward!'

'It's better than the alternative.'

'Which is what?'

'Oblivion,' said Asmethyum simply.

'It was oblivion that I was aiming for on the bridge,' Dimmot reminded him.

'Oblivion for all Mankind, fool. Not just for you.'

The old man was right about responsibility, of course. Throughout his life Dimmot had bemoaned his fate, blamed the world, cursed his luck. It was only when he'd sat in the darkness of a broom cupboard and done something that no other man or magician was able to do that he'd had a feeling of self-worth. It was a profound, if short-lived, emotion, and Dimmot realized that many people felt it daily, and some throughout their lives.

Merlin and Griswold knew it, but then they'd earned it.

For Dimmot it had been a first time, and as such it was so sweet that it hurt.

'All I ever wanted was to be a musician,' he whispered.

'I know,' said Asmethyum. 'But, for better or worse, you're

something much more than just a musician. That's why you were sought out by my son and that's why Fate has brought you here.'

'What does getting out of here entail?'

'Simple,' said Asmethyum. 'Make a Wish.'

Chapter 39

'And now,' said Nemestis, spreading his hands expansively towards the heavens, 'the time has come. Time to celebrate. Time to terminate. Time to invite our guests.'

They turned from the corridor into a vast hall. The floor was, not surprisingly, marble and through the distant windows Merlin could see clouds and blue sky. Marble pillars and arches supported a staggeringly large marble dome and potted aspidistras lined the floor along each wall.

A large, cumbersome and remarkably vulgar ball, made of tiny mirrors, hung from the centre of the dome and spun sluggishly on its chain. Against one long wall was a raised stage, decked with more potted plants, heavy velvet curtains and . . . music stands.

Seeing the Enchanter's look of mild bewilderment, Nemestis waved a hand expansively. 'A faithful reproduction with a few touches of my own. Built to overlook the Thames on the site of the Savoy Hotel. Round about Mr Dimmot's time, as it happens! I call it the New Savoy Hotel.'

When the Enchanter refrained from asking why, Nemestis continued jovially, 'Call me sentimental if you like, but I stayed at the Savoy, during the war. Second World War, that is. Nineteen forties, y'know. That was mainly my doing.'

'By all accounts a dismal failure,' murmured the Enchanter.

'You've been listening to Nostradamus, I'll bet. On the contrary, old friend, merely a practice run. Experiment in mass programming, one of several.'

He turned to Scarbald.

'Right, cretin. Go to it.'

The gnome sneered a grin and trotted into the middle of the

floor. From the grubby folds of his tunic he dragged a small oblong box dotted with buttons and little windows.

Nemestis leaned towards Merlin and whispered from the corner of his mouth, 'He's very proud of this trick. Took him nearly three hundred years to perfect it. A little polite applause would be appreciated.'

Scarbald pushed one of the buttons. The windows lit up, flashing a regular, random-looking sequence.

Merlin fidgeted, gave his cloak a shake and pulled it about him. He wished he could have cast his inner eye about the building to search for Griswold and Dimmot, but the best he could do was to leave a trail in the hope that Griswold might find a way to escape his captors and follow it. He dare not resort to magic now.

Right now magic could destroy three thousand years of hidden work.

He knew *how* he'd been brought to this point in time and he knew why. Nemestis wanted to watch the Enchanter suffer as his beloved Mankind died out.

But how could the demon possibly have found him so far back in the depths of time, when Merlin had arranged for history to bury him in obscurity long ago?

Had he bungled?

And if not, then who?

'Thy little lights are most impressive,' he sneered, briefly clapping his hands.

'Your sarcasm is of no interest,' replied Nemestis. 'Watch.'

As they watched, the gnome glared intently at the flashing lights for a few seconds, then he stabbed a warted finger at the buttons.

A patch of pale blue light appeared in the air before him, spreading until it was an egg shape six feet high by three across hovering silently a few inches from the floor. The humming rose slightly in volume and pitch.

A second patch of light appeared several feet away, expanding like the first.

Another appeared.

Then another.

Inside the first balloon of light a shadow appeared, rapidly swirling and taking shape until, with a sound like something bursting in reverse, a figure snapped into existence and the light around it vanished.

One after another more lights appeared, forming into figures until the room was filled with the sound of popping. Frozen figures appeared all around.

Scarbald gave a snuffle of delight.

In minutes over a thousand figures appeared until the room was still.

The gnome turned and glanced at Nemestis with raised eyebrows. The demon nodded. Scarbald gave one more casual stab at the box and the room burst into pandemonium.

Every creature came instantly to life, greeting those near it or moving towards colleagues across the room. Roars, screeches and hisses filled the air. So did the stench of a thousand evils.

As Merlin stared about him, taking in the living obscenities shuffling and hopping before his eyes, his blood ran cold.

'I see that you are impressed, old friend,' Nemestis smiled.

'Thou hast dredged up the creatures of the Netherworlds,' intoned the Enchanter.

The noise from a thousand demonic throats thundered about him and the unspeakable forms milled about them in a gruesome dance of mutual recognition.

'Well, of course,' answered Nemestis. 'Two hundred warlords from the darkest regions of Hell. Eight hundred of their commanders, each with a million demons under his command, just waiting to leave their myriad dimensions and sweep across your little planet.'

He grinned. 'One thousand in all. And will they be pleased to see *you*.'

He took a pace forward and gazing casually at the floor, raised a hand lazily in the air.

A wave of silence flowed across the hall and every eye turned towards him.

On seeing him some of the creatures grinned friendly grins. All of them waited in eager anticipation.

'Friends,' he said in a voice that resonated implacably to the farthest ears in the hall.

'Welcome. You, who have come from the farthest . . . and darkest . . .'

A respectful titter ran through the hall.

'. . . corners of the galaxy at the behest of our Lord and Master, Lucifer, Prince of Darkness . . .'

Through the crowd ran a thousand murmurs, growls and mumbles approximating the phrase, 'Praise be to Lucifer.'

'. . . are here today to bear witness to humanity's final hour. By this time tomorrow the Balance of the Cosmos will be in our favour. All will be chaos. Evil will reign supreme.'

A collective sigh arose from every throat, and the air crackled with triumph.

'Tonight we celebrate! Your rooms await. The freedom of the hotel is yours, until eight o'clock this evening when we all meet in this hall for dancing, drinking, debauchery and general devilment.'

He grinned as the visitors shrieked with laughter at the joke, and winked at the Enchanter.

Merlin stared back impassively with his hands folded before him.

The demon raised his hand once more for silence. His voice rang out softly.

'There is one more item to mention before we disperse. Of all the lands on all the worlds, this green and sickeningly pleasant one has been more of a thorn in our collective sides than any other. For thousands of years the pinnacle of piety has resided in the kingdom we have come to know and hate. A piety held together by a fragile succession of men of magic and occasionally religion. Of all those men the one who has pricked our ribs most bloodily . . . stands with me here.'

He turned and raised a hand towards Merlin.

'Creatures of Hell, those of you who have in times past suffered his wrath, those of you who have fallen victim to his wizardry, those of you who were unable to break the barriers imposed by his magical banishments from this world . . . I give you . . .'

'Merlin! Merlin the Enchanter.'

A voice from the back of the great hall bubbled with nasal fury as its owner rose up on its hind legs, its claws clenched with rage.

'I'd recognize him anywhere.'

A roar of anger erupted and, all around, creatures who knew better shuffled back with fear in their eyes.

The wizard returned a thousand stares with calm indifference.

He focused his attention on the creature who had spoken.

'I underestimated thee, Phobious. I'd have sworn that my magics had destroyed thee beyond any hope of reincarnation. I must try harder next time.'

'What next time, Merlin?' replied the creature. 'You're at our mercy and our mercy is extremely strained.'

Contemptuous, though slightly nervous, sniggering skittered through the crowd.

'Thou speakest brave words, Phobious. From a distance.'

Before the creature could answer, Nemestis interrupted. 'Enough,' he murmured. 'Like you, my friends, the Enchanter is my guest. Like you he will have the privilege of witnessing the Last Trump.

'And, like you, he will go on to reside for all his days, such as they are, in the fires of Hell, although, unlike you, he will not feel quite so at home therein.'

The wizard turned his gaze up to Nemestis' eyes with contempt.

'I carry my own hell within me, demon, and it shall pleasure me soon to visit my hell upon thee and thine iniquitous lackeys. I might even dare to expend some little energy in so doing.'

'A bold speech, old man. In which case, when the time is come I shall willingly afford you the opportunity to pit your skills, meagre though they be, against mine.'

'I am overwhelmed with gratitude,' said Merlin.

He smiled an absent-minded little smile that said, 'Sorry, lost my train of thought. Did you say something?'

And Nemestis made an error. For an instant a glint of hatred sparked in his eyes. In that instant the minute weakening of his iron will allowed the seed of a Wish to squeeze its way into his unconscious.

'In fact,' he added as an afterthought, 'I think it might be rather enjoyable to see you and Mr Dimmot locked in mortal combat first. The winner to be the one who dies. The loser to have his soul methodically dismantled by my good self over a long period of, say, one thousand years. Sound good to you?'

'Well?' croaked Asmethyum. 'Did you get through?'

'I've no idea,' retorted Dimmot. 'How am I supposed to know?'

'Your senses, boy! Your senses would've felt the shift in the fabric of the space–time continuum. Did you feel a shift in the fab—?'

'I wouldn't know if the space–time bloody continuum turned itself inside out. Anyway, you're the one who's supposed to know about these things. Didn't *you* feel a shift in the whatever?'

'It's *your* continuum, fool. *Your* reality, not mine. I can't feel your reality. Gods, don't you know anything?'

'Do you know what a minor seventh with a flattened ninth is?' screamed Dimmot.

Asmethyum scowled and stared into the distance. Then he sat down tiredly on nothing substantial and said, 'I suppose we'll just have to wait and see, then.'

Griswold awoke to the smell of perfume and the gentle slither of silk sheets across his body.

It had been an interesting interval and extremely demanding. In fact he'd had more than a little trouble in maintaining the balance between supply and demand.

'Just a short rest, mistress, if you please,' he'd managed to gasp.

Amanda had given a pout and a sniff and graciously conceded and, vowing to resume his search for Merlin and Dimmot shortly, Griswold had closed his eyes for a few seconds.

He opened an eye and saw stars.

He sat up with a jerk, slid around a bit and grabbed the headboard to steady himself.

Staring through the window he saw blackness sprinkled with little spots of starlight. For one hopeful second he imagined that he was still in Guinevere's chamber, waking from some wildly ludicrous dream. He glanced round the room and his hope vanished.

The smell of perfume came from a hanging ball, which dribbled smoke from the mouth of its lifelike and ugly bronze face.

The woman, Amanda, was not there.

A wave of relief swept through him, immediately followed by one of alarm.

She was gone and it was night time. He'd slept through the day. Fool, fool and thrice horny fool, he thought.

Scrambling from the bed he gathered his clothes from various parts of the room and slung them on, casting his eyes round for a decent weapon.

I wonder what a bazooka looks like, he thought, peering hopefully under the bed.

Amanda's room was surprisingly bereft of weaponlike objects. Neither hairpins, brooches nor any manner of sharp things decked the dressing table or the bedside cabinet. Nothing in the way of clubs or knuckle dusters.

'Ah, well,' he murmured. 'When needs must.'

He grabbed the smoking ball and yanked at the rope, tearing it from the ceiling.

Hefting the rope in one hand he stepped out through the door into the sound of distant music.

Chapter 40

It was a mixed party.

It was also very noisy. With just over an hour to go before midnight, the clatter of hooves, the scratch of claws and the flop of paws echoed off the vast marble floor while thunderclaps and the roar of mini-hurricanes resounded round the ballroom. Smoke issued from nostrils, steam rose from strange bodies and occasional puffs of talc spiffed into the air as guests vanished on the spot, taking the quick way upstairs to the loo.

The music, provided by an orchestra whose fingers would have outnumbered their owners, pro rata, if they'd been a local group, swirled and rippled through the ears in a distinctly unEarthly manner.

The trumpeter was particularly impressive.

Wandering through the dancers, Nemestis, in a cloak of black bordered with white ermine, with Amanda clinging to his arm, and Merlin and Dimmot at his side, smiled a smile of quiet triumph.

Merlin's face was impassive, unreadable, Dimmot's slightly bleary and a similar colour to the pink drink he held in his moist hand. The glass, though 90 per cent proof, half empty, and his third, was bleak comfort.

It appeared that his Wish had come half-true. Although Asmethyum was left in the strange prison cell without bars, Dimmot had been invited to join Nemestis and Merlin for the celebrations. The demon had said something about no vestige of Mankind being left behind. Dimmot didn't exactly understand what he meant, but Nemestis' smile filled in the gaps.

Two creatures on their left writhed round their host sinuously, grinning wide, conspiratorial grins.

'Congratulations, you lucky devil,' laughed the man. 'Cut it a bit fine though.'

'The eleventh hour, Ssirias,' agreed Nemestis.

'The hour of glory iss ssoon upon uss,' smiled the woman.

'Indeed, Hessia,' Nemestis smiled. 'You may kiss me.'

The woman's beady eyes glittered. With a hiss of delight she twined her arms round his neck and slid her cold, thin lips against his. Her man-shaped companion laughed a silent snake's laugh as, to Merlin's disdain and Dimmot's horror, she succumbed to her passions and let her human-like body dissolve into its natural form.

Nemestis was undisturbed as the face and hands became three flat diamond-shaped heads joined to the one body.

He was unperturbed as three little forked tongues flicked out and attempted to explore his mouth and both ears simultaneously.

And he was quite unsurprised when the two tails that had been the woman's legs wrapped around him, the tips stroking their way along predictable paths.

He reached up and pulled her away from him.

'Enough,' he said.

The serpent resumed her human form and pouted with disappointment.

'Enough for now, Hessia. Perhaps we will savour our triumph later,' he said.

He gave the couple a smile and moved on.

'Hissing hussy,' snapped Amanda sulkily.

She wore a sleek-fitting gown of shiny, overlapping scales that were basically white and pink when the colours stayed still long enough to be recognized. It was a full-length gown if one defines a full-length gown as one that reaches up from the floor to a point two inches below one's breasts. The designer had quite rightly felt that to cover them up would be to diminish the effect of the sapphire pendants hanging from the pins which pierced Amanda's nipples. If the straps that criss-crossed between them contributed anything to their support, it was superfluous since they stood up perfectly well on their own, being far more firm than breasts of that age had any right to be.

A smug smile lit her face and she clung more tightly to Nemestis' arm.

'I notice that she didn't do anything for you in spite of her sneaky, snaky tricks. Nobody does any more, do they? Only me.'

Nemestis continued to nod and wave to his guests with a smile playing on his lips. Then he stopped and looked down at her.

'You are correct in part, sister.'

Above his smiling mouth his eyes glinted coldly.

'Nobody does any more.'

He turned and walked off through the guests, waving to a nearby group of guards to keep an eye on the Enchanter, leaving Amanda shaking with rage.

A pair of centaurs and a brownish creature not quite describable paused in their dancing to stare respectfully as her pendants gave a tasteful impression of two criminals kicking in their nooses.

Without giving the spectators a glance Amanda glared at Nemestis' departing back, her full red lips a mouse's navel, her eyes flecked with venom.

'Your womanly passion is wasted on such as he,' said Merlin quietly. 'His heart and his soul have long since succumbed to the coldness that denies both love and hate, both desire and passion.'

'A lie, old man,' snapped Amanda. 'I still have the power to stir his passion. He's had much on his mind of late.'

'What did he mean by "the eleventh hour"?'

Amanda looked down at the Enchanter with disdain.

'Time has run out for my brother. Should he fail to destroy the miserable remnants of Mankind within the next two days, Lucifer will recall him to Hell and send a replacement. To learn from Nemestis' mistakes and to start from scratch.'

'And your brother?'

Amanda stared into the distance and gave a shrug.

'No more Nemestis,' she said. 'But then again, it won't happen. Tonight is his night of victory. Eternal glory will be his. And, once again, he will be mine. He cannot fail.'

'No?'

'No. Nothing and no one can stop him.'

'There are those that would try,' said Merlin.

'Who, for example? Your knight without sword or armour? Or that griping primitive from the dark ages?'

She pointed her slender chin at Dimmot.

'Here, d'you mi—?'

'Or you, Merlin, with your powers stripped like the skin from your bones?'

She turned away and began to glide through the crowd.

'Enjoy yourselves while you may,' she called over her shoulder. 'Especially the floor show.'

'What's s'special 'bout the floor show?' whispered Dimmot, maintaining his balance with difficulty.

'I gather that that is when yon minstrel . . .' he nodded towards the trumpet player who was lounging against what passed for the piano, '. . . will loose upon the world the lethal powers of his musical genius.'

Dimmot stared at the trumpet player for a second. He looked harmless.

'What's *he* gonna play that's so lethal?'

'Why, the Last Trump. Thou must have heard of it.'

Chapter 41

In the year AD 3797, on November 29th at midnight precisely, following a day of holocaust throughout the planet Earth, in which the peoples of every nation suffered all manner of terrible visitations upon their bodies, minds and souls by the creatures of Darkness, there came a moment, long predicted and long feared, the moment that would precede Man's final hour and his descent into the fiery depths of Hell, lifeless, soulless and beyond hope of redemption. The moment in which would sound the dreadful notes of the Last Trump.

Encyclopaedia Esoterica,
revised edition AD 5008,
Appendix 2

The Last Trump is, of course, nothing new. Stretching through the mists of Time, tales concerning the end of the world abound in all shapes and forms. Many of those tales speak of the moment when a trumpet, or variation of same, will blast out across the landscape and, with its final notes reverberating around the skies, the world will come to an abrupt and tumultuous end. What form this end will take varies according to the local folklore of the storytellers, and the whim of the musician, but basically the cause and effect are the same in every case.

Even James Dimmot, though not a student of anyone's folklore, had heard of the Last Trump. He stared intently at the chap on the bandstand whose job it would be to play the terminal notes.

Hope welled up within him. With the hope, and more than enough alcohol, came an idea silly enough to make his already weak knees grow even weaker and his mouth become dry.

He drained his glass in one gulp, leaned towards Merlin and mumbled, 'How much time do we have left?'

'No more than an hour.'

'Tha' should be enough,' said Dimmot and he turned towards the bandstand.

'Where goest thou?' called the wizard to his retreating back.

'I'm gonna do what I do best,' said Dimmot in an unusually firm voice. 'I'm gonna play piano and I'm gonna drink liquor.'

Then, he added in the silence of his own mind, I'm going to save the world. He sniggered. Jus' call me Bond, James B—

'Oh, yeah,' he turned back and, bringing his face close to Merlin's, whispered, 'nea'ly forgot. I have it on good author'ty that the best thing for you to do right now is to . . .' His brow furrowed in deep concentration. '. . . "seek again the source of your wizardly power". Y'know, like you did once before, only you didn't quite make it, cos you had to get me an' ol' Gris'old out of trouble. Anyway, good author'ty, break through this time, power beyond y' wildest . . .'

His voice trailed off as he turned away and wove a dubious path through the dancers. Staring doggedly ahead and trying to ignore the sight of heavy-loined reptiles with claws on their heels and elbows, and beautiful, blue-bodied women sprouting numerous snaky tails from their buttocks, he headed for the stage.

The Enchanter stared after him through narrowed eyes. Then, keeping a new and impossible hope shut firmly out of sight in the depths of his soul, Merlin wandered off to find somewhere quiet.

The three guards looked from one to the other uncertainly, shrugged and trailed behind him.

Dimmot arrived at the stage to find Scarbald standing in front of the bandstand, having convulsions. The gnome's glazed eyes bounced loosely about in his face and each limb was spasming independently. For some reason everyone was keeping well clear and no one seemed to want to help him.

Dimmot was hoping his affliction might be terminal as the music came to a crashing halt. Everyone stopped dancing and, to Dimmot's amazement, gave the gnome a thunderous round of applause. Scarbald stood gasping for air with an ecstatic grin on his face. It was several seconds before Dimmot realized that Scarbald had been dancing. Keeping out of his way was obviously a matter of prudence rather than indifference, just as applauding his performance was considered preferable to courting the risk of disfigurement by those eager teeth.

Dimmot approached cautiously.

There's my ticket onto the bandstand, he thought. This requires a diplomatic approach.

'That was very impressive,' he said. 'Pure Ginger Rogers.'

He was favoured with the gnome's equivalent of 'Thank you', a smile of smug hatred.

'The band are very good,' went on Dimmot, 'although they don't do you justice, of course.'

Scarbald directed a sniff of contempt towards the stage.

'If I got the chance, I'd show those buggers how to play music worthy of a dancer of your talent.'

Scarbald eyed him suspiciously for a long minute while Dimmot tried desperately to radiate sincerity.

The gnome turned his gaze towards the stand where the trumpet player stood with his back to the crowd, drinking from a bottle with two spouts.

Without warning Scarbald grabbed Dimmot by the scruff, shoved him towards the stage and thrust him bodily up on to the bandstand. Then he scrambled up beside him and glared at the trumpet player, as if willing him to put his drink down and turn round.

Which he did.

With a casual wave and a hollow gurgle that translated loosely as, 'Hey, Scarbald. Hi, man,' the trumpet player swivelled on his toes and gave the two men a grin.

Two grins actually, one from each of two vertical mouths, side by side.

'Ah,' said Dimmot. 'That explains it. I wondered how you managed to play two horns at once. Some of those harmonies were incredible.'

'Ah gots the advantage, man, I'll give you that. You a music player?'

'Piano,' said Dimmot.

'Ma name's Moog.'

'Dimmot.'

The two beings shook hands gravely, while Scarbald gave a derisive sneer and drummed his feet impatiently on the stage.

'You wanna play a bit o' piano wid us?'

'Cert'nly do,' said Dimmot and he gave Scarbald a large wink.

The gnome spat knowingly at Dimmot's feet.

The piano keyboard was invented back in the early dark ages and it remained a perfect vehicle for artistic expression among the human race for many centuries, with virtually no alteration to its basic structure.

When word got round that human beings were doing great things with the harmonies of the cosmos, fingers of all shapes and numbers got involved and the keyboard became diversified beyond recognition.

The pianist on stage was one of the old school. He'd studied under the spirits of Chopin, GherXes, and Hindemith/CR3prig in his time and, having only five fingers on his right hand, he confined his playing to a keyboard with an everyday conventional layout. Dimmot felt that he could live with the overall shape, which dropped away to right and left to form a vertical arch, even though it meant reaching round and playing the end notes at full stretch. It also meant that he'd have to play by feel. Since playing while unable to see the keyboard or anything else, other than through an alcoholic haze, had become standard practice, this was no hardship.

Running his fingers over the keyboard he gave a silent prayer of thanks as the sounds proved to be identical to those he used to play eighteen hundred years ago.

He glanced briefly at the most daunting audience he had ever faced in his life. As one person they broke into a wild applause that held more than a hint of what would happen if the musical guest artist failed to satisfy their expectations.

Planting feet that were trying frantically to go through very fast running motions firmly on the floor, he gave Moog a nod.

'You throw it 'n' I'll catch it,' he said.

Giving him two flashing grins the trumpeter raised his hand to start the band.

'Blue Moog,' he called. 'One, two, one two three FOUR!'

Some things never change, thought Dimmot happily.

He swallowed deeply from the bottle and passed it on. The

band were resting between numbers as dance bands do, swapping evergreen in-jokes and lubricating their overworked throats.

That Moog the trumpeter was the only wind player in the band had little bearing on the enthusiasm with which the bottle was rapidly being emptied. They'd played three numbers with an astonishing degree of rapport, while Scarbald gave his impression of two rabid dogs sharing an epileptic fit. The crowd, already sky-high on anticipation, screamed its appreciation.

Now, sitting in a loose circle round their instruments, with the gnome between them, they passed the bottle from hand to hand, wiping lips and jowls with relish.

James Dimmot began to talk. He talked fast and animatedly. He talked about his life, his music, his past, his wives, coming back to his music, the kick he was getting from playing with such talent as was on the stand that night, and while he talked he waved his arms, stood up, walked about and generally endeavoured to disguise the fact that, when Moog passed him the bottle, he'd take his slug and pass the bottle straight to the trumpeter.

Try playing thad on y'r plumpet when you're pissed to the eyeballs, he thought, less than lucidly. Never could be done. Can't be now. Jus' like th' music, pal, some things never change.

Then it was time to play again.

'You gonna finish the set with us, Dimmot?' asked Moog.

'Wouldn't miss it,' retorted Dimmot. His feelings were mixed. He knew that Moog had to be slapped down before he could do whatever harm he was meant to do, but he didn't relish watching the trumpeter make a prat of himself.

Us musicians deserve bedder'n'at, he thought.

He turned his gaze towards Scarbald.

'Go to it, Ginge,' he mumbled.

Scarbald gazed back. Then, having made several successful grabs at the passing bottle, he gave a snarl, slid gracelessly over the side of the stage and disappeared with a thump. Dimmot heard the scrabbling as the gnome crawled under the stage with seconds to spare before falling into a deep sleep, full of nightmares, exclusively of his own making. Then the band took off at a frenzied pace with Dimmot sweating to keep up and the crowd breaking into another orgy of ghastly athletics.

It soon became clear from the way Moog's trumpet soared and

sang that he was not in the least affected by the same alcohol that was tracing well-worn paths through Dimmot's system and heading with practised deliberation for his brain.

'Dammit,' he mumbled as his fingers flew across the keys and his eyes took on an all-too-familiar lack of focus.

'It'll have to be Plan B.'

What Plan B would entail he had no idea, but he knew it would have to involve him using violence. He realized with a sinking feeling that he might not be up to it. Violence was something that always happened *to* him.

The music, which in reality was getting louder and louder, began to fade from the remains of Dimmot's consciousness, leaving him suspended in a vague, rapidly darkening world of roaring silence. His head drooped forward until his face came to rest on the keyboard, creating a chord of such awful dissonance that the crowd went wild and the band rose to new heights of creativity.

As Dimmot slipped smoothly into stupor he wished that Griswold would turn up and start laying about everyone in sight, but it was only a half-hearted wish with a small 'w'.

He didn't hold out much hope.

Chapter 42

The guards trailed nonchalantly behind Merlin, laughing and chatting amongst themselves. The dreary little would-be magician from some distant land was less of a threat than the aspidistras in the ballroom. He'd take a few steps, wheeze a bit and lean against the wall, take a few steps, wheeze, lean.

He didn't look fit to last the evening. Why Nemestis bothered assigning them to keep an eye on him was beyond them. The little man stopped once more and squinted up at them towering over him.

'I'll rest here a while if 'tis all right with thee,' he whispered hoarsely. 'I would deem it a charity if thou'dst stay close, lest I succumb to the faintness that threatens me. Thy master would be displeased if I . . .'

He tottered to a nearby seat and sank heavily into the plush cushions.

The tallest guard sighed impatiently. With the celebration well under way there were far better things to do than babysit this withered old cadaver. If he'd had a choice . . .

'All right,' he murmured, not knowing that he and the others had just changed jobs from restrainers to lookouts.

'My thanks,' said Merlin. 'I shall see that th'art rewarded as befits.'

Meaning that, should the unfortunate necessity arise, they would die quickly and painlessly.

The Enchanter closed his eyes while the guards stood around and did what guards with time on their hands do. They talked, passed wind, sighed with boredom and let their concentration slip.

Merlin breathed deeply, guiding his thoughts down, down into his unconscious, leaving his body on the surface, deathly still and silent. Unnoticed by the guards his breathing soon became as shallow as the surface of water and his features relaxed in peaceful repose. He descended through the depths of the labyrinth to where the door that he'd faced only once before stood in front of him.

The two pendants beat a wild and vibrant tattoo on Amanda's breasts as she spun round in horror.

Sir Griswold was no longer in her bedchamber.

Having left him to sleep off the effects of their indulgences she was convinced that he would not surface until well into the early hours, when she'd top off the night's celebrations by waking him with a kiss . . . for starters.

That mortal must have the constitution of a centaur, she thought desperately.

Confirming an age-old proverb about the tendency of history to repeat itself, however obscurely, Amanda dropped to her knees and peered under the bed.

She rose, trembling.

'Damn!' she snarled.

'Damn!' she snapped, lurching to the dressing table. Grabbing up a perfume jar, she swung back her arm and hurled it, intending to smash it against the wall. The jar, with malicious inaccuracy, flew through the window and, executing an arc of far greater radius than if thrown by any human arm, sailed gracefully down to fall with a tiny plop into the Thames.

'DAMN!' screeched Amanda.

Shaking with rage she fought to gather her thoughts together. When she did, she rather wished she hadn't.

Oh, Lucifer! If Nemestis found out that she'd been hiding the knight in her chamber . . .

As the thought was too horrendous to contemplate she left it unfinished and swept out of the room. Slipping along corridors and trying to avoid being stopped by passing guests, she peered round doors and down stairways.

If only she had a fraction of Nemestis' powers she could locate Griswold with no trouble, damn him.

What she was going to do if she failed to find him before he did some damage, she didn't know. After ten minutes, three flights of stairs and increasing desperation she began to glow with a thin sheen of moisture which, in other circumstances, she'd have used to provoke men or beasts to unheard-of heights of desire.

Right now she was scared to Heaven and desperate enough to do something silly.

She turned and fled along the corridors and down the stairs four at a time with her little criminals dancing their deathly jitterbugs.

She skidded to a stop, heaving for breath, at the door of the hall of statues.

'If I can't find him, I know a creature who can,' she gasped.

In the distance the swell of music and the insistent thump of the bass pounded softly in her ears. She glanced round, making sure that no one was in sight, unlatched the door and went through. The statues were silent and, except for the occasional stirring in their sleep, quite still.

Hurrying silently across the soft carpet she came to a halt before her latest acquisition.

'Bathym,' she hissed. 'Wake up, you wretch.'

She grabbed a marble-covered leg and shook it as one might shake an oak tree.

She slapped it.

'Wake up, damn you. I need your help.'

A slight cracking sound made her glance up. The statue was opening one eye with difficulty.

Bathym's words came out thinly sandwiched between the sliding slabs of his jaws.

'What do you want?' he intoned ponderously.

Amanda stared up desperately.

'I need you to find someone for me.'

The statue glanced down at her heaving breasts and glowing skin.

'I wouldn't have thought you'd need *me* . . .'

'This is important, fool. The knight, Griswold. The large, shaggy one. I . . .'

'Oh, him. Yes, I remember Griswold. Friend of Merlin the Enchanter.'

'That's the one. You must find him.'

'Again?'

'Pardon?'

214

'Never mind. Where is he?'

'If I knew *that*, I wouldn't need you, fool.'

'Oh, you don't just mean get him, you mean *find* him as well.'

'Yes.'

'I usually only go and get people from known locations. S'part of the deal. Usually.'

'Well, I'm sorry.'

'What do you want me to do with him when I find him?'

Amanda frowned. She hadn't thought that far.

She sighed. What a waste.

'He must disappear for ever. Anywhere, anywhen, as long as Nemestis can't find him.'

'Ah,' said Bathym knowingly. 'I suppose my reward will be quite substantial?'

'Yes. You may have me for a whole night.'

'Rather have my freedom.'

'What!'

'No offence.'

Amanda stared at him, aghast. This was turning out to be a hell of a day. First Nemestis' snide remark, then Griswold walking out on her, and now this cretin . . .

She glared up at Bathym.

'All right then, damn you!'

'I have your word?'

'Of course. Just get on with it.'

'Consider it done. Assuming that I *can* find him. Perhaps if I had some help?'

'Name it.'

With a sound like rocks groaning, Bathym raised his arms and embraced the hall in general. Amanda looked round to see all the statues awake and staring down at her in anticipation.

'Who better?' said Bathym.

In the stark silence of his prison the ancient being who called himself Asmethyum wondered if it was really worth the effort.

Three thousand years, he thought dismally. And for what? A two-hour lecture on the harmonic development of twentieth-century blues. His own fault really. He shouldn't have asked.

James Dimmot, with a captive audience before him and a

215

burning, and somewhat desperate, enthusiasm behind him, had shown no sign of flagging.

'. . . which brings us to your minor seventh with the flat . . .'

At that point the door had opened and the stick-like figure of Nemestis stood, starkly outlined against the light.

'Mr Dimmot, you've been cooped up here long enough,' said the demon. 'Would you care to join me?'

Since then Asmethyum had sat alone in the darkness, pondering the nature of irony and wondering why he had been left out when James Dimmot had made his Wish.

He was still pondering when his ears caught the sound of someone testing the solidity of the door.

Metaphorically, that is.

Merlin opened his eyes, took a breath and rose to his feet. He no longer feigned frailty, but spoke steadily and quietly to the guards lounging against the walls.

'It is time to return to the festivities. Be so kind as to take me back.'

'You all right, old man?' asked the head guard without much interest.

'I am better now. Much.'

Down in the tunnels of the Enchanter's mind a door swung lightly to and fro on its silent hinges. Through the doorway a room of unfinite boundaries could be seen to be quite empty.

Metaphorically, of course.

In the Hall of Statues the air was becoming a little heated.

'Doesn't *anyone* know how to find missing persons?' growled Bathym.

All of the forty or so entities there were highly accomplished at their crafts.

'I'm a bringer of storms and pestilence,' said one with a shrug. 'I don't deal in fiddly little things like people.'

'You find him, I'll teach him a thousand tongues or turn him inside out,' said another.

'I just deal in virgins,' murmured another.

'This is all very unsatisfactory,' grumbled Bathym. 'Our freedom depends on this.'

'Then the answer is simple,' said the only one who was into multi-dimensional mathematics and space–time logistics.

'Yes?' chorused the rest.

'We split up.'

'And?'

'We take a floor at a time and search every room until we find this Griswold fellow. Then we meet at the banquet hall, hand him over to Bathym to do whatever Bathym does, and *then* we go our own ways,' he concluded smugly.

A murmur of assent went round the room. They split up.

Chapter 43

A hush fell over the great banquet hall of the New Savoy Hotel, London, broken only by the half-conscious mumblings of the only being not holding its breath.

Dimmot, gripping the empty bottle, sat slumped across the keyboard. The band had switched off the power and were sitting around radiating musicianly indifference.

All eyes turned towards the stage as the lights dimmed, leaving the bandleader Moog standing alone in a grim, smoke-grey spotlight.

High above the crowd on a balcony which circled three walls Sir Griswold flattened himself against a pillar and watched intently.

He noted with relief the tiny figure of Merlin. He also spotted Amanda, trying vainly to hide some unaccountable agitation. There was Dimmot, prostrate at an altar similar to the one which the little man had at his abode and, standing before Nemestis, a host of the most awful-looking monstrosities Griswold had ever seen.

By God, he thought, the skinny devil *could* bring the flies to life.

Griswold peeled himself off the pillar and crept along the balcony towards the platform, the heavy bronze ball on a short rein for instant use.

The stench of evil, sweating bodies drifted into his nostrils.

He hoped that the Enchanter would be able, and inclined, to adjust the odds a little in his favour. He crept closer to the platform. Below him the crowd parted as Nemestis strode to the front of the stage. He turned to address the crowd, his face alight with triumph.

'The time is now,' hissed the demon quietly. 'The millennia to come will ring with tales of this moment. Across the depths of space, in every dimension, through Eternity, nay Infinity! Mankind, detested enemy of Evil, is about to gasp his final breath.'

Behind him, shielded from all eyes by the shadows and the demon's glistening black cloak, James Dimmot was stirring.

'Sons and daughters of Darkness,' intoned Nemestis. 'Taste with me the sweetness of victory. Bear witness to my triumph. Rejoice in Man's demise as the notes of the Last Trump rend his ears.'

His audience growled in anticipation.

Dimmot gazed about him blearily. He saw Moog standing alone in the spotlight and registered Nemestis' words. His forehead wrinkled as he put two and two together to make a terrifying, if somewhat hazy, four. Taking a firm grip on the bottle, he rose unsteadily to his feet.

In the midst of the crowd Merlin stood with his head bowed as if in defeat, his shaking hands folded before him. Around him the creatures slavered through cruel lips. From somewhere in the distance the sound of a gigantic clock began to chime.

The green-clad figure on stage placed a lazy hand to his trumpet and lovingly held it up to gleam in the spotlight.

Looking down on the scene Griswold tried to comprehend exactly what was going on. Whatever was about to happen had to be for the worse, yet Merlin stood unmoving, making no attempt to do anything about it.

Was he truly powerless? Was there some reason why he should stay his hand?

Griswold stared intently about the hall. Every creature was waiting for something. The sounds of the clock's chimes resounded in the knight's ears, intoning a death knell in his mind. A decision was needed and it seemed that he was the only one in a position to make it. But what decision?

The chimes continued their steady countdown to midnight.

Bong . . . bong . . . bong . . . bong . . .

The creature on the platform slowly raised the trumpet to his lips.

Bong . . . bong . . . bong . . . bong . . .

Suddenly James Dimmot rose to his full height, wielding a

219

bottle over his head and screaming, 'Oh no, you don't, you bastard!'

Bong.

Merlin looked up in horror as the little man lurched towards the trumpeter. The Enchanter's face was white, his lips drawn back from his teeth, yet he seemed unable to speak.

Bong.

A concerted roar erupted from the crowd and Nemestis whirled about, his hand raised in a gesture that was all too familiar to Griswold. The demon was about to hurl a bolt of something dreadful at Dimmot.

Bong.

Griswold knew that time had run out. He gave the bronze ball one swift twirl and sent it hurtling with unerring accuracy towards the platform.

Bong.

The ball struck Dimmot with a resounding thud on the back of his head. With a sigh and a hurt look in his eyes he dropped to the floor.

Moog stared down at him, perplexed. Then, with Nemestis yelling, 'Now, damn you! Now,' he put the two mouthpieces to his lips and blew.

The notes rippled chromatically up adjacent scales, tripling and tumbling in their frenzied race to reach the top, where they hovered, a screeching semitone apart. One scale descended, followed by the other, doublets against triplets, rhythm against rhythm, until they lurched, growling, into the belly of the instrument before rising up again. The fanfare was so terrifying in its harshness, so relentless in its conflicting sheets of sound, that even the creatures in the great hall cringed.

Dimmot, mercifully unconscious, stirred only slightly beneath the onslaught, but on the balcony, Griswold fell back against the pillar, his hands clamped over his ears, sweat gushing from every pore of his body.

The notes of the Last Trump soared through the open windows of the Savoy Hotel, London and swept into the skies and across the face of the Earth, unhindered by mountains, forests or cities, for the notes were not of the Earth or created by Earthly means.

Wherever they rang out people fell to their knees, hands to

their ears, black despair in their hearts and escape into oblivion uppermost in their minds.

The notes of the Last Trump swept round the Earth three times, then vanished as if they'd never existed. The planet was silent.

In the hall of the Savoy Hotel a single voice spoke softly.

'Here beginneth the last lesson,' said Nemestis.

Up on stage Moog began to pack his instrument into its case, humming casually to himself. The creatures in the audience began to shuffle, casting uncertain glances at each other.

Nothing seemed to be happening.

Why the anti-climax?

Nemestis glanced about him.

'Cretin,' he intoned evenly. 'Where are you?'

From beneath the stage came a snuffle and a hic as Scarbald crawled out from the blackness. The intensity of his malignant glare was softened by a certain glaze in his eyes and slackness of mouth.

Nemestis sighed. 'Have you *no* sense of occasion?' he groaned.

Scarbald belched, grinned and looked up at the demon questioningly.

'We wish to witness Man's demise,' said Nemestis grittily. 'If that's all right with you.'

The gnome's face lit up with understanding. He fumbled in his pocket, pulled out his control box and squinted at the buttons. After a dramatic flourish, followed by a slight pause for effect, he stabbed. The silence was instantly shattered as the floor of the hall vanished. Scenes of carnage filled its place as though appearing on a vast television screen.

In the bleak suburbs and green-treed villages of England, pale-faced office workers and ruddy yokels rose from their beds and ran amok through the night. They slashed at anything that lived with breadknives and they clubbed screaming heads with axes and hammers.

On the plains of blisteringly hot countries, armies engaged in the current wars abandoned their highly trained teamwork to fight amongst themselves, cutting each other to bits with laser-powered machine guns.

In the Third World continents, starving people threw themselves and their children in the paths of rampaging gangs who beat them to eagerly awaited death.

With screeches and growls the audience leapt with joy as the scenes unfolded beneath them. They grovelled on the floor with glee as people of all colours and hues fought with each other across the face of the Earth.

They glared through vicious eyes, alight with lust, as women threw themselves from anywhere high and men ripped at their own throats with anything that would cut or tear.

They clung to one another, screaming with laughter, as men blew out their brains with lasers or boiled them with sonic guns.

In their midst stood Merlin, shaking with fury, his face set in an expression so close to evil that he was indistinguishable from those around him.

Up on the balcony Griswold, staring with horror and incomprehension, turned away, retching against the wall.

What the hell was Merlin up to?

The terrible pictures continued to unfold while the audience drank in its fill of suffering.

Nemestis nodded to Scarbald, who scuttled to the centre of the floor and began to manipulate the controls in earnest. The pictures split into two separate frames and the demons bounded from one to the other, drooling, their bodies smoking and steaming with passion. Eyeballs gleamed and stood out on stalks, scales flaked from trembling bodies.

Scarbald stabbed.

The pictures split into four and a renewed yell went up.

Scarbald paused . . . and stabbed.

Sixteen frames. The crowd applauded.

He gave a flourish, as though conducting an orchestra, and stabbed once, twice, three times.

A concerted scream. A hundred frames.

He pirouetted on one toe and caused the floor to split again, this time into a thousand frames, each showing individual episodes of the carnage befalling Mankind.

With a final flourish the gnome raised his gnarled hands slowly and majestically over his head, and the pictures rose from the flatness of the floor, swelling into three-dimensional holograms. The demons shrieked with delight and bounded in and out of the pictures like children in a cold shower. The images burst on their thrashing bodies, scattering into shimmering fragments, while across the walls their shadows were mingled, merged and shattered by the lights of the ghastly holograms.

Only Nemestis, Amanda and Merlin remained unmoving, as though commanding a domain of stillness in the eye of a hurricane.

Nemestis said, 'It's time to send my commanders on their way. Watch carefully, Merlin. You're about to see *real* genocidal mania at work.'

He stepped into the maelstrom of shimmering creatures and illusions, as Scarbald, on cue, hit another button.

The sounds of Mankind's death throes ceased.

The screams of Nemestis' creatures died rapidly away.

Everyone stood motionless amidst the flickering pictures.

All eyes turned to Nemestis.

The demon smiled.

'My friends. The Earth is yours for the taking. Summon your armies from the dimensions of Hell. Deploy them across the face of this hated planet that they may gather the souls of Man into their noble maws.

'But remember what I have told you! They can take only the souls of those who have yielded to despair and died at their own hands. Ours is not to destroy, but to gather Man's soul for posterity, so that desolation may shine like a grey-smoked beacon from Earth's surface 'til the end of time.'

The gaze that he turned on every creature in the hall was alight with such a dreadful passion that all tongues remained still, and the blood of even those ghastly beings ran cold. Only Merlin was able to return his gaze. As their eyes locked, Nemestis cried out to the demons, 'Begone!'

The hall burst into life. Demons sped into the night in a dozen different ways. They vanished in puffs of smoke, they flew through the windows on leathery wings, they spiralled through the floor, disappeared into pinpoint holes in their navels, turned into indescribable things which streaked through the walls.

A few individualists left by the door.

Soon the hall was empty of all the monstrosities save the warlords.

Throughout the countries of the world the demon commanders

began to appear in the holograms. They were turning their faces to the skies, eyebrows arched, eyes ablaze, clawed hands raised aloft, intoning spells that would bring forth their troops.

Within minutes the skies above the planet were boiling and churning. Where there were clouds, they poured forth like scalding steam. Where the skies were clear, lightning flashed and multi-coloured sheets filled the air.

The legions of Hell burst upon the Earth.

Chapter 44

Dropping from the skies, thrusting up through the earth, appearing from nowhere in shivering balls of fire, they began to wreak a terrible wrath upon the souls around them.

Some grew enormously and, with terrible slurps, sucked crowds of screaming souls into their slavering mouths. Some were all but invisible, mere shimmering patches of light slithering across the terrain, drawing from the dead the grey-shadowed wisps that were Man's link with the cosmos. Others raised great clawed arms and swept them about, magicking the souls away from their owners and into the blackness of their own beings.

'How does it feel to taste the bitterness of defeat, old friend?' smiled the demon.

For a long while Merlin stared into the holocaust.

Then he spoke.

'I will be better placed to tell thee if ever I suffer defeat,' he replied. 'But I feel that thou'lt have first hand knowledge ere the night is gone.'

'You foul and foolish little man,' hissed Nemestis. 'What hope of victory have you against me? Your powers have gone, while mine are vast beyond your comprehension. I have only to suck your puny being into my mind and I can crush you into nothing, a forgotten memory. I have only to command the sun, the moon, the planets to visit their gravities upon you and you will be torn asunder, atom by atom, as though drawn and quartered by raging stallions. Indeed, I have only to raise my hand and I could sear your body to a crisp, you gnat. You mayfly. You . . . nothing.'

'So many options, oh powerful one,' said Merlin. 'Thine omnipotence is awesome. I trust thou wilt not be hampered by choice, for the time to choose is at hand. Look.'

He pointed towards the shimmering holograms.

'Thy dream is about to crumble, thy triumph to fall apart like the walls of a castle built of sand.'

The wizard's face was alight with a cold glow of triumph as Nemestis turned to stare through narrowed eyes, his gaze darting from scene to scene.

Had Merlin's mind snapped?

Nothing was amiss. Wherever he looked all was going according to plan.

Men were killing, either themselves or others, and the souls of the newly dead were wrested from them, quickly, efficiently and beautifully.

No, the Enchanter was simply demented, a fitting and delightful bonus to an already exquisite experience.

And yet.

What was this?

Nemestis frowned and caught his breath as a faint chill touched him.

In the midst of one of the pictures was a man, not young, not old, a nondescript figure, just one of thousands. Seconds ago he'd been on his knees, head sunk to the ground. As the demon watched he'd raised his head and climbed to his feet. Now he stood amidst the mayhem with his face to the night sky. He was smiling. A wan Harold Lloyd smile, as though oblivious to the slaughter broiling about him.

Nemestis' jaw dropped, revealing his dry, black tongue.

The man stood still for a while, then, as if snapped back to consciousness, he glanced about him, first at the churning bodies of men, and at the demon that was flailing a hundred fiery tentacles about him, methodically gathering souls by the score. Then he cast his eyes about the ground and picked up a heavy, club-like chunk of wood. With a silent cry that was an unmistakable and furious 'NO!' he rushed towards the demon, stumbling over debris and bodies in his eagerness. His face was aglow, as if he'd been released from the black depths of despair and had found enlightenment.

Nemestis glanced in disbelief, ignoring Merlin, Scarbald and Amanda, each staring at the scene with totally different expressions. His black eyes darted from picture to picture and,

226

like a fast-rising tide, the coldness of fear spread up his body, catching his breath so quickly that he gasped.

Other pictures were telling similar stories. Men and women were stopping in their tracks, their weapons stayed in mid-strike, the animal expressions melting into wonderment and joy.

They were turning upon the demonic creatures and confronting them with puny hands and weapons.

Nemestis at last grasped a grain of the unbelievable. He turned to the Enchanter.

Merlin's face was serene, its terrible coldness tempered by the merest smile. He pointed at the man with the club. The man's arms rose and fell like pistons as he smashed the flaming tentacles into the ground, sending fountains of bubbling fluid arching into the air. The grey shadows of men's souls, released from their grip, floated away, bobbing on the turbulent air before disappearing like clouds into the warm sun.

While he laid about him the man's lips moved as if he were singing to himself.

Nemestis reached out, grabbed the open-mouthed Scarbald by the throat and lifted him from the floor.

'Give me sound, cretin. There,' he hissed, pointing at the man.

Scarbald's fingers fumbled at the keys and the sound from the hologram burst about their ears. The man's words were punctuated with his gasps of exertion as he pounded at the flowing limbs.

'. . . And thy heart knows bitterest defeat,

'Then from darkness there will come a burning light,
From the silence there will rise the word to fight,
From the cold will blaze the fire of hope and love,
Each builded from the other . . .'

'As below, so above.' The voice of Merlin the Enchanter chorused the man's final words.

Nemestis' head snapped round.

'What!' he said in a voice whose customary resonance had given way to a deadly flatness.

'And there's more,' said Merlin.

He pointed here and there, and from each picture came the sound of people chanting the poem recited to their ancestors seventeen centuries before. The chants filled the room, overlapping at first like the ripples on a pond, rapidly becoming engulfed in their own torrent as men, women and children sang out in a million different rhythms, pitches and tempi.

'It worked,' said a trembling voice at the Enchanter's elbow.

Dimmot looked about him blearily, eyes full of wonderment and tears.

'Little Mankind is struggling for the shore. Does this mean we've won?'

'Not quite,' said Merlin softly. 'There is one final requirement to complete our victory. I'm afraid the cost will be high.'

Dimmot's hands began to sweat, but pride puffed out his puny chest.

'What must we do?' he asked.

'Nothing, my friend. We have done all we can. I only hope it is enough. It now falls to the forces of Darkness to secure their own defeat.'

The room was awash with the sound of Earth's people chanting in all their different tongues.

Nemestis turned blazing eyes towards Merlin.

'What have you done?' he whispered.

'We've set a bug to kill a virus,' replied Dimmot.

The demon glanced at him and back to Merlin.

'Primitive symbolism,' explained the wizard. 'Meaning that the seed of rebellion, planted in a hundred million innocent souls, and having traversed the centuries through the Mind of Man, has finally reached its one source of nourishment. That which thou thyself hast provided. Now it is bursting into bloom.'

Dimmot grimaced.

'And you say *I'm* primitive!'

The face of Nemestis smiled, but his voice trembled as he spoke.

'It seems that we are lost.'

He turned to the stage.

'Mr Moog, may I prevail on your services once more? Kindly sound the retreat. At once.'

228

The trumpeter gave Nemestis an impassive glance and casually began to unpack his instrument.

Dimmot leaned towards Merlin and whispered, 'Now what?'

'Now the minstrel will recall the lackeys from the conflict before they are tempted to retaliate and give Man the chance to build strength from this adversity.'

Seeing Dimmot's frown of confusion he explained.

'It is vital to Nemestis that men do not see this victory as being of their own making. From such belief will come their strength to fight anew, their will to win the next battle.'

Dimmot surveyed the terrible carnage. With some effort he forced the words from his lips.

'But if Man is defeated? What then?'

'Even if the battle is joined and Man is destroyed, his martyrdom will immortalize him in the eyes of his mother . . .'

'The cosmos?'

'. . . and his father.'

'The need to survive!'

The Enchanter nodded without taking his eye off the demon.

'Thus it will be clear that the child they created is a worthy adversary against Evil. So, in time, they will create more. The fight will go on.'

Dimmot watched the trumpeter assembling his instrument.

'Well, do something. Stick his lips together.'

'It will not be necessary.'

Dimmot gingerly felt the back of his head. He was certain that the throbbing lump there was all part of the cosmic scheme of things, just like Nemestis' sudden U-turn and Merlin's refusal to act one way or the other.

He wished that things could be a bit simpler and wondered, not for the first time, where Griswold was.

On the stage Moog placed the trumpet to his lips and blew a long, slightly flat note that drifted towards the open window, sharpening to its correct pitch as it gathered momentum. Another note joined it and together they sped out into the night. More followed, trilling resignedly and whipping away across the countryside of southern England, spreading in all directions, breaking out into the sunlight on the far side of the Earth to call home the denizens of Darkness.

'My God, that's the saddest sound I've ever heard,' said Dimmot.

'Even the forces of Evil know anguish and despair,' replied Merlin.

'I could even begin to feel sorry for the bastard.'

'Don't,' said the wizard.

Across the face of the planet creatures pricked up their ears, looked towards the sky and reluctantly began to withdraw.

Griswold looked down from the balcony, realizing that he would soon be needed at Merlin's side. He scoured the hall for creatures carrying suitable weapons.

For a long while Nemestis watched impassively with his hands clasped behind his back. The holograms reflected the increasing confusion. Creatures which had appeared from nowhere were disappearing into nowhere. Wherever there were people there were corpses. And no one really knew why or how. They knew only that some sort of victory was being denied them.

He turned to the Enchanter.

'I have lost the battle, thanks to yourself, but the war will not be abandoned. You, Merlin, cannot live for ever. Indeed, you won't actually live to see the dawn, but that's another matter. Suffice to say that my tactics were sound and my successor will merely have to go one step further than I to ensure that your . . . bug . . . be squashed wherever it raises its little head. And there will be no Merlin the Enchanter to thwart the destruction of Mankind.'

Instead of glaring with anger the Enchanter gave Dimmot a wink and Nemestis a sly glance.

'My demise is of no import and my presence will not be required. Even now Mankind is carving his name in the annals of immortality.'

Before their eyes the holograms showed creatures of Darkness turning to snap at their pursuers before vanishing.

In the hall the warlords growled approval.

Nemestis whirled about, his cloak casting a glittering swathe around him.

'Silence,' he barked. 'Go home to your far dimensions and await further . . .'

A roar of encouragement interrupted him.

Across the Earth demons were beginning to retaliate and do demonic things to Mankind. Fire roared from flared dragonian nostrils, engulfing the frail human bodies as they clawed and struggled over each other, some trying to escape, others trying to reach their enemies.

Gigantic leathery wings whoofed through the air over city skyscrapers, over village greens and jungle villages, scattering the inhabitants as demons swooped down on them in their scores.

Mighty rock-muscled arms bunched and heaved, toppling buildings on to the crowds, plucking airliners from the skies and dragging ships beneath the waves.

Slithering creatures traversed populated areas, leaving deep trails of slime, beneath which humans struggled for life as their body tissues dissolved and fell from their bones.

'Oh, God, no,' whispered Dimmot, closing his eyes.

'I told thee the cost would be high,' said Merlin thinly.

Chapter 45

Why the Last Trump failed to achieve its goal is not known, though there are as many theories as there are theorists. What is certain is that the forces of Evil grossly underestimated Man's will to survive. The holocaust that followed lasted several days, during which time the people of Earth were reduced to one-fifth of their original number, while the Evil that had invaded the planet was heroically and systematically decimated before retreating into the Darkness from whence it came.

Encyclopaedia Esoterica,
revised edition AD 5008,
Appendix 2

'NO!' roared Nemestis. His clenched fingers dug razor-sharp nails into his palms until drops of blood spattered the marble floor. Around him the demons shrieked encouragement as the scenes on Earth became more grotesque, the violence more terrible.

'Scarbald,' he screamed. 'Bring them back! Destroy them if you must, but bring them back.'

With a silent snarl Scarbald stabbed at the control box, his fingers dancing across the keys until they became a blur. The room began to fill with demons plucked from the corners of the Earth.

One couldn't tell from Scarbald's expression if he was enjoying himself, but even after seeing the state of the first arrivals, he made no noticeable effort to improve his method of transportation.

The fortunate ones were dead on arrival. Those that weren't smouldering their last seconds away or screaming as they melted into bubbling puddles, stared with fascinaton at the interesting rearrangement of their body-parts before lapsing into terminal shock.

In the confusion a lone figure dropped silently and unnoticed from the balcony, snatched a double-headed axe from a demon and clove its owner's head into two equal parts. He dragged the corpse behind a pillar and sidled through the darkness to the Enchanter's side.

'Thine entrance is timely,' murmured Merlin. 'For once.'

Griswold smiled a grim smile. 'Then 'tis time to act?' he asked.

'Indeed. First . . .'

'Good,' said Griswold and, before Merlin could continue with, '. . . the gnome and his box of spells', he leapt towards Nemestis with the axe whirling.

The demon turned just as the axe hissed towards his head.

But it didn't land.

Nemestis raised his open palm towards Griswold and a beam of cold blue light flowed from his hand. The axe shuddered to a halt, as if striking rock and the shock reverberated up the shaft, rattling the knight's teeth in their sockets. Frozen within the beam Griswold strained to break its hold. Nemestis stared at him in amazement.

'What is *he* doing here? How did he escape?'

Without waiting for an answer the demon brought his other hand up, intending to send a bolt of lightning to burst Griswold asunder.

Then several things happened in quick succession.

Amanda, who'd been attempting the singularly difficult task of maintaining a low profile, gave a scream and flung herself between Nemestis and Griswold, unaffected by the beam except for the remarkable things that it did to the lines and contours of her glowing limbs.

An 'oft and plentifully' situation, if ever I saw one, thought Dimmot sourly. Then he threw himself at the demon, tripped over his own feet and crashed to the floor.

Nemestis glared at Amanda, weighed up the facts and, reaching more or less the same conclusion as Dimmot, growled, 'You!'

Before he could unleash a bolt at his sister, the squat and ugly shape of Scarbald scrambled between them, shielding her with his body and upraised arms, unaffected by the beam except for the

233

remarkable things that it did to the crags and fissures of his glowing stumps.

The control box in his hand gave out a dull gleam as he held it between himself and Nemestis' deadly fingers.

After a few seconds' disbelief Nemestis recognized a standoff when he saw one.

'All right,' he snapped, lowering his hand. 'But the knight stays where he is.'

The gnome nodded, but there was a faint look of wonder on his face. For one moment he'd had the most powerful demon, short of Lucifer, over a barrel. The bastard had been helpless. If Scarbald played his cards right, when this game was over, he would have to cash in on this realization and become the most powerful gnome in the history of gnomekind. Perhaps he'd even marry Amanda, with or without Nemestis' consent. Or Amanda's.

The warmth of power flowed through his stubby limbs.

He stepped confidently out of the beam.

At that moment the huge mirrored ball chose to strain its chain beyond its breaking point and hurtle towards the spot on which he stood. In the split second before it arrived Scarbald glanced up in time to glimpse the fragmented images of a hundred little Scarbalds growing rapidly bigger.

His silent snarl of rage was rammed down his throat as the ball hit first him then the floor around him with an ear-rending crash, sending a starburst of glass skittering across the marble. A billion glass shards, which would have happily shredded any normal living body, bounced off him, landing with dull tinkles amid their colleagues. The control box flew from his hand, skidding over the glass to stop, cracked and lightly smoking, inches from Dimmot's upturned face.

For a brief instant Scarbald stood as erect as his stature allowed with an expression of fury distorting his features. The enormous eyes pulsated then glazed over as he toppled back on to his rump.

'It appears,' said Nemestis, 'that even misfortune has conspired against me on this night.'

He peered searchingly into Merlin's eyes.

'So it appears,' agreed Merlin.

'Pick up the box, wizard, and bring it to me.'

'I will not.'

234

'Then the knight dies.'

Before Merlin could reply Dimmot grabbed the box and scrambled to his feet. The smell of terror, manifesting in his armpits, rose to his nostrils.

'Here. Here it is,' he said, holding out the box. 'Don't hurt him,' he added in a small voice.

Nemestis took the box in one hand and cast his eyes over it. His face became quite devoid of expression as he tossed the ruined instrument to the ground.

The holograms had begun to fade and waver, but it was clear to those watching that the demons would eventually be overwhelmed and destroyed.

Immortal tales of Man's triumph were already in the making.

There was no more that Nemestis could do.

'All that is left is for you to die,' he said.

He pointed a hand towards the control box, spread his fingers and brought them together as if crushing a tomato.

On the floor at his feet the box buckled with a sound of grinding metal. Threads of smoke trickled from the fascia and, through the cracks appearing in the box, rays of insipid light peeped into the darkened hall. In seconds the box was a crumpled ball of metal.

The holograms winked out abruptly, leaving the hall even darker and more silent.

'Thus will I crush you, wizard,' hissed the demon.

He dropped his hand and the beam encasing Griswold vanished. The knight lurched towards him with his axe still raised and the voice of Merlin thundered across the hall so powerfully that every creature froze.

Even Nemestis looked surprised.

'Hold, Sir Griswold!'

He gave Griswold a glance. The merest flicker in his eyes told the knight of Merlin's feelings regarding his courage and loyalty. The merest twinkle told him that the action was about to start.

'Stay thy hand, lad,' said Merlin quietly. 'This battle belongs to me.'

In a voice that was chiding, but with an undercurrent of contempt, he addressed the demon.

'I challenge thee, monster, to single combat across any terrain where battle may take us, into any dimensions we may be drawn

235

and by any means we may employ. In return for offering myself to thy sadistic pleasure I ask that my friends be unharmed and returned to their own times.'

'No!' shouted Griswold and Dimmot together.

'I agree,' said Nemestis. He paused, then added, 'In part. Single combat it shall be. When and wherever . . . it shall be. By whatever means . . . it shall be.'

He leered a leer of undistilled evil that consumed his face with a malicious rictus.

'But there the agreement ends.'

His hands snapped out towards Griswold and Dimmot. Fingers of unbelievable strength seemed to grip them by their throats, though they were several feet away from him. With eyebrows arched above flashing eyes like the wings of a vampire, Nemestis scowled down at them.

'You wish to remain. Remain you shall.

'Destroy them!' he roared out and, lifting his hands high above his head, he thrust them towards the crowd. Griswold and Dimmot rose from the floor, as if on invisible wires, and tumbled through the air into the crowd where they sank, struggling, out of sight.

The warlords leapt over the remains of their commanders, and flailed towards Griswold and Dimmot, screeching for blood and any bits of soul they could get their claws on.

As horror stabbed through Merlin's defences Nemestis whirled about and sank his eyes into the Enchanter's mind, paralysing his will before Merlin could pull himself together.

'Ha, ha. Never fails,' sneered the demon. 'And now . . . you.'

Beneath the mass of demons Griswold bellowed with rage and swung his axe. And Dimmot, squealing and kicking, tried to focus his mind on Wishing that someone would come along and bring this horror to an end.

The acrid breath scalding his eyes and the unearthly screeches tearing at his ears and the grip of cold, needle-sharp claws on his body, made it rather difficult to concentrate.

Impossible, in fact.

Held in the grip of Nemestis' attack Merlin struggled to bring his fear under control. Unable to move a limb or turn his head, he could not search for Griswold or avoid Nemestis' talons as they slowly and steadily glided towards his eyes.

Deep inside him a voice whispered urgently, but the Enchanter was unable to reply. Ashamed that he'd been caught by so simple a ploy, Merlin the Enchanter tried in vain to bring his will to bear.

The demon's fingers crept closer.

Two feet. One.

The deadly nails were inches away from Merlin's eyes when a figure appeared unnoticed on the balcony. With a slight crackle and a pause to dislodge his great, double-edged sword from a cranny in the past, Uther Pendragon leaned over the balustrade and gazed down blissfully at the mêlée.

He was clad in leather battle-armour and carried a heavy shield, which was, of course, superfluous, but Uther always liked to dress for the part.

Spotting Merlin standing toe to toe with a nasty piece of work and noting the threatening talons, he recognized a typical example of psychological dominance. Never mind, soon straighten that out.

'MERLIN!' he bawled at the top of his voice. 'BY THE WIND O' MY . . .'

Nemestis' head whipped round in an instant.

'Uther Pendragon!' he snarled. 'I don't believe it!'

The bolt of lightning from his fingers tore through the balcony, exploded against the ceiling and sent tons of scorching masonry tumbling down on the monsters beneath it.

The old king disappeared from sight.

With a smile of satisfaction Nemestis brought his attention back to Merlin.

But, to a wizard who had clocked up a hundred and fifty years of survival against all the odds, an instant is enough.

Suppressing his amazement at Uther's appearance, Merlin shut down his defences with a resounding clang.

He gave Nemestis a cold smile.

'Heh, heh! "Never fails",' he sneered and then he vanished.

As Uther reappeared beside Nemestis with a shimmer and a shuffle round to get his bearings, the disembodied voice of the wizard snapped at him.

'Don't just stand about, you old fool. Go and help the lad.'

Uther paused for just long enough to give Nemestis a warm and evil grin, then he scuttled off, yelling, 'Up and at 'em, my bullies,' his sword singing reassuringly.

The air, already bristling with magics and demonics, crackled anew with the appearance of a hundred assorted warriors, as different from one another as two thousand years of human warfare would have one expect. Every one was of the same transparency as their monarch, for each was the spirit of one whom life had forsaken, though in spirit they all had a common desire. In death, as in life, they were warriors, heroes, leaders of men. The stuff of glory.

They set about the demons with relish.

Red-haired Vikings in horned helmets and animal furs laid about them with great iron spears. Romans and Celts traded coarse encouragement as they cut and parried. A crop-haired sergeant appeared and leapt to his monarch's side, his sword flashing.

'Good man, Belkin,' roared King Uther. 'Get stuck in and enjoy yourself, old son. This way.'

He bounded away, his once-ageing limbs unhindered by the creak of time. Carving his way happily into the monstrous crowd with Belkin covering his back, he reached Griswold just as the knight was going down under the weight of something yellow-fanged and furry.

With a blood-curdling cackle the old king swung his sword high over his head.

When you've got access to Infinity, you can do wonders with ordinary, everyday actions. You can slice the end off a limb, drop out of the present, back or forth, and pop back for another slice. Drop out, pop back, ad infinitum, even stop to get your breath back, not that you'd need it.

Thus were demons diced into minute sections in a flash, or filled so full of holes that they briefly resembled walking fountains.

Thus did massive-boned heads turn to mush in a flicker, or two creatures of Darkness drop simultaneously to the floor in tiny, wet pieces under the blows of a single blade.

Thus did a hundred warriors become a thousand.

The overall horror of a mass of creatures fighting to the death was, perhaps, tarnished a little by the sight of an athletic chap with a silly feather in his hat prancing around, vainly trying to get three opponents to take him on at once, and a splendidly overweight Amazon in scanty black leather laying about her with a broadsword.

Had Dimmot been able to see Rose Falworthy's undulating lines so incredibly garbed, he would have taken time out from screaming hysterically to cringe with embarrassment. He would have been even more appalled to hear her strident rendition of the 'Ride of the Valkyries' soaring above the screams of the dying.

By the bandstand, Nemestis stared about him, bemused.

Merlin had reappeared on the other side of the hall and was striding through the mass towards him.

He had underestimated the wizard, Nemestis thought. It was obviously time to employ a more resourceful method of bringing him to his knees.

Spending no more than a second to wonder why demons were tumbling to the floor, as if being felled by invisible weapons, Griswold scrambled to his feet. Grabbing Dimmot by the arm, he shoved him through the passage that had somehow appeared in the midst of the demons. Reaching the nearest wall, he pushed Dimmot against it and turned to face the enemy. His axe hummed, slicing through a wart-studded belly.

Over his shoulder he hissed, 'If you have any more magics like that, my friend, employ them now . . .'

He parried a thrashing talon and drove the spiked end of the axe into a leathery throat. Brown, foul-smelling fluid gushed on to the floor around them.

'. . . if you wish to see the dawn.'

Dimmot wondered what he was dribbling about.

'Why can't Merlin help?' he whimpered.

'Merlin has a more vital task,' said Griswold firmly. 'For the present we are on our own.'

James Dimmot cursed his life, his misfortunes and, most of all, his constant fear. He longed to have Griswold's strength and courage. But he was not the stuff of knighthood, not SAS material by any stretch. He was just a terrified little bugger about to die a miserable death.

Griswold, panting for breath and beginning to give ground,

shouted, 'The door to your side. Run for it while I hold them off. If you cannot save us, at least save yourself.'

Dimmot glanced across the room. For what? he thought, catching a glimpse of Merlin and Nemestis striding through the writhing mass towards each other. To escape and wander through an alien world alone, knowing that the only real friends he had ever had were dead, thousands of years from home?

He thought of the words that Merlin had spoken to him, how long ago, a hundred years, a thousand? The time didn't matter. The words would be true for ever.

'Man's greatest glory lies in the strength of his will.'

Dimmot clenched his hands into bony fists. I'm long overdue for suicide, anyway, he reasoned grimly. But at least I can go down fighting like a man. He glared with fond regret at the broad, straining back in front of him. And even *that* big oaf can't stop me this time, he thought.

He stepped out into the field of battle just as Griswold swung the axe across his body with every ounce of his furious strength.

Dedicated musicians are pretty much the same everywhere. They share a confirmed lack of interest in anything other than their music. Non-musicians, world affairs and the acquisition of power hold no charm for the dedicated musician. By the same token non-musicians, men of the world (any world) and those who would rule others tend to dismiss musicians, quite rightly, as unthreatening and of no consequence. So they are generally given carte-blanche to ply their art unhindered.

Musicians will play at the drop of a hat and they share a universal pride in playing their best under the most demanding conditions.

So, when the doors to the hall burst open and a host of creatures, of a common red-marbled hue and a statuesque appearance, poured in, shouting, 'There he is,' and made a bee-line for the large, shaggy-haired human with the axe, pushing aside the occupants of the room as they did so, the band on the stage stirred and looked up with interest.

And when it became clear that two opposing factions were about to lay claim to the shaggy-haired human, they strolled over to their instruments and switched on the power.

And, when the mass violence took a distinctly indiscriminate turn (with some unaccountable slaughter, source unknown, being perpetrated in its midst), the band, being strong on tradition, launched into a rousing syncopated number worthy of the most dedicated saloon-bar pianist to accompany, at great personal risk, the most lethal of bar-room brawls.

Unnoticed, Scarbald climbed to his feet. He was several minutes into his dance routine before he began to feel that, somehow, he was being outclassed all round.

A short lie-down was needed, then he'd come back and show 'em. He tried to spit contemptuously on the floor, dribbled on his foot, and wove a dazed path through the mayhem and out, more by chance than judgement, through a convenient door.

Uttering an oath as unaccustomed as it was foul Griswold buried his axe deep in a scaly chest, releasing a spillage of green organs. He snatched the victim's one-handed blade and scooped Dimmot from the floor with considerably less care than one should adopt on the recently brained.

'Clumsy ragwort,' he snarled.

Dragging the little man by one arm and using the sword to hold off two more attackers, he backed towards the nearest door. When he was within reach of the door his feet became entangled with Dimmot's. He crashed to the floor, struggling to rise, but Dimmot was sprawled across him. He gritted his teeth and prepared to fend off the talons that threatened to tear them both to shreds, but, as they converged on him, the two creatures began to jostle each other until they stood over him exchanging blows and the most awful language. Squinting his eyes against a rain of drool and venom Griswold saw that the creature, who made a great deal of cracking noises as he fought, was also short of a finger.

'This one is mine,' snarled Craggus. 'Find yourself another meal.'

They locked limbs and staggered about, wandering off out of reach. Oddly enough Craggus appeared to be trying to defend Griswold rather than slit him open, which was, of course, ridiculous. Confused, Griswold struggled to his feet, wiped his eyes and, grabbing Dimmot by the scruff, dragged him towards the door. Across the hall a battle swayed to and fro. Griswold wondered what they were all fighting about.

The door was bolted.

Griswold threw his weight against it, but to no effect.

He turned, ready to fight his way to another means of escape, when a voice in his ear shouted above the din, 'No, my tiger. This way.'

Griswold had never heard of a tiger, but Amanda's tone of voice told him all he needed to know. He followed her back to the door, waited while she waved her fingers at it and plunged through after her with Dimmot slithering over the floor behind him.

Chapter 46

In the midst of the battle, untouched and unreachable by anything around, Merlin the Enchanter and Nemestis the demon stood mere feet apart. Suddenly they were in their own small world. The boundaries were but a few steps in any direction. Their sky could be touched with a moderately energetic leap.

'A neat trick, don't you think?' said Nemestis.

'A cheap one, certainly,' replied Merlin. 'If this paltry magic is the extent of thy powers, my task will merit me little.'

The demon chuckled darkly and the membrane surrounding them yielded to the movement with a shudder that rippled through all three dimensions at once, hinting at one or two more.

'Tell me, wizard. The mirror-ball. That *was* your doing, was it not?'

'It was.'

'A somewhat indirect approach. But, then, you've been highly devious from the start. Before I destroy you I would like to know why.'

'Since thou wilt not live to reveal the truth I will explain, though any creature of moderate intelligence will have guessed my reasons by now.'

'Go on,' replied Nemestis softly. He was beginning to look a little pale.

'Thy war was against, within and for the mind of Mankind. With thy victory Man's very soul was thine for the taking. The last hope of redressing the Balance would be gone for ever. Since the final victory must be seen to be Mankind's, while the task of redressing the situation has fallen solely to one who is known throughout history as being, in part, alien to Man, the secrecy of that person and of the extent of his powers is essential.'

'As I thought. Admirable. Not until you quoted from that second-rate poem did even I conceive that something was amiss, but when the ball fell by your magic, I realized that I had both lost and won. It was not Mankind who had defeated me, but Merlin the Enchanter. When I return to my domain with the truth . . .'

'I cannot allow that,' said Merlin. 'Therefore, let us forsake the academic and bend to our task.'

'As you wish. Prepare yourself for a long and interesting death.'

The paleness of Nemestis' skin had increased. His body began to undulate as if he were slowly flexing his muscles. His outline became translucent, growing in size and throbbing with an energy that seemed to come not from inside himself, but from all around him. Merlin's skin crawled as the throbbing waves touched at his body, taunting gently, like a child preparing to tease.

He set his jaw and gathered his strength and his will.

Not yet. Not yet, said a voice deep within.

'What ails you, Merlin?'

Nemestis' voice came to his ears as if from the empty air. It had taken on a slightly gritty tone.

'Why don't you attack me? Is this another of your devious tricks or has your nerve gone?'

The demon's face was slipping out of focus. It was also changing. The smooth, green-black lines were becoming ragged and the colour was draining away. Beneath his cloak the slender limbs grew, stretching his tight-fitting clothes into grotesque shapes.

The wizard said nothing.

Beneath Merlin's feet the floor heaved and he was almost thrown to the floor. Nemestis moved towards him with a strangely shuffling gait and the wizard knew that he could maintain his inaction no longer.

With a few apt words he rose from the floor and edged away from the demon, intoning a protective spell. Nemestis' eyes glinted and a grin broke across his changing features.

'At larsshhed,' he croaked in a voice that didn't quite seem to come from his throat. 'The Enshanderr fiedsss bac.'

With a languorous wave he tossed a stream of fire in Merlin's direction. The flames crackled to within inches of his face before veering off to spit against the shimmering wall and send a shower of sparks sizzling round about them.

'Well done, Meryin. I commendd yo' skillsss. So fah!'

Merlin shook his cloak, as if to rid it of stray sparks.

'Thou'st seen nothing yet, walking stench,' he sneered.

His cloak swirled around, enveloping him and suddenly shrinking to nothing. Behind what had been Nemestis the demon he reappeared with a laugh of derision.

His laughter died as the creature stared at him without bothering to turn its head. Instead it melted its features and remade them to point in his direction.

Tight-lipped, Merlin swept his hand across his body faster than a mortal eye could follow. The hiss of forged steel seemed to follow its path and the demon's head lifted from his body as if struck by an invisible blade. With a grunt of triumph Merlin leapt through the air to unleash another blow.

But Nemestis was not there.

Instead a barely intelligible rasp forced Merlin to whirl about.

The creature with its head intact on its ponderous, sloped shoulders leered a drooling leer.

'DOO CAN BLAY A' THAD GABE, BERLIB,' it rumbled hollowly. The cell echoed each word with a new wave of reeling movement.

Merlin saw that the floor seemed to have melted to swamp and the being was having to wade through it to get to him. Then it raised its arms and he realized that it wasn't the floor that was melting.

'DIME FO' THE PARDI DRICKS TO END, MERYIN. NOW TH' SERIOUS BIGNETH SDARDS.'

The arms, head, legs, the whole body of the thing was merging into one glutinous blanket, spreading to embrace the walls, floor and ceiling, flowing towards the wizard, seeking to engulf him.

Ah, said the voice inside Merlin's mind. *So this is how it would be.*

The words of his enemy merged into a rumbling intonation, unintelligible to the ear, but the thoughts that gave birth to the words reached his mind and told Merlin all that he needed to know.

'I will make you part of me, wizard. Soon you will feel the

245

essence of my soul in every cell of your body. Your senses will yield, shrieking, to the tortures of the damned as a thousand years of my life's history soak through them like hemlock through a gauze. Your soul will be saturated with the blackest of my motives, the most base of my desires from centuries past.

'I will do more than destroy you. Far, far more. You will become what I have been, what I am, what I ever more will be. You will become evil! And then you will leer, cold-eyed, at the Earth-born spawn of the cosmos and you will see them as do I; puny creatures of unclean, gross flesh, fit only for destruction.'

The blanket was now all round Merlin, black and limitless as though he were peering into the depths of space, seeing no horizons, no boundaries.

It seeped through the air towards him.

'It will be our pleasure, Merlin, to be the instruments of that destruction. Mine and yours.'

And the voice deep within the Enchanter's mind murmured, *Rambles on a bit, doesn't he? I think it's about time for a spell.*

I have the very thing, replied Merlin. Do I have thy permission to use thy powers to the limit, no matter what that limit may be? he asked of the voice's owner.

You were fated to decide Man's destiny from that sunlit day when sheep graced the warm meadows with bleating and a maiden gave comfort to a lonely old man beneath the green leaves of a world so very far from his own. I trained you long and cruelly in your childhood, in order that you might have the strength to control those powers in times such as this. I created the doorway in your mind to my powers, wherever they were, and arranged it so that you would eventually find me. My powers are yours to draw on whenever the need arises, my boy. I'll be off and leave you to it.

'Wait,' said Merlin, voicing his thought aloud. 'Thou can'st not desert me now.'

You've no need of me now, my son. I'm glad I got to see you, though I wish we could have had more time. Never know, we might meet again. Still, must go. Got a book to finish.

Mumbling vaguely about being overdue for his deadline, Asmethyum wandered out of Merlin's mind and skipped, with surprising agility, across the stepping stones traversing the river of Time, en route to his own dimension.

The gap that had filled a large part of the Enchanter's heart for most of his life returned.

The blanket looming over him paused and gave a tremor, as if suddenly nagged by suspicion.

'To whom do you speak?' it boomed.

Ignoring the question, Merlin took a breath deep into his body. With the breath the awareness of the power within him grew. Like the blanket hovering about him the power tumbled and swirled within him, filling his mind's eye with a vision of an immense white nimbus striving to burst.

Unlike the blanket, which was a hundred shades of black and which crackled faintly with hatred, Merlin's inner cloud was gleaming white, glinting with pastel shades of all colours. Where the blanket churned, the cloud danced; where the blanket became shadowed, the cloud sparkled.

Merlin gathered the power about him, savouring the flow of it round his body, more tangible than any force he'd yet had the privilege to command. His previous powers seemed like mere trickles of sweat upon the eyelids compared with the total immersion that he now felt.

This was the magic that would be contained only by an unbendable, unbreakable will.

The Enchanter prayed that he was equal to the task.

As the evil wrapped itself about his body like a second cloak, covering him totally, first in one cobweb layer, then folding and refolding upon itself, Merlin's outline was obscured, woven into a mound of creeping, diabolic fabric.

Now we will merge, came the thought from the awful being.

The wizard had battled so many souls in his life. The only regret that death held for him was that he might have neglected his friends, his king and queen, his fellow men. He'd fought with a single-minded vision of victory, so strong that fear had never been granted the chance to enter his thoughts.

Now, as Nemestis' grotesque manifestation explored the surface of his skin, the Enchanter fought down terror and strove to make animal snarls of the whimpers hovering at his lips.

'What you feel now is only the beginning,' said the demon.

Merlin fought the urge to cringe as atom-thin tendrils threaded their way under his skin. Slithering between his very cells, they

247

burrowed deep within him, a myriad rivulets flowing with dreadful purpose. Every ounce of his will was needed to prevent him from fighting against the flow.

Instead, the Enchanter let the terrible power fill him, committing himself totally with the aid of the most courageous spell ever given to a man of wizardry, a spell of purest essence which, if ever put into words, would have read thus:

> Come to me, essence of Evil.
> Seek in me thy dark purpose.
> Visit upon mine being thine iniquitous intent
> And I shall take thee in.
>
> Fill my mind with thine own black thoughts,
> My heart with thy most base desires,
> Imbue my soul with the life that is thine,
> And I shall take it in.
>
> These things done, abandon thyself
> To thine ostensible victory.
> Languish with thine thoughts
> And as thou lies on pillowed triumph,
> Gazing with heavy-eyed malevolence upon my plight,
> Then will thou see that thou truly hast
> been taken in.

Chapter 47

The passage leading from the Savoy banqueting hall was dark, dank and increasingly steep.

Griswold shifted Dimmot's dead weight on his shoulders.

'Where are you taking us?' he grunted at Amanda's glistening back.

'To somewhere safe,' she replied over her shoulder. 'My brother will not look for you there.'

Griswold noticed that they were walking deep into the heart of rock.

'Why not?' he asked.

'Because he trusts me.'

The passage wound round and down. Griswold noted the torches burning smokily at intervals and the smoothness of well-worn rock under his feet. He turned his senses a little more keenly to his surroundings.

On his shoulder Dimmot dreamed of a great iron bridge and large flakes of icy snow filling the night sky. The ominous chimes of a great clock rang through his dream. He found the sound familiar and comforting and wished that the dream was real.

Amanda turned a corner and they walked through an arch to enter a vast cavern. At once the dankness ceased to exist and was replaced by a feeling of dread.

The floor of the cavern was no more than a ledge of rock a few feet wide circling the walls.

Glancing over the edge Griswold saw that the cavern dropped away into the blackness with no sign of ending.

'Come away, my stallion,' whispered Amanda, clasping his arm. 'It would not do for me to lose you now.'

The temperature had dropped noticeably, but in spite of her

less than sufficient clothing, she showed no sign of feeling the cold.

'This way,' she said.

They followed the ledge to one side, skirting the cavern. Their footsteps were all that could be heard. Griswold sensed somehow that, though the ledge was well worn, theirs were the first footsteps to break the silence for a very long time.

'What is this place?' he asked quietly.

'This is where our adventures begin. Yours and mine.'

Amanda came close to Griswold, her eyes gazing into his. Her lips were but a kiss away. Her chest heaved.

'Beyond the ledge is an arch. Beyond the arch a thousand worlds beckon. We can reach those worlds, travel their roads, sail their seas, cross their skies. Make love under their moons.'

Her upper lip glistened. Her breath was unusually warm.

'Drop him off and we will go on.'

Griswold was not a man to do blindly as he was told, but a few moments' rest would benefit them both. He lowered Dimmot gently to the ground and leant him against the wall.

He flexed his shoulders to bring the nourishing blood back to them and raised himself to his full height, stretching his arms high over his head until the joints cracked.

Amanda was watching him with a frown drawn across her beautiful features.

'Well, go on,' she urged. 'Drop him off and we'll be on our way.'

Griswold frowned.

'Over the edge,' she explained testily.

In the banqueting hall the battle was raging nicely. The band ducked flying bottles with practised adroitness and without missing a beat. The floor had become suitably covered with ganglia and spilled body fluids.

Craggus and Bathym, fighting back to back, conversed over their shoulders.

'They went that way,' grunted Craggus, nodding towards the door. 'Get after them while I hold this bunch off. And Bathym . . .'

'Yes?' growled Bathym.

'When you send the knight off to his destination . . .'

'Yes?'

'Leave a finger behind. Just for me.'

The osmosis was complete.

The essence of Nemestis was suffused throughout Merlin's being, his body one with Merlin's, his mind one with that of the Enchanter.

His soul, that sadistic spectre of many thousand years' black cruelty, squirmed lazily throughout Merlin's own, merged so totally that no distinction could be found, no shred of evidence to belie that just one soul existed.

Only one living being was able to detect him.

'Dost think that thine insidious meanderings will gain thee aught?' scowled Merlin, fighting to subdue the nausea rising within him.

'Oh, indeed I do,' replied Nemestis within Merlin's own thoughts.

He did the ethereal equivalent of cracking his knuckles.

'We are one, you and I, and now you will come with me through a thousand millennia. You will visit the dimensions that have crossed my past. You will learn the bleak coldness of a hatred long burnt out by the passage of Time and you will feel that same hatred at its height, knowing that your fate will be to feel that same coldness, just as I do. You will suffer the purgatory of eternal indifference that is the price of immortality. But more than that. You will share it for all Eternity with me. Then you will die.'

The membrane around them melted and dissolved into the foetid, blood-drenched air, leaving one being standing in the centre of the hall.

Around him the battle ceased.

Demons, spirits and statues backed away from the Enchanter, staring wide-eyed, their weapons lowered. Many mouths went very dry, many loins became quite wet.

To the eyes of those around, the form of the wizard shimmered from within and a vague, horribly familiar figure could be seen writhing beneath his skin.

Not so much a figure as the essence of one.

For many seconds a dreadful silence sang through the air. Then the merest whisper tickled each ear, rapidly becoming an icy draught that plucked at the clothes and made the eyes water. The draught turned to a roaring wind which poured across the room from all directions, tearing at tendrils, hair and leathered wings and sending creatures staggering. It converged on the wizard and vanished into his body, as if drawn from the far reaches of Earth.

Snakes of lightning flashed and crawled across his skin. His hair lashed about his face and his cloak crackled and snapped like a topsail in a hurricane. The translucent features were contorted with pain and from under the closed eyelids crept a dull red glow as if from distant fires in the night.

Spirits and demons alike did not want to be around if Merlin were to open his eyes.

Within him, oblivious of all but his own lust for Merlin's defeat, Nemestis, second only to Lucifer and Archduke of the blackest reaches of the galaxy, knew no such fear.

In a voice that rolled thunderously through the Enchanter's body the demon roared his scorn.

'You think that the power of your contemptible father will help you? That withered cadaver was within my power for over a thousand years, helpless, mine to crush or destroy as I wished. You are no more a threat to me than he was.'

His laugh was the grating screech of a thousand vultures swooping on their prey, tearing at Merlin's nerves and singing a Siren's terrible song within the Enchanter's teeth.

'I brought you here by my mind's power with no more effort than it takes me to breathe. So shall I cast you like a rat in a terrier's jaws, across the tides of space and time and into the depths of my black, bleak reality. With each inch of every light year, with each second of every century, you shall feel the depth of my evil.'

As the meaning of Nemestis' words broke over him, understanding swept through Merlin like an icy wave and a scream of anguish burst from his body, searing his fire-parched throat. He turned his face sightlessly to the heavens.

'Father!' he cried. 'Thy power is not enough. We are lost!'

'INNDEE–EEE–EED YOU ARE–RE–RE–RE!' boomed Nemestis triumphantly. And his voice filled Merlin's reality, throbbing, violating the Enchanter's mind with gross, rhythmic shudders.

'YOU TIN–Y, IN–SIG–NIF–IC–ANT SCOUR–UR–UR–GGGE. FE–EL MY PRES–ENCE–NCE–NCE. FE–EL MY POW–ER–ER–ER–ER!!!'

Against the roar of the cyclone the voice of Nemestis filled his mind.

'MER–RL–LINNN,' screamed Nemestis. 'YOU ARRRE LOST–TT–TT. NOW YOUU WILL BEGG MEE FOR MERCY–YY–YY. MERC–YYY IN THE NAMME OFF LUCIFERRR–RR!!'

'Ah,' sobbed the Enchanter. 'Thou who speakest of mercy in the name of one who is merciless. An offer most apt, but one I must refuse, for I have just such a one of my own.'

And in his mind's eye he created a tiny symbol.

He held it before him and brought forth a different one.

Then another.

And another.

'WHATT ARE YOU–UU DOING–GG–GG?' Nemestis' voice came out of the wind, edged with contempt. YOU CAN SEE–EE NOW THAT NO MANN CANN STAND–DD–DD AGAINST–TT–T MEE.'

Merlin's body shuddered as the forces in him struggled for supremacy, but he held firm, focusing his thoughts on the picture forming before him.

'That much is clear to me now,' he sobbed. 'It is not the power of man, demon or any living being that I seek.' More symbols appeared, linking together in an ominously mathematical manner. The picture expanded rapidly as the symbols increased, joining, linking, jostling to find their ordained positions.

'WHAT ISS THISS–SS WE SEEE BEFORE–RE USS–SS?' cried the demon irritably.

'An old ally who knows no friends,' gasped Merlin. 'A slave who would be master.'

From the depths of his memory an unforgettable and deadly spell was being recreated, piece by dreadful piece, unmoved by

253

the storm about it, sliding into place like the scales of a malevolent predator.

Between the wizard's eyelids the fire crackled. His fingers clawed at the air, white-knuckled, as the forces of magic and evil, locked within each other, battled for supremacy.

'Thou hast entered in, intending to destroy. Thine intent is now thy jailer and thine executioner,' intoned Merlin.

The last symbol of the Formula slid into place.

And the demon laughed happily.

'ISS THISS–SS ANNOTH–ERR OF YOURR FEEEBLE SSPELLS–SS, WIZ–ZARDD?' he hissed. YOU WISH–HH TO *SSCARRE* MEE TO DEATH–TH?'

The Formula might be mindless, but it was no fool.

At the instant of its birth, it turned lifeless, abstract eyes this way and that, absorbing, calculating, assessing the odds of its survival.

It saw two entities.

One it recognized as its host.

He that both created it and destroyed it.

That one must be avoided at all costs.

The other one was new.

It reached out.

Nemestis gave a gasp of surprise. For a moment the absence of feeling that had filled him for many centuries seemed to plummet to a hitherto unknown depth, carrying him to where even his cold soul shivered with trepidation.

The grim piranha of doubt took its first tentative nibble at the toes of his triumph.

Chapter 48

Griswold was not an easy man to annoy. Of the few things guaranteed to enrage him, the most effective was the questioning of his loyalty.

'You misjudge me, mistress,' he hissed. 'This wretch is my friend.'

Amanda stared aghast. 'His friendship is worthless to you.'

'But mine is everything to him and you would have me betray him.'

'Am I not worth betraying all men for? Am I not the essence of your dreams?'

Griswold stared deep into her beautiful eyes.

'You are your brother's sister. 'Tis your good fortune that you are a woman.'

He bent to lift Dimmot back on to his shoulders, but Amanda clutched at him and threw her arms about him.

'All right. Bring him with you, but please don't leave me.'

'You are left. You have no place in my life.'

'Without me you are dead. Both of you.'

Griswold pushed her away and hefted Dimmot up.

'So be it,' he said over his shoulder. 'We are going back.'

He'd not taken two paces when from the darkness ahead came the merest whisper of a sound.

Snuffle.

Peering ahead, Griswold was in mid-stride when the force of Amanda's fury hurled him against the wall so violently that he left Dimmot suspended temporarily in mid-air before he eventually crashed to the ground.

Griswold hit the wall with a sickening thud, lurched away and rolled across the rocky floor, coming to a stop with one arm dangling over the edge of the ledge.

With eyes blazing and pendants shivering Amanda advanced towards him. A wisp of smoke dribbled from her fingertips.

'You dare to deny me? Only one man has ever done that.'

She raised her smouldering fingers and pointed them at the unconscious Griswold just as Scarbald shuffled out of the darkness. With a snuffle and the slightest hint of a hic he placed a restraining hand on Amanda's arm.

He stared long and hard at Griswold, then raised his eyes to hers.

'Oh, all right,' snapped Amanda, lowering her hand. 'But make sure it's painful and very bloody.'

The gnome grinned gratefully and swivelled his eyes around the cavern. A boulder nearly as high as himself stood against the wall.

Ignoring the muffled groan of James Dimmot returning to consciousness, Scarbald approached the boulder and placed his hands lovingly about it. He caressed it gently for a few seconds then gripped it in his fingers.

Dimmot woke, sobbing with the pain that was splitting his head and the blinding lights that were searing his eyes. One thought filled his mind, one single desire, fired by the agony shuddering through his body.

He was going to smack Sir Griswold des bloody Arbres right on the hooter.

Just once was all he asked.

He squinted through the flickering white flames and saw Griswold lying just a few feet away. He rolled on to his stomach and, with teeth gritted and clenched fists trembling, crawled towards him.

Then he caught sight of Scarbald.

With terrible strength the gnome was lifting an enormous rock above his head. He shambled towards Griswold. Beneath the shadow of the boulder his eyes gleamed dully. His lips dribbled thick fluid on to his stained tunic.

As Dimmot gazed in horror Griswold strove to raise himself up on one arm, shuddered and fell back, his head rolling loosely.

The gnome took one final step towards him, sucked in an

ecstatic breath and braced himself to smash the boulder down on Griswold's head.

Dimmot knew what he must do.

The choice was made.

Not by chance, not by destiny or ill-fortune.

But by the look in Griswold's eyes as he stared up at the gnome. To the very point of death he glared his defiance with no vestige of pleading, no trace of fear.

Dear God, I could have done with someone like him when I was a kid, thought Dimmot.

He scrambled up on legs barely able to hold him, eyes wide with fear, and staggered towards Scarbald. Flinging his arms round the gnome, Dimmot heaved him towards the edge of the ledge. The boulder slipped from his hands and fell with a ground-shuddering thud. For an instant Scarbald's feet scrabbled at the rock surface and held, but Dimmot continued to push, his lip grazing painfully against Scarbald's harsh, warty cheek, his legs finding strength in the look of disbelief that the gnome threw him.

'Believe it,' groaned Dimmot. 'Believe it, you little prick.'

With the last shred of his strength he drove his feet into the rock.

Locked together, Dimmot and Scarbald toppled over the edge into the abyss.

Chapter 49

Merlin and Uther stood to one side while the monarch's heroes wandered professionally through the carnage, searching for signs of life. The occasional swish of a blade or the thud of an axe on skull punctuated the heavy air.

In the centre of the floor, amid the remnants of his army, Nemestis sat with legs spread-eagled, pale and dead-eyed. The face that had remained smooth and alive for centuries now hung slack and grey like ancient curtains. A spider's thread of dribble on the lolling tongue drifted down to roll off his stomach on to his leg.

'He came so close,' said the Enchanter. 'Had his vision not been clouded by malice when he found us, he would have seen the First Unborn for the threat that they were. They would have perished then and there, their destiny unfulfilled.'

'What're you going to do with him?' said Uther.

'He will return to the hell from whence he came.'

'Feet first, of course.'

'I think not. Without the key to free him from his "rest", or the potion to preserve his physical being, he will remain thus for all to see until the cells of his body decay and fall. Creatures of Evil who have never seen me will quake at the name of he who brought upon Nemestis the living death.'

Uther wiped his blade on a recumbent tunic.

'Nothing like getting yourself a reputation,' he said approvingly.

'All part of one's armoury,' said Merlin.

'Talking of reputations,' said Uther mildly. 'You didn't do yours much good, turning up late for young Dimmot. Gave me a proper run around. Still,' he added reflectively, 'it had its compensations.'

'Dammit!' Merlin slapped his forehead. 'I forgot them.'

'You *have* been rather bus—'

'Where are they? Griswold and James Dimmot?'

Uther pointed with his chin to a door in the far wall. 'They scooted out that way. With some woman. Half nak—'

'Oh, gods. We must find them. Come.'

With a flash and a faint smell of ozone, the wizard spun in an ever-decreasing circle, vanishing into nothing three feet from the ground.

Uther grunted, dropped out of the present and caught Merlin up as he rounded the bend leading to the cavern. They hurried along the tunnel until voices slowed them in their tracks.

'Get on with it, fool,' said a woman's voice. 'Carry him to the farthest, darkest corner of the universe, where no man will find him, and leave him there to rot.'

'And then may I go on my way?' murmured the demon Bathym.

'Yes! Now do it,' hissed Amanda.

'Yes, Bathym,' said Merlin, stepping silently out of the darkness. 'Do it. If thou think thou canst escape my wrath and my vengeance.'

Amanda and Bathym turned and stared unbelievingly.

'You!' hissed Amanda. 'You have eluded my brother?'

'More than that,' said Merlin tonelessly.

'I think I'll be on my way,' murmured Bathym.

He backed off a few steps until he came up against the point of King Uther's sword.

'You stay here, friend,' said Uther amiably. 'We may need you shortly.'

Merlin stepped towards Amanda and stared up at her coldly.

'Stand aside, woman, and pray that the lad is unharmed.'

He knelt beside Griswold's still form and passed his hand over the knight's body, feeling for any wounds in Griswold's life force.

Amanda watched with a faint sneer playing about her lips.

'Do what you can for him, old man, while you can. When Nemestis comes for you, your time will run out so quickly it will leave you breathless.' She sniggered. 'Literally.'

'Thou hast thy brother's needle-sharp wit,' said Merlin.

He passed his hands once more over Griswold's forehead and chest, this time releasing the healing force of his powers into the other's body.

259

'Perhaps thou shouldst join him and trade jests as to the means of my demise . . .'

With a yawn and a stretch Griswold opened his eyes and gave Merlin a tired smile.

'. . . though I feel thy ribaldry will be a little one-sided.'

The edge in the Enchanter's tone and the coldness in his blue eyes brought a shiver to Amanda's body. She turned and edged back along the tunnel. Griswold levered himself up to restrain her, but Merlin held him back with a touch.

'She is of no consequence to us. Nemestis may have her.'

They watched as Amanda hesitated, then turned and ran silently into the darkness.

Merlin turned to Griswold, who'd got to his feet and was standing unsteadily.

'Art thou all right, lad?'

'I'm well, but . . .'

'Good. Our task here is finished. It's time to go home, while I still have the power. Drag Dimmot out from wherever he's hiding and we'll be on our way.'

Griswold stared at the ground with pain in his eyes. His lip trembled.

'I've failed thee, Merlin.' He nodded towards the abyss. 'Dimmot is gone.'

'Then,' snarled a woman's voice from the darkness, 'you'd better go and get him back.'

'Oh, oh!' murmured Uther.

They turned to see a female figure emerging from the tunnel. It appeared to be divided into segments. As it stepped into full view they could see clearly the expanses of bare flesh separated by skimpy black leather.

Merlin, Griswold and Bathym stared aghast.

'Who on Earth are you?' whispered the Enchanter.

'The angel of death,' mumbled Uther under his breath.

'That's right, your majesty. Yours if anything's happened to my little Jamie,' snapped Rose Falworthy.

She turned to Merlin.

'You're the cause of all this, you and that whiskery oaf of yours.'

Griswold opened his mouth to protest. The look in Rose's eyes shut it again.

'And if my Jamie's in some sort of trouble,' she said, waggling her sword persuasively under the Enchanter's nose, 'you'd better sort it out right now!'

A sliver of light from the main hall pierced the gloom of the tunnel as Amanda trod stealthily towards the door. The noise of battle had ceased.

She eased the door open and peered through.

On the stand Moog wove two sweetly bitter counterpoints over the band's fairly accurate, if unEarthly version of 'One for My Baby and One More for the Road', that Dimmot had shown them in the interval.

The hall was awash with death and they were all deeply content.

(The keyboard player had crossed out Chopin and Hindemith/CR3prig in his phone book and replaced them with the name given to him by Dimmot. 'You wanna play *real* mean Earthy blues,' Dimmot had advised him sincerely, 'you gotta go a long way to beat *that* bloke.' The keyboard player had thanked him and promised that when he got home, the first thing he'd do was give the spirit of Richard Clayderman a call.)

Body fluids of all kinds covered the floor, some crawling with their own parasitic life-forms, some billowing acrid smoke as they ate into the marble. On the surface bobbed assorted pieces of meat and, rising from the gore like rugged islands in an evening ocean, the steaming remains of Nemestis' warlords, who only a while ago had leapt with joy at the sight of Man's death throes.

The smell of death filled Amanda's flared nostrils, bringing a sigh of exquisite revulsion to her lips.

Craggus and the other enmarbled demons who had survived the battle were gone. Having found Griswold, they felt they were entitled to exercise their option of leaving Bathym to do whatever Bathym did and headed out in search of the magical equivalent of a sand blaster.

Belkin and the leaders, fighters and heroes had strutted off, arms round shoulders, to compare notes and wait for the old king in a nearby dimension.

The hall was empty of life, save for the band, the odd remnant of aspidistra clinging to survival and a lone figure sitting in the centre of the devastation.

With a moan of relief Amanda glided across the floor towards her brother. Crouching on her haunches, she gazed into his eyes. Something other than death stared out at her, unseeing and unheeding. Something other than life held the whole of the demon's body cramped and rigid.

Except for his horns. They lay like two black slugs on his temples, flaccid and wrinkled.

'Nemestis,' she whispered in horror. 'Nemmi. It's me.'

The thin chest rose almost imperceptibly as the lungs within took the demon's only breath for another hundred years.

Amanda's lips quivered uncontrollably and a screech of fury broke from them. Her pendants jiggled wildly until one broke loose and fell with a browny-green plop into the liquid at her feet.

The band winced and lost the beat, gave a collective sigh and began again from the beginning.

Very quietly.

Amanda stared at Nemestis' lifeless face, her breasts rising and falling as she fought to bring her breath under control. After a while she turned her green eyes coldly towards the door from where she'd come.

'My congratulations, Merlin. You've done what no creature has ever done before. Some day I shall see you again and learn the source of your powers. Perhaps let you share mine,' she added with a smile that would freeze an inferno.

She turned back to Nemestis. The aura of power that had been a part of him all his life was gone. No trace of his immense will could be felt, no atom of strength.

She gazed long and thoughtfully into the eyes that had held her in their power and had viewed her desires with disdain.

'But now my brother needs me and I must satisfy his need.'

She took Nemestis' face in her hands, pushed him gently back into the gore and covered his cold lips hungrily with her own.

'As oft and as plentifully as I can,' she murmured.

The band played on.

262

Epilogue

. . . legend indicates that James Dommit is meant to have disappeared and/or committed suicide, date and reason unknown, having made no impression on history whatsoever.

Encyclopaedia Esoterica,
revised edition AD 2845,
Appendix 758

In fact, James Dimmot was a living person. A Wisher of enormous, but unharnessed talent, he played a crucial role in the salvation of the Earth and the prevention of the Eternal Dark Age, when the Forces of Evil attempted to destroy the last outpost of Man and, subsequently, the Balance of the Cosmos.

He was a small, frightened and insignificant man who faced the ultimate responsibility with his last act and found greatness at his last breath.

Anyone who knew him, however briefly, could consider themselves privileged.

I do.

Encyclopaedia Esoterica,
revised edition AD 2845,
Appendix 758A
(not for publication)

In a room on a far distant world in a fairly distant dimension is a man.

He is indescribably old.

Ancient. Not as white as he was but still a bit pale.

He is, of course, a writer. Has been for a long time.

And he has a secret.

'Hope this means something to you, Dimmot, wherever you are. It's the least you deserve. Sorry it couldn't be more.'

Here, one could say that Asmethyum takes the page that he's just written in the Book, otherwise known as the *Encyclopaedia Esoterica*, and tears it out carefully, before the ink is dry, ensuring that no trace is left for prying eyes. He stares at it for a while, then crumples it gently and tosses it into the crackling fire.

For those who believe in Mankind with a capital M, however, it goes like this:

Asmethyum focuses on the amendment that he has just created within the nexus of multi-dimensional forces of which space, time and mind are but a part, and before which pale to insignificance the magics and sorceries of all save that which created it. He gazes sadly at it for an immeasurably short moment, then, before it can be absorbed and recorded for all eternity, he erases it from existence.

James Dimmot can wait no longer. He feels as if he's been waiting for centuries for something to give his life some purpose.

He sits on the snow-swept parapet of Tower Bridge at 2 a.m. on 13 January 1987, slippered feet dangling over the Thames. Below him assorted blocks of ice flow down to the sea, bobbing and chuckling amid the effluent, for it is the worst and the coldest winter for many decades.

The grey gabardine raincoat that is his only other clothing does less to protect him from the icy blizzard than does the lethally high alcohol content in his bloodstream.

The chimes of Big Ben begin to sound the hour, a vaguely familiar death knell.

But James Dimmot is unconcerned. With a peculiar feeling of déjà vu, he flings back his head, simultaneously draining the last dregs from the bottle and toppling backwards into the drift of snow piled high against the balustrade.

With his feet lodged on the rail above his head and the snow soaking through his splayed raincoat, he lies there for some time, thinking.

Well, fantasizing really, with ridiculous pictures forming in his brain, 90 per cent proof of course, but interesting all the same. Dim impressions of demons, spirits, ancient beings. A sort of wizard-type chap. And a grotesque, hate-driven creature that fills his vision before it falls away into endless blackness, leaving him staring up into the face of some creature called Botham, who is carrying Dimmot in his arms. The arms are as hard and cold as mortuary slabs.

'I'll nev'r wash another crickid mash, s'long s'I liff,' mumbles Dimmot.

As the pictures fade from his memory, he becomes aware of sounds, melodies and harmonies, drifting and swirling through his mind. Some of the sounds are brilliant, some exhilarating, some horrifying.

He hears a massive choir weaving ten thousand counterpoints, every voice singing the same song independently of the others.

He hears the raucous, syncopated rhythms, the harsh, dissonant harmonies mirroring untold violence and mayhem.

And, above it all, the sound of two muted trumpets spinning and curling sensuously in a melancholy embrace.

It is alien music that he didn't know he knew.

Music never heard in twentieth-century London before.

He thinks of Bach at the height of his complexity, punk rock at its most horrific, Miles Davis double-tracking.

'Now those,' smiles Dimmot glassily, 'are my kind o' flies.'

It is time to do something worthwhile with his life.

He'll do something with music. Powerful, magical stuff, music. With music you can tell the world that life is worth living.

With music you can say, 'Mankind is spelt with a capital "M" and don't you forget it!'

He drags his body painfully to its feet, wondering how it could have got so bruised and battered by falling into a snowdrift. He pauses, squinting into the blizzard, as if trying to remember . . . anything.

With a shrug and a grunt, he weaves a purposeful path back to his cold flat, leaving, as the only sign of his passing, a thin layer of skin from buttocks frozen to the unfeeling ironwork.

A warm breeze drifts above the fields of Camelot causing sparkling leaves, feather-soft plumes and hastily erected bunting to flutter limply.

'Art thou ready, Sir Griswold?' calls Sir Lancelot du Lac.

Griswold replies with a lazy wave of his gauntlet and gathers up his reins.

Settling the lance comfortably under his armpit, he casts a glance at the stand on his right, whereon sits Queen Guinevere enthroned amid a select crowd of the court retinue. To his left most of Camelot stands watching casually from behind a line of the king's guards, under the eyes of Sergeant Belkin.

The queen is watching him with a somewhat quizzical expression. One would not think that less than an hour ago her vanity had been smarting under his misunderstood remark regarding her looks.

At the far end of the arena Lancelot keeps his lance erect and turns his white-liveried horse towards the stand.

Griswold looks at the crowd and raises his eyebrows. Lancelot never misses a chance to make a speech.

The crowd shrugs.

'Thy Majesty, my Queen,' calls Lancelot in a voice deepened more by conscious effort than by nature.

'Today it saddens me to . . .'

Out of sight behind one of the tents surrounding the area, two shadowy figures, barely more than shimmers in the sunlight, watch the proceedings and converse quietly.

'You're really pushing your luck, Merlin,' murmurs Uther. 'Tampering with the flow of Time . . .'

'Be still, old man. The moment is at hand.'

'He shouldn't be brought back yet. You know the consequences.'

'A particular course of events was decreed by me for the glory of King Arthur and the good of Mankind. It was due to go down in the history books as such. When the pup intervened with his clumsy platitudes, that course of events was turned from its path. We have to regain that path in the only way we can. The consequences must fend for themselves.'

In front of the tent Lancelot's eloquence is waxing and the crowd's interest is waning.

'. . . this woodcutter's son whom I did willingly take under my wing many years since . . .'

'Well,' says Uther. 'Bathym wants it on record that he's doing this under protest.'

'Yes, yes, yes,' snaps Merlin. 'He has my word, tell him that.'

The crowd is becoming restless.

'. . . so I ask for the last time, Sir Griswold, that thou kneel before thy queen and apologize. What sayest thou?'

As the crowd turns its collective gaze on Griswold, the two shadows move closer to the arena, invisible to all but a bony dog, scavenging for titbits. The dog, dimly aware that *beings* are lingering at the edge of his dimension, slinks off looking thoughtful.

Griswold looks towards the stand. Guinevere stares back, her face expressionless. With a sigh, Griswold raises his hand, gives the queen a wave of salute and snaps down the vizor of his helmet.

The crowd cheers.

'He is obscured from sight,' hisses Merlin to Uther. 'Now, before they are met.'

Uther gives a nod and vanishes.

Lancelot snaps down his own vizor, wheels his horse about and lowers his lance. For a moment the two knights pause to bring their mounts under control, then give them their heads and thunder towards each other to the sound of the crowd's crescendo.

In a nearby reality a brief conversation takes place.

'Merlin says . . .'

'I heard him. I still don't like it.'

'Bring the lad.'

And the Griswold who, seconds before, had been sprawled unconscious at the edge of a yawning abyss, is whisked back in time to a place in which Nature had never meant him to be, at least, not more than once.

The momentary hole in the fabric of time, signalled by an inaudible 'splop' and a faint touch of grey streaking across the clear blue sky towards the arena, goes unnoticed by the people of Camelot. The only sign that something untoward has occurred is Sir Griswold's horse faltering, as if momentarily burdened with a double load, and a muffled yelp of pain from behind the closed vizor.

The knights' lances cross and Griswold's, which had been perfectly placed to skewer Lancelot just beneath the chin, slews off target. The reins slip free of his left hand and Lancelot's lance glances his shoulder, sending him tumbling from the saddle to crash with a metallic thud to the turf.

As he rolls to a stop, the sudden intake of a thousand breaths is punctuated by the clatter of his falling lance and the pounding of Lancelot's horse coming to a halt.

Griswold sits up with difficulty, stares for a second at his left gauntlet and pulls it off.

Where his little finger had been is a clean, pink stump. He tips up the gauntlet and shakes it.

By the tent Merlin turns an ice-blue gaze upon the returning Uther.

'What mischief was that?'

Uther shrugs. 'Did the trick, didn't it?'

'A simple turning of the lance was required. Not dismemberment.'

Griswold climbs to his feet as Lancelot dismounts from his horse and strolls towards him.

The crowd holds its breath.

Merlin turns to leave. He is not due to return to Camelot for another two days, remember, and the laws of space and time can become rather vindictive if they are overstretched *too* often.

Taking Uther by the arm, he says quietly, 'Come. Our task is done. The mistake redressed. I take it the lad will come to no further harm,' he adds evenly.

'He'll suffer from illusions brought about by living two parallel lives for some weeks . . . well, years. But that's on your head,' Uther reminds him.

'So be it. History will prevail. I will look after him. Wilt thou be around if I need thee?'

'I have a newly formed army of heroes who need a world to fight for and a newly devastated world that needs heroes. I have a plump, newly laid consort whom I would make my queen, although she's a bit reluctant at present.'

'That's never stopped thee in the past,' replies the Enchanter.

'Anyway,' Uther continues, 'my days will be filled with royal plans and kingly deeds for the next thousand years or so.'

He lays a hand on the Enchanter's bony shoulder. The striped tent glimmers faintly through his broad and mischievous grin.

'You know where to find me,' he says and fades from sight.

'Oh,' he says, poking his head back into the present, 'nearly forgot. The reason you turned up late . . .'

'Yes?'

'You went off half-cocked.'

'Half-c—'

'You didn't allow for Uranus, Neptune or Pluto.'

'Who on Earth are they?'

'No idea. But that talking book of yours said they "weren't due to be discovered by Man for at least another thousand years", so they were only mentioned in the small print. Said a spell for flagging eyesight wouldn't come amiss.'

Merlin watches him disappear with a quizzical frown, shrugs impatiently and turns back to look at the arena.

Griswold is gazing impassively as Sir Lancelot strides up and stands before him.

'So, young Griswold,' says Lancelot in a voice that he ensures will reach all ears. 'Thy words have been thine undoing. Thy skill has been tested against mine and found wanting.'

He turns and raises a hand to Guinevere. She waves back somewhat absently. She has a feeling that things were meant to turn out differently, but she doesn't know quite why.

Lancelot goes on, 'Now all of Camelot knows who is the better man. For this reason I forgive thee in the name of our queen and, for this reason also, I will grant thee mercy.'

He leans closer and speaks quietly so that only Griswold can hear.

'And when I have her panting for the victor's favours tonight I will not concern myself in the slightest that her eyes are crossed and her teeth protrude.'

The burning pain pulses through Griswold's hand, leaving it limp and useless, but his right hand works well enough. He closes the fingers of that hand into a massive fist.

'You treacherous prick,' he says and, wondering vaguely where he's heard that last word before and what it means, he brings his fist up in a sweeping arc.

In the sunlit silence the hills of Camelot echo flatly to the sound of Sir Lancelot du Lac's neck snapping.

'Oh, my God,' groans Merlin.

'Ribwash. Thou art ribwash,' smiles the crowd prophetically.

269

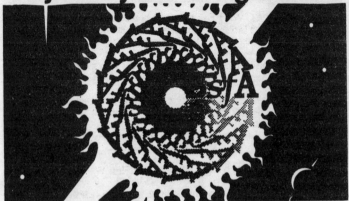

Who Goes Here?

BOB SHAW

War was one game Warren Peace didn't want to play. So why had he joined the Space Legion? Warren knew he'd got to escape, but to do so meant a hair-raising and hilarious journey into the forgotten past ...

£3.99   0 575 05678 9

The Weird Colonial Boy

PAUL VOERMANS

Nigel is a drongo – a wittering, spot-faced pillock whose only, lonely passions are music (it's 1978 and the Sex Pistols are riding high), sex (unconsummated) and tropical fish.

Then one of his fish finds its way into another dimension (don't ask) and Nigel follows it ...

'A wild comic romp' – *New Statesman*

£4.99   0 575 05715 7